THE REVISIONIST

BY THE SAME AUTHOR

P.S.

Out of Time

Not a Free Show

Wanting a Child (Coedited with Jill Bialosky)

THE REVISIONIST

A NOVEL

HELEN SCHULMAN

BLOOMSBURY

Published by Bloomsbury, New York and London
Distributed to the trade by St. Martin's Press

Cataloging in Publication Data is available from the Library of Congress

ISBN 1–58234–172–9

Originally published in hardcover in the United States by Crown Publishers in 1998

This paperback edition published in 2001

10 9 8 7 6 5 4 3 2 1

Design by Leonard Henderson
Printed in the United States of America by
RR Donnelley & Sons Company, Harrisonburg, Virginia

To Bruce—who else?

ACKNOWLEDGMENTS

For their generosity, support, and *patience,* I would like to thank: the Corporation of Yaddo, the Virginia Center for the Creative Arts, the New York Foundation for the Arts, *The Paris Review,* Elissa Schapell, J. K., Dani Shapiro, Rick Moody, Sloan Harris, Karen Rinaldi, Miriam Kuznets, the excellent Elizabeth Gaffney, my wonderful family, the cast and crew at Columbia University, and always, the memory of Lee Goerner and Eric Ashworth, who believed in me before I knew who I was.

"This was loneliness with noise, unlike the kind I had at home."

William Matthews

from "Cheap Seats, The Cincinnati Gardens, Professional Basketball, 1959,"
The Atlantic Monthly, December 1994

1

David Hershleder was tired. It had been a long, hard week, perhaps the longest of his foreshortening life. He was thirty-nine and a neurologist. He knew from long, hard weeks before. Why should this one be different? Days in and out this go-around were as similar and as varied as days usually were at the hospital. Tuesday he'd had grand rounds; he'd supervised students on Monday and Wednesday; spent Thursday reluctantly with his handful of private patients. Whatever time he could squeeze out of the rest of the week was devoted to the EEG lab and his research. Maple Syrup Urine Disorder: a form of mental retardation, mysterious in that the primary symptom is the patient's piss smelling like a squeeze of Aunt Jemima. Dystonia: involuntary movements that often lead to sustained, bizarre poses, something like the freeze-tag of Hershleder's youth. There was his predecessor's pet project, the death studies (he'd inherited the data when Dr. Lawrence Edelstein himself ended up a Labor Day highway statistic), and Hershleder's own follow-up, brain birth: When does human life begin? His hypothesis: If "death" is no longer defined by cardiac malfunction but by the cessation of cerebral activity, then human life itself can only begin when those same cerebral neurons commence firing.

The ramifications, ethical and otherwise, of his inquiries were endless, but at this time, this exhausted, worn-out time, and for most of his adult life, ethical ramifications were of less interest than theory itself. And even that—the pure elastic beauty of science when it was decoded and made available to the willing Hershleder mind—was less seductive than it had been in his youth.

Lately, Hershleder's flirtation with aberration, originally so intoxicating, was proving to be wearing. His romance with the opening and closing of the eye of God, the observer, once so rich and satisfying, had begun to cool. And yet his professional life, with all its twists and turns and inevitable frustrations, was all-consuming. Often he felt as if he was whirling wildly, like a teenage girl burdened by an uncontrollable popularity; as far as work was concerned, Hershleder's dance card was dizzingly full.

While he was no stranger to primary studies, most of his work involved secondary sources, a synthesis of the literature at large. He was a reader, Hershleder, a looker-upper. It pleased him endlessly to sort through graphs and papers, to pore over charts and brain maps, to gaze at a photographic study of an anencephalic monster as if it were some stupendously horrible work of art. No matter how vile the disorder, Hershleder was helplessly drawn by his own desire to puzzle the mess in question out. He would dally eagerly with anything two-dimensional. It was that third dimension—the depth of breath and bone and brain—that scared him half to death. Hershleder was allergic to his patients.

When giving one of the privates—a nice guy, a forty-five-year-old attorney with a wife and twin daughters—a diagnosis of glioblastoma multiforme, Hershleder had said, "There's good news and there's bad news."

He'd had to say something. Dealing directly with people had never been his forte. The words just spilled out of his mouth.

"Bad news first," said the attorney, like a true attorney, Hershleder thought.

"You have a malignant brain tumor," said Dr. Hershleder.

After a lengthy discussion of possible treatments and procedures, the attorney insistent that the good doctor visit him with an inviolate pronouncement of the days and weeks and years—please, God—left to his humble existence, as if he, Hershleder, were capable of doling out the remaining chapters, the attorney had asked wearily, "So what's the good news?"

"The good news, the good news . . ." the exhausted Hershleder struggled. Was there such a thing? Had he not thrown that phrase out unthinkingly, in an impulsive effort to improve his bedside manner?

"You could have had a glioblastoma *multi*-multiforme," Hershleder said, nonsensically.

The attorney nodded, grateful to learn that it was possible to be worse off than he was.

In the privacy of his own mind, Hershleder came to another conclusion: The good news is it could have been me. Then he berated himself over the selfishness of the thought.

Now, as Hershleder swiveled around in his black leather chair, his eyes just open enough to note with pleasure the rich array of different woods that forested his office—the cherry of his chair, the mahogany of his desk, the ebony of the brain-shaped paperweight he was awarded as chief resident years before—Hershleder made a noise. He threw his head back, his comb-over falling dark and curly and long on one side of his head, his pink scalp peeking out the other, his white neck exposed, and he made the sounds of a tired man. He made the sounds of his father.

"Aaacch," rose from the throat of David Hershleder, at just the same timbre and pitch as it had coughed its way up the esophagus of Irv Hershleder, his father the doctor, and of Chaim Hershleder, his father's father, the dress store owner. But the grandfather had died long before Hershleder's little ears had whorled and formed—he was four months in utero the day of the funeral—enough so that they could record the phlegmy arpeggio that would someday become his legacy. Hershleder had heard his own father's sighs only intermittently during his childhood, as his father was often absent for the same reasons most fathers were absent in the fifties, in the sixties—he certainly hadn't heard them frequently enough to make an absolute case for monkey-see monkey-do. So this sigh of sighs, it was part of his inheritance. Still, at first his mother believed she could wean it out of him. "Dovidil, please," said Mrs. Hershleder. "That sound, that sound! It could kill you."

His poor mother. Mrs. Hershleder had spent much of her life with her hands over her ears, to block out *this* annoyance as well as an entire cast of others: the screech of her screaming children, her whistling kettle, the cackle of her busybody sister, the sound of her own loneliness echoing, echoing against the walls of her bones so that she simply vibrated with deprivation, with lack of intellectual connection, lack of romantic touch.

Hershleder's earliest recollection of his mother was when he was a toddler and they had just moved into Stuyvesant Town, a redbrick haven of the middle class. Before that they lived in Queens, a garden apartment, a yard, a green-and-white ticked awning. But he had been too little to remember that—he'd only seen the pictures, heard the stories. Magically, he'd been raised as an only child—the youngest, a boy—even though he'd had two sisters. It was Fifteenth Street and Avenue C, apartment 5F, where Hershleder developed memory. That morning, he and his mother were alone, together, in the living room. He was buckled up in one of those harnesses, strapped to the playpen like a mental patient so that he would do no harm to the furniture (new slipcovers), no harm to himself (a coffee table with sharp corners). He remembered looking up from his toys to see her, the lovely total *her* of his being, standing in the middle of that messy room with her long, thin hands over her ears; how thin her hands were, the skin so translucent you could see through it like smoked glass. She was whispering, "I can't stand it."

What was it? baby Hershleder had wondered, the squeal of the television, the gunshot of a car backfiring? Was it Mindy and Lori (his sisters) and their morning squabble over some cloudy pink angora sweater? Or was it what he feared most, that his three-year-old presence was what Mrs. Hershleder couldn't stand?

It wasn't until years later, after her death, that Hershleder realized that with his gabby sisters mostly away at school, with his father forever on call, Mrs. Hershleder's beloved piano permanently lent out to some neighbor's child prodigy, that instead of all that noise it was a certain kind of silence that his mother couldn't stand. She couldn't stand the fact that there was no other sound in her world at that moment that satisfied her but that of her boy's breathing, Hershleder's own rise and fall not enough to fill the chambers of his mother's empty heart. When that same mother heard that "aaach" rise from her own boy's throat time and time again when Hershleder was in the throes of puberty and adolescent angst, it made her sick. That's when she, who had been reading Freud in the spare moments of all that waste of her young womanhood, threw in her vote for nature over nurture, left his father and went back to school to save herself.

She pursued a degree in Holocaust Studies. Because she was a survivor, the war was the most significant chapter of her own small insignificant history, a period of time, a series of events, that she had not recovered from, and so she frantically invested in this course of study in her later years, when she couldn't bury her memories any longer. She wanted, she told Hershleder, some small understanding of what had happened to her.

She was trying to explain her devotion to her work. She was trying to explain her one-hundred-percent preoccupation, the hours in the library, the dishevelment of her clothes, her hair, the apartment: the dishes rotting in the sink, the laundry on the chair. She was trying to explain her *descent.*

But it had been hard for Hershleder to listen. He'd been a boy, frightened by the pain of his living mother.

Now, perhaps, Hershleder might be old enough to want to hear her. Maybe.

But she died, *she died!*—Hershleder couldn't believe sometimes that his mother had died—before obtaining her Ph.D., before getting another lover, before filling the painful silences with some music of her own.

Aaach.

This was the tragedy of his life. He was making his father's sound again.

His father's sound; was his mother right, was it hereditary, the product of some errant gene, like Lou Gehrig's disease or colon cancer? Hershleder had been a boy who wanted to please his mother. As a man, it horrified him to find that this terrible trait of his father's, like some alien animal, lived inside his throat.

Making that sound was breaking one of the many will-not-do vows Hershleder made in childhood that he was incapable of keeping as an adult. For one, he wore a suit and tie every day of his life, almost. Just a few nights prior he had said sternly to his own boy, "When I was your age," and then the ghastly, "Because I'm the father." What's more, his family lived in the suburbs! Perhaps the biggest crime of all, he had allowed the two of them, his funny-looking offspring, the freckled fruit of his loins, to be born; he sentenced his children to life spans of their own.

How many nights had Hershleder lain awake as a child, had he sat up in bed as a teenager smoking cigarettes, smoking pot, wondering why his parents had forced his appearance on this earth? Wouldn't it have been easier for all concerned, especially in his teen years, and considerably less painful, if he had been left to float in the cosmic pablum of unassigned elements, random energy—for this is how he had pictured pre-life as he called it then: a bubbling, contented porridge, a fertile oatmeal of atoms and what-have-you? But when push came to shove he had given in to the same quest for immortality as his own parents must have done—that and the tearful nagging of his biological clock–watching wife. Perhaps this was the definition of maturity, Hershleder thought, knowing that you are trapped by the same traps as your parents.

Now Hershleder rubbed his palms across his cheeks as if he were washing his face awake.

"Dude," said Inge.

She was in the doorway. His chief lab technician. She was Norwegian, her hair as white as her coat, bones so big, Hershleder, the observer, was constantly aware of her skeleton. Cheekbones so loud and prominent, they looked like the wingspan of a small, powerful bird, and when she chewed a sandwich or on the soft tissue of her inner lip—as she did now—those cheekbones appeared to be rhapsodically in the midst of flight. *Handsome* was the only adjective for her, the only adjective in the world, except for *frightening.*

She was learning English, the vernacular.

"TGIF," said Inge. She placed a stack of EEGs, each as thick as the yellow pages of a town the size of Ithaca, New York, on his desk.

"TGIF," said Hershleder.

"To be read," said Inge.

"I know," said Hershleder.

Her eyes were two bright blue gas jets. Flamethrowers. She cracked a Nordic smile.

"Party-hearty, Kimosabe," said Inge, her giant, perfect shinbone connecting to her giant, perfect knee, and then onto her femur, that ivory tusk, sending an electrical message singing up into her hips: wiggle, wiggle.

As she walked out of his office for the weekend, Hershleder was visited by a vision that he was instantly ashamed of; he could picture her skeleton a millennium later on display at the American Museum of Natural History under a sign that read THE SHIKSA GODDESS.

Inge had been in this country only about a year and a half and had providentially found her way straight to Hershleder. Age-wise, she must have been hovering somewhere near thirty. She'd come here to be with a younger boyfriend, an ex-frat boy, all-American whiz kid she'd met while eating at a luncheonette outside a scientific conference center in Oslo. He accounted for the "party-hearty." Hershleder had met this boyfriend, a jovial, football-playing sort, at the hospital Christmas party. Louie. He was a boy genius, a rocket scientist, literally—he did research for NASA—with a neck the size of Hershleder's waist. Of course, Inge herself was no slouch in the brains department. As far as Hershleder was concerned, she was the brightest bulb in the socket in Neurology, including two of the attendings and the chief resident. Inge was the finest technician he had ever had in the EEG lab. Lately, she had taken to running things.

Hershleder reached across his desk for the phone. It was a long reach, a large desk, a mahogany desk, a doctor's desk, covered with files and old unread EEGs, reference books, several half-drunk cups of sludgy coffee. A layer of ash as delicate and gray as antique lace had wafted across his papers; officially, Hershleder had quit smoking nine months before. This present dusting of desk and suit clothes was only a minor setback. It occurred to him that if he blew his work clean, disorder and chaos would fly, resulting in more disorder and chaos, and so he did not blow but lifted the receiver and tapped into one of the service's many outgoing numbers. One of the buttons on the phone bank was a direct line to his heart.

She'd been christened Eliza Isabella, but no one ever had the chance to wrap a tongue around that queenly moniker. Her brother Spencer called her "It" from the day she was born. "Itty" was a parental attempt to soften the blow. Itty, his wife, his wife! And their two dastardly children. All it took was a light press of a finger pad and father and family were almost instantly reconnected, a high-fidelity umbilicus, a finger in a light socket, a filial defibrillator ready to shock them all back to life. The receiver up, the finger lifted in anticipation like a pianist's, and then the imp, the shadow of the bad boy Hershleder never was but always dreamed of being, the hookey player, stretched awake inside him. Why not take his time? If he called Itty now, he'd be wedded to taking the 4:40 back to Larchmont. Why not stretch it out a bit, that isthmus between work and homework, between doctorhood and fatherhood, between being tired and being tired?

The receiver crashed like a hipbone into an arthritic socket. The sleeve of his white doctor's coat swept across the desk. Hershleder swiveled 180 degrees, looked out his coveted and bitterly fought-over window into the romance of the East River. The patients, who were usually in and out of the hospital in a matter of days or weeks, got the windows; most of the doctors who spent the best years of their lives in that gloomy facility got the inner, lightless offices. Hershleder was a lucky one. Sky and water were the same color. Metal. For a few hours more, there would be no horizon, which was what he liked. Bellevue. Beautiful View. Endless gray, no boundaries, no differentiation, just pure boring calm. He threw back his head, closed his eyes. His father's sigh climbed the walls of his throat. "Aaach," said David Hershleder. "Aaach."

He was tired.

• • •

"You look like hell," said David Kahn. "You look like shit warmed over."

The Kahn-man ordered them both another round. They were surrounded by oxidized copper walls, tall, dull, steel tabletops, and high, skinny black chairs that encouraged all potential sitters to stand. They were surrounded by standing secretaries and standing nurses and medical-supply salesmen leaning against the bar, all of them starting their weekends early, with a bang. The Davids were drinking Seven-and-Sevens. They'd been drinking them since high school, when the only kid who would sink low enough to drink with either one of them had unfortunately been the other. A geek drink for the geek boys—Kahn and Hershleder. Now Kahn was richer than God. He was in securities. "A financial genius!" said Kahn's mother. He was the only one left on the Street making money. What did it matter, Hershleder thought, that he could buy me out twice over? He's still a loser. My best friend. "Aaach." This one bubbled up like gas.

"You sound like an *alter kocker,*" said Kahn.

"Thanks," said Hershleder. "Thanks a lot."

Kahn manipulated the frost on his glass with his swizzle stick. He swiveled his gaze around the bar. Ample buttocks in tight short skirts. A few seersucker summer blazers. Not his crowd. He hunched forward in his Italian jacket and looked Hershleder in the eye.

Kahn had been an ugly boy, carbuncular and jug-eared, but he was not an ugly man. Most men weren't ugly, really, that's what Itty said. They just got old enough to look like someone's father. They grew into their weaknesses, and the result was oddly comforting, the way that a weakness in character can be comforting when you find it in someone you admire. "We like people for what's wrong with them," Itty said. "We like them because they're lazy, or they lie, or forget to call their mother. We like them when they've been dumped or fired. We like them when they confess to cheating on their wives and then appear to suffer horribly for it. We like people when they suffer." Itty repeated herself. She was a talker, Itty. She said a lot of things.

"Take Kahn," said Itty. "He grew into his lack of chin. It makes him more likable. If he were as arrogant as he already is and he looked like a sex god, everyone would hate his guts.

What we like about him is that he's chinless, and yet somehow, against all odds, he's won."

"He's won?" said Hershleder.

"You know what I mean," said Itty.

Kahn had no chin, that was for sure. In high school there had been no hiding it; in college he had grown a beard to conceal its absence. At business school he had shaved the beard, revealing once again that his lips did a gentle slope toward his neck. But he still had his hair, Kahn, a great black mess of it, and what had been scrawny on a boy, his long gawky body, his primatelike limbs, was now considered fit and trim—Kahn worked out three mornings a week with a personal trainer.

Hershleder had never been as bad off. As a boy he was a bit too tall, ungainly, but sensitive-looking. Big brown eyes, his nose a little long, maybe, long enough to look smart, serious, Jewish. He seemed easily destroyed. Gentle. The kind of face an older woman might take into her hands.

Later in life this stood him well. Homely-handsome. A hippie-wimp in college, an "eighties man" in the eighties. Who knew how he'd fare once he was able to look back on the nineties in retrospect? Luckily, he was a doctor. As soon as a certain type of girl grew out of her bad boy–loving phase, as soon as she got down to business, went on a husband search, Hershleder's popularity took off. Women, babes who wouldn't give him the time of day at twenty, began, as thirty loomed closer and closer, to leave cute and anxiously available messages on his phone machine: "David, this is your long-lost pal Jodie Fish. Jodie Fish, from camp? We had rice pudding at the cafeteria at work today and it made me think of you . . . Well, Proust had his madeleine, right? Give me a buzz sometime, 555-1324. Jodie Fish, Camp Trywoodie, 1967, Summer of Love." And then to herself as she was hanging up: "Oh God, I can't believe I said that."

The two of them, he and the Kahn-man, finally got to see a little action then, to call the shots. "Revenge of the Nerds," said Kahn, and he threw his hand up for a high five when either one of them got lucky.

While Hershleder was in med school and Kahn was still a trainee at Bear Stearns, they had shared an apartment in a tenement near the hospital. It was your typical walk-up: peeling linoleum on the staircase, Chinese takeout menus strewn across the ground-floor vestibule. There was a bathtub in the kitchen that Kahn thought was the coolest thing on earth. Whenever they had parties he'd make Hershleder lug ten-pound bags of ice up the six flights to their apartment; they'd dump the ice in the tub, add a case or two of beers, the green bottlenecks studding the ice like faux emeralds.

It had been *fun,* the half-eaten pizza in its box lying permanently on the floor like an historical landmark, the glimpses of each other's girlfriends' chassis (a breast, a back, a meaty thigh) as they passed in and out of the rooms of the railroad flat to get to the kitchen, to get to the bathroom, to answer the phone. More than once Hershleder had come home exhausted after a weekend on call to find Kahn and some Debbie frolicking in a tub full of froth, letting Calgon take them away, drinking Cold Duck out of the bottle. This was

Kahn's big come-on line: "Let the theme of the evening be bubbles."

They'd lock each other out for the night, make the moves on the other guy's woman. They'd conduct a monthly tour of their refrigerator, offering nonexistent prizes to any guest who could guess the nature of the mystery food inside. And they'd go wild trying to get girls to play a grown-up game of Twister ("It's retro," coerced Kahn) and even spin the bottle. Then came Itty, and the long-awaited party was abruptly over. Kahn never forgave him. It took Kahn six more years to marry, nine more months to divorce. Now he was happily, terminally single.

"So what's up with the It-girl?" asked Kahn, looking at the floor. It was terra-cotta tile. A few weeks before, the bar had been a mock Southwestern road stop.

"Nothing," said Hershleder. "What should be up with her?"

"Hershey," said Kahn, in a human voice.

Hershleder was touched. He waved over the waitress and ordered another round. "On me this time," said Hershleder. Since he had made a buck, Kahn was sure everyone liked him only for his money. Hershleder of the paltry grants, staff salaries, Hershleder with the "artist" non–wage-earning wife, Hershleder with the two lesson-attending children (art, piano, ballet, drama, soon the shrink bills pouring in) always took the check. To prove a point. That Hershleder wasn't out to use Kahn, that he, Hershleder, was just stuck with him.

"Thanks for the drink, man," Kahn said.

"De nada," said Hershleder.

A waitress appeared, refilled their nut bowl, took away their glasses, and set down another round.

"I love the way you do that, Sunshine," Kahn said to her, and the kicker was that this same crudely hit-upon waitress actually slipped Kahn a hint of a smile. Hershleder couldn't believe it. How did Kahn manage to get over with a line as limp as that? He tried to catch Kahn's eye, but Kahn had immediately trained his focus on the complimentary snacks. With one finger in the nut bowl, Kahn started to hunt out the sesame sticks. Next he'd go after the almonds, the filberts, and the Chex Mix. By the end of happy hour, Hershleder knew there would be nothing left but peanuts.

"So did you read the paper today?" asked Kahn. He popped a sesame stick into his mouth.

"Do I ever have time to read the paper?" asked Hershleder.

"Snapple went up. Two points. I told you," Kahn said. That index finger was back in the bowl again, roiling around, ferreting out.

Hershleder averted his eyes. "You told me," said Hershleder. Two points of Snapple could have paid for two sets of orthodontic work. Two two-month sessions of summer camp. Sleepaway.

"More," said Kahn, sorting out the almonds. "David Josephson, remember him? He made the paper. The fucking *New York Times.*" One by one he hoarded the almonds in a pile by his drink.

Another David.

Hershleder remembered Josephson from visiting Kahn at

Dartmouth. An egghead. The kind of guy who read so much, he'd forget to eat and sleep. You'd find him in the lonely room he rented at a frat house, slumped over his typewriter in an academic coma. This was who Kahn chose to hang out with, a smart guy. Kahn figured that maybe some of it would rub off on him. He also had a heart, Kahn, a small one. Hershleder remembered Kahn bringing Josephson some PB&J from the food co-op for lunch; the guy was so high on reading Bakunin, he'd forgotten a person had to take in sustenance of a more basic order.

Now that Hershleder thought about it, Josephson's behavior seemed borderline psychotic. Hadn't there been an incident when, too enraptured with his studies to get up and go to the bathroom, Josephson had urinated in his pants? Or was that just a jealous rumor? Josephson was clearly an academic success, although just as clearly he wasn't the type to succeed at the things Kahn or Hershleder or any of the guys were dying to succeed at, the things you really went to college for: to get fucked up, to get lucky, to have your latest road trip turned into a legend. A nosedive into the books made sense for a boy like him. Josephson should have been a Talmudic scholar.

"So," said Kahn, "this schmuck Josephson, he translated some book—man, does it sound boring—a thousand-page engineering study on the mechanics of the death camps. No history or nothing, just blueprints or whatever engineers do."

"Drive trains," said Hershleder.

"Funny," said Kahn, yawning. He put a pretzel on the flat

of his palm, slapped his wrist with his other hand, and caught it on his tongue. The pretzel flashed golden.

"So he translated it, he didn't write it, why is the article about him?" Hershleder was feeling a little bit competitive. With some studied nonchalance: "Wasn't he socially retarded, or am I remembering some other guy?"

The Kahn-man rolled his eyes. "Because this study proves that the Holocaust occurred," Kahn said. "Duh-hey now."

There was a piece of unswallowed pretzel on Kahn's tongue. Hershleder looked away again. At the floor he looked, and spotted a blob of Russian dressing that almost made him retch. A stepped-on french fry was smushed up against his wingtip. Everything within eyesight was disgusting. He tried to kick the french fry aside, which only made matters worse. He closed his eyes.

"Got a little trouble down under, Hershey?" asked Kahn, noticing something was up. "That waitress, huh? Another round and I won't be able to stand up. Pup Tent City," Kahn said.

"The Holocaust," said Hershleder. "Josephson."

"This French asshole who wrote the study, he thought the Holocaust never happened, conspiracy theory, something us Jews dreamed up. I mean, didn't they ever show *Night and Fog* at his grammar school?" Kahn downed his drink.

"A revisionist," Hershleder said, nodding.

His mother, in the final days of her life, had been increasingly troubled by revisionists. She had stumbled upon an advertisement in her university newspaper challenging the scholarly community for documentable proof. As Hershleder remembered it now, she'd been outraged. "Forget it, Ma," he'd said. "They're just a bunch of nuts. Don't waste your time."

"Waste my time? Waste my time?" said Mrs. Hershleder. "This is about not wasting my time, for once." Then, more softly, "Don't be like me, darling. Promise."

He'd promised. It was easy for him then not to be like his mother.

Kahn ran his fingers through his hair; it flip-flopped wildly. "So this revisionist, he sets out to prove this drek he calls a theory, and guess what? He proves himself wrong. The fuckwad. He ends up proving what he set out to disprove, if you get my meaning." Kahn leaned forward, eyes coming at Hershleder like the headlights on the A-train. "This is news. This is why that loser Josephson makes the paper, because some anti-Semitic Frog thought that Europe in the thirties and forties was a great big holy party, a giant, fucking bar mitzvah. Then changes his mind, Jesus Christ!" Kahn's eyes looked really crazy.

"Talk about denial," said Hershleder, recoiling. He hated when Kahn got riled up.

"You're telling me," said Kahn. "Talk about rewriting history." Kahn paused. "And now that he finally accepts what the Nazis did, does he approve of it or what?"

"How would I know?" said Hershleder.

Kahn leaned in closer. His eyes were lit, but his face was pale as soap. "So what's up with the It-girl, Hersh?" asked the Kahn-man.

"Nothing," said Hershleder. "Not a thing."

"You're telling me," Kahn said.

• • •

Hershleder put Kahn in a cab—Kahn, who'd actually scored that waitress's phone number; Kahn, who had to get home because he had a date that night with a new babe.

"How old is this one, Kahnny?" asked Hershleder. "Nineteen?"

"You got the sense of humor of an uncle, you know that, Hersh?" Kahn said in disgust. "You're goddamn *avuncular.*"

He was in a hurry. He was cooking this new babe dinner. He needed time to buy some fresh pasta, to whip up a batch of cilantro pesto. Kahn, raised on frozen blintzes and TV dinners in Co-op City, had started taking classes in the last year or so at the Culinary Institute and had developed into quite a cook, or so Kahn said. How could Hershleder know? The only meal Kahn ever made for Hershleder was dressed-up Ramen noodles, and once, after Kahn's divorce—when Hershleder had come over in a bumbling effort to comfort him—Kahn had poached a salmon fillet for Hershleder by wrapping the fish in silver foil and running it through the dishwasher. But Hershleder hadn't been to Kahn's place in years. He'd been safely ensconced in the suburbs. Mostly he'd talked to Kahn on the phone; once in a while, a rare while, they would meet like this, for drinks.

Kahn schlepped to Westchester to the Hershleders' for all the holidays that Kahn didn't schlep to the Bronx to see his mother, *trayf* stuff like Christmas Eve. He was a fixture in their lives. The kids were crazy for him. He'd enter their calm, messy house like an eggbeater, flinging his coat around, heading straight for the kitchen, where he would rummage through the refrigerator, take the lid off every pot. He'd fix himself a drink, start in at once about one of his latest sexual exploits, as if there weren't children in the room—which was why Hershleder's kids loved him so. Kahn told a great dirty story. His pockets were usually filled with the kind of stuff parents wouldn't let their offspring near: Garbage Pail Kids cards, plastic Ninja warriors, anything that could rot your teeth. Once the kids stopped crawling all over him, Kahn would tell tales about all the money that he made. What he bought with it. How whatever he bought drove the chicks crazy.

No one, including Itty herself, knew why, but she adored him. Kahn was the epitome of everything she couldn't take. "Die Yuppie Scum," said Itty whenever she signed off the phone with him. And then in her mock-mother voice: "Make sure you wear a sweater."

• • •

It had been a hundred years since Hershleder had taken in a late-afternoon movie, a hundred years since he had gone to the movies by himself. It was 5:45. There was a 6:15 train Hershleder could still make. But why give in, why do something as inevitable as being home on time for dinner? At heart he was a rebel. Hershleder walked up the avenue to Kips Bay. There, there was a movie house. He could enter the theater in daylight. When was the last time he had done that, gone from a dazzling summer afternoon—when the air was visible and everything looked like it was in a comic book, only magnified, broken down into a sea of shimmering dots—into the dark, cool mouth of a movie theater? It was a dry July day. It was hot out. Who cared what was playing? Porno. Action. Comedy. All Hershleder wanted was to give himself over to something.

He was drawn to the box office as if the bored gum-chewing girl behind the counter was dispensing pharmaceutical cocaine and he was still a young and reckless intern—the kind he had always planned on being, the kind Hershleder was only in his dreams. She had big hair. Brown hair, sprayed and teased into wings. She had a dark mole beneath her pink lips on the left-hand side of her face. It looked like the period that marks a dotted quarter in musical notation. She was a beautiful girl in an interesting way. Which means if the light were right (which it wasn't quite then) and if she held her chin at a particular angle (which she didn't—her chin was in a constant seesaw on account of the gum) when she laughed or when she forgot about pulling her lips over her teeth (which were long and fine, almost canine), she was a lovely, Cubist vision. The planes of her face didn't add up to anything organic but lived splendidly and independently and her eyes were hazel, impressionable, and changeable.

Hershleder bought two tickets from this young girl without seeing any of this, the wonder of her extraordinary face. He bought two tickets out of force of habit. He entered the building, passed the two tickets toward the ticket-taker, and realized that he was alone.

Back at the box office, the girl wouldn't grant Hershleder a refund. She said, "It's a done deal, doll." But she smiled at him.

Hershleder gave the extra ticket to a bag lady who sat under the marquee, where the sidewalk was slightly more shaded than the street, where the open and close of the glass doors to the air-conditioned theater provided the nearest thing to an ocean breeze that she would feel on this, her final face.

Hershleder the blind, Hershleder the dumb—oblivious to the thrill of a beautiful big-haired girl's lyrical smile, a smile a musician could sight-read and play. Blind and stuck with an extra ticket, Hershleder gave it away to the old lady. He wasn't a bad guy, really. Hadn't the old woman once been somebody's baby? Wasn't it possible, also, that she was still somebody's mother? Were there ever two more exalted roles in this human theater? This woman had risen to the pinnacle of her being; and she'd fallen. She suffered from La Tourette. Hershleder held the glass door open for her; he'd been well raised by his own mother, a woman with a deep residing respect for the elderly.

"Bastard," said the old lady, smiling shyly. "Cocksucker."

Hershleder smiled back at her. Here was someone who spoke his language. Hadn't he seen a thousand and one patients like her before?

"Fucking Nazi prick," the woman said, her voice trailing low as she struggled to gain control of herself. Her face screwed up in concentration; she wrestled with her inner, truer self. "Faggot," she said through clenched teeth; she bowed her head now, trying to direct her voice back into her chest. The next word came out like an exhalation of smoke, in a puff, a whisper: "Motherfucker."

The old lady looked up at Hershleder from beneath hooded lids—in her eyes was a lifetime of expressions unfortunately not held back, of words unleashed, epithets unfettered. There was a locker room of vile language in her head, but her face seemed apologetic. When Hershleder met her gaze, she fluttered her lashes, Morse-coding like the quadriplegic on Ward A, then turned and shuffled away from him.

• • •

It was delicious inside the theater. Cold enough for Hershleder to take off his jacket and lay it flat like a blanket across his chest. His hand wandered across his crotch, stroked his belly. In the flirtation of film light, Hershleder felt himself up under the curtain of his jacket. There were a couple of teenagers in the back of the house who talked throughout the movie, but what did Hershleder care? It was dark, there was music. Stray popcorn crunched beneath his feet. A side door opened and he got high off the smell of marijuana wafting on a cross breeze. An old man dozed in an end seat across the aisle. A beautiful girl on-screen displayed a beautiful private birthmark. A bare-chested man rolled on top of her, drowning Hershleder's view. Above warplanes flew, bombs dropped, the girl moaned, fire fire fire. Something was burning. On-screen? Off-screen? The EXIT sign was the reddest thing he'd ever seen. It glowed on the outskirts of his peripheral vision. Time passed in a solid leap, as in sleep, as in coma. When the lights came up, Hershleder was drowsily aware that much had happened—but what? Couldn't the real world have jumped forward at the rate of on-screen time in quantum leaps of event and tragedy and years? The movies. Like rockets hurtling a guy through space.

It was a way to make the hours pass, that's for sure, thought Hershleder. For a moment he had no clue as to what day it was.

• • •

Grand Central Station.

Hershleder waited for information. On the east wall was a huge photo essay, Kodak's, presenting the glories of India. A half-naked child, his brown outstretched hand, an empty bowl, his smile radiant. A bony cow. A swirl of sari, a lovely face, a red dot like a jewel amidst the light filigree of a happy forehead. A blown-up piece of *poori:* a bread cloud. The Taj Mahal . . . *In All Its Splendor.*

The lobby of Bellevue looked something like this. The women in their saris, the homeless beggars, the drug addicts who punctuated the station like restless exclamation marks. Inge had told him that at the hospital, in the ground-floor women's bathrooms, mothers bathed their babies in the sinks. Hershleder could believe this. There, like here, was a place to come in out of the cold, the rain, the heat.

The signboard fluttered its black lids; each train announcement inched its way up another slot. Hershleder's would depart from Track 11. There was time for half a dozen oysters at the Oyster Bar. He headed out past Zaro's Bakery, the bagels and the brioche, the pies of mile-high lemon frosting.

Cholesterol—how it could slather the arteries with silken ecstasy! (Hershleder had to watch himself. Oysters would do the trick—in more ways than one. What was that old joke . . . the rules of turning forty: Never waste an erection, never trust a fart.) He hung a left, down the curved, close passageway—the tunnel that felt like an inner tube, an underground track without the track, an alimentary canal, a cool stone vagina. Vagrants sagged against the walls, sprawled beneath the archways. There was a souvenir stand. A bookstore. A florist. Daisies, bright white for Itty, beckoned from earthenware vases. This was a must-stop on his future trek to Track 11. Hershleder picked his way across the map of curled-up bodies; he sidestepped globs of spit, puddles of stinking urine. The passageway smelled like a pet store. The horrible inevitable decay of everything biological, the waste, the waste! Hershleder did a little shocked pas de bourrée over a pretzel of human shit, three toe-steps, as lacy as a dancer's.

• • •

They slid down easy, those Wellfleets, Blue Points. Hershleder leaned against the polished wood and ordered another half dozen. Not liquid, not solid—a fixed transitional state. A second beer. So what if he missed his train? There would always be another. Death and taxes. Conrail and the Erie Lackawanna. The fact that oysters made him horny.

They tasted cold and wet. Peppery. Hershleder wasn't one to skimp on hot sauce. The shell against his upper lip was blue and smooth; his lower lip touched lichen—or was it coral? Pinstripes made up his panorama. The other slurpers were all like him. Commuters. Men who traveled to and from their wives, their children, "The Office." Men with secret lives in a foreign land: the city. Men who got off on eating oysters, who delayed going home by having yet another round of drinks. They all stood in a row at the bar the way they would stand at a row of urinals. Each in his private world. "Aaach," said Hershleder, and tipped another briny shell to his lips. His mouth was flooded by ocean.

Delays, delays. A lifetime full of delays. Hershleder the procrastinator, the putter-offer. Hershleder of the term papers started the night before, the grant proposals typed once into the computer, the postmarks fudged by the hospital's friendly postmaster. He was the kind of man to leave things to the last minute, to torture himself every moment that he did not attend to what needed attending to, his tasks, but also the type to always get them done. While in his heart he lusted after irresponsibility, he was never bad enough. Chicken-shit. A loser.

Hershleder's neighbor at the bar was reading *The New York Times.*

"Hey, Mister," said Hershleder, sounding like he was seven. "Would you mind letting me look at the C section?" Now he spoke like a gynecologist.

The Neighbor slid the paper over without even glancing up.

Hershleder turned to the book review.

Josephson. A picture of the sucker. A picture; why a picture? Hershleder wondered. It wasn't even Josephson's book. He was just the translator, that schlep was.

Josephson had not fared well over time, although to be fair, the reproduction was kind of grainy. Of the three Davids,

Josephson seemed to have the least amount of hair. A hook nose. A high forehead. He still looked brainy. That forehead hung over his eyes like an awning at a fancy club. Hershleder read the article for himself.

> A 1032-page study of the Nazi gas chambers has been published. . . . The study is by Jacques LeClerc, a chemist who began his work doubting that the Holocaust even took place. . . . The book, written in French [translated by that bald rat Josephson!], . . . presents as proof, based entirely on technical analysis of the camps, that the Holocaust was every bit as monstrous and sweeping as survivors have said. . . . It is also a personal story of a scientific discovery during which, as Mr. LeClerc writes in a postscript, he was converted from "revisionist" to "exterminationist."

Exterminationist. What a hell of an appellative. Hershleder shook his head at no one in particular. Exterminationist.

Is that what he himself was?

His beloved mother, Adela Hershleder, along with her sister, smuggled out of Germany by an intrepid cousin right after Kristallnacht. They were small girls, little kids, with tiny bendable bodies, easy to hide—they'd actually traveled over the border as luggage, together, bouncing around in the same trunk. Her mother, Hershleder's grandmother, had been rounded up and sent to the camps; after the war, word got back to the family that she'd been raped by some prison guards and in the aftermath had thrown herself onto an electrified fence.

This story was told to Hershleder in secret by the same intrepid cousin, Ida, years later, after she'd moved to Israel, when she was visiting the States. Ida had cornered him in the hallway, between the bathroom and the Seder table, the matzo stuffing still between her teeth. His own mother had never said a word. For years Hershleder had thought that only he had been entrusted with this information, and he'd carried it like the weight of the world until his sister Mindy retold the event at the shivah after his mother's funeral.

Exterminationist. Is that what he was?

His mother's father, a diabetic, had died of an infection shortly before their escape; no physician had the courage then to treat him. His grandmother's six brothers and sisters had been incinerated in Hitler's crematoria. The friends, the extended family, even the neighbors they didn't like—all gone. No one left, but fabled cousin Ida, who died in 1979. On the other side of his family Hershleder's father's father, Chaim, and his grandfather's brother Abe came to this country from Austria as refugees after World War I, the sole survivors of the sweeping tragedies of Europe that did away with their entire extended family.

And here was Hershleder, the beneficiary of all that compounded survival. Hershleder the educated, the privileged, the beloved, the doctor! Hershleder the first-generation New York Jew, Hershleder the bar mitzvahed, the assimilated, Hershleder with the shiksa wife, the children raised on Christmas, bacon in their breakfast, mayonnaise spread across their Wonder Bread, the daughter who once asked him if calling a person a Jew was really just another way to insult him.

He was lucky; his ancestors were not. What could you do? Isn't this the crux of it all (the history of civilization): those of us who are lucky juxtaposed against those of us who are not?

Mindy and Lori, his sisters, married with children, each active in her own temple, one out on Long Island, one on the Upper West Side. Irv, his father, retired now, remarried now, donating his time to the Jewish Home for the Blind. Were they any more Jewish than he was? Wasn't it true, what his own Jewish mother had told him, that what mattered in life was not religion per se, but that one strived to be a good person? Wasn't he, Hershleder—the researcher, and on Tuesdays and Thursdays the healer, the father, the husband, the lawn-mower, the moviegoer (he did show that bag lady a good time), the friend to Kahn, to Josephson (at least in theory)—a good person?

My God, thought Hershleder, just imagine being this chemist, this LeClerc, having the courage to disprove the very tenets upon which you've built your life. Hershleder knew this kind, he had seen them before: LeClerc's accomplishments were probably less about bravery than they were about obsessive compulsion; LeClerc was probably a man who practiced a strict adherence to facts, to science. After all, Hershleder had spent much of his adult life doing research. You let the data make the decisions for you. You record what you observe. You synthesize, yes, you interpret, but you don't theorize, create out of your own imagination, needs, and desires. He knew him, LeClerc, LeClerc the compulsive, the truth-teller. They were alike, these two men, certainly not in their orientations, their beliefs, but in their behavior; they were rational, exact, methodical. Science was their true religion. Not the ephemeral mumbo jumbo of politicians, philosophers, poets.

Hershleder and LeClerc: They told the truth, when they were able, when it stared them in the face.

Hershleder folded up the paper and left it on the counter, its owner, his neighbor, having vanished some time ago. Hershleder exited the comforts of the Oyster Bar and headed out into the festering subterranean world. He stopped at the florist to pick up those daisies, two dozen, a field of them, a free-floating urban meadow. He held the bouquet like a cheerleader's pompom in his hands.

"Daisies are wildflowers," said the florist when he wrapped up those hothouse posies in a crinkly paper cone. What did he think, that Hershleder was a poster child? He'd been to summer camp, away to college. Didn't he live in the suburbs and have a wife who cultivated daisies of her own? Daisies smell awful, but their faces are so sunny and bright, so fresh, so clean, petals as white as laundry detergent.

As he made his way to Track 11, Hershleder had a musical association: "Daisy, Daisy, give me your answer true." He had a poetic association: "She loves me, she loves me not." He had a visual association: the daisy stickers on the leaded glass windows that faced his yard, the plastic daisy treads that his mother had suctioned to the bottom of his bathtub so that he, Hershleder, her precious boy-child, the third-born and most prized, the object of his sisters' ire, wouldn't slip, hit his head and drown. The big bright patent-leather daisies that dressed the thongs of his own daughter's dress-up sandals. The golden yolk, the pinky white of Itty's eyes when she'd been crying.

Hershleder walked through the vaulted, starred amphitheater of Grand Central Station with a sensual garden, his human history, flowering bitterly in his hands.

• • •

"Smoke," hissed a young man in a black concert T-shirt. "Thai stick, dust, coke." The young man stood outside Track 11. Hershleder had seen this dealer there almost every day for months and months. Hershleder nodded at him, started down the ramp to the train tracks, then stopped. He had been a good boy. At Bronx Science he had smoked pot, at Cornell he'd done magic mushrooms once in a while at a Dead show—then usually spent the rest of the night in the bathroom throwing up. For the most part, he'd played it safe: a little blow on a prom night or some graduation, but no acid, no ups, no downs (well, that wasn't true, there were bennies in med school, Valiums after), no needles in the arm, no track marks. No long velvety nights of swirling, hazy rock songs. Drugwise, he was practically a virgin. Hadn't this gone on long enough?

Hershleder backtracked up the ramp.

"How much?" asked Hershleder.

"For what?" said Mr. Black Concert T-Shirt.

For what? For what?

"Heroin?" asked Hershleder, with hope.

Mr. Black Concert T-Shirt looked away in disgust. "Smoke," he hissed. "Thai stick, dust, coke."

"Thai stick," said Hershleder. Decisively. "Thai fucking stick," said Hershleder the reckless, the bon vivant.

Even though he was in danger of missing his train (again), Hershleder went back into the lobby of the station and officially bought cigarettes. He bought Merit Ultra Lights, thought better of it, backtracked to the kiosk, and traded in the Merits for a pack of Salems.

• • •

The john was small enough that if you were to sit, your knees would be in your armpits and your elbows in your ears. Hershleder and his daisies floated in a cloud of smoke, mentholated, Asiatic; the chemical smell of toilets on trains and airplanes permeated all that steam. The resultant odor was strong enough to etherize an elephant, but Hershleder the rebel was nose-blind to it. He was wasted.

The Metro North rumbled through the tunnel. Outside the scenery was so familiar, Hershleder had it memorized. First the rude surprise of 125th Street, all those broken windows, empty eyeholes, the flash of graffiti, of murals, loud paint. The decals of curtains and cozy cats curled up on cheery sills pasted to crumbling bricked-up tenements, the urban renewal. Then onward, the Bronx, Riverdale, Spuyten Duyvil. The scramble of weedy green, the lumberyards, factories, houses that line the train tracks in the suburbs. At night, all of this would be in shadow; what he'd see would be the advertisements for *Cats,* for Big Mac attacks, for Newport cigarettes: usually of a man gleefully dumping a bucket of something over an equally gleeful woman's head. The lonely maid still in uniform waiting for the train to carry her home two towns away. A couple of emasculated teenagers without driver's licenses. A spaced-out commuter who had stumbled off at the wrong station. Hershleder knew this route by heart.

In the train car itself, there was always the risk of running into one of his neighbors, or worse yet, the aging parents of a chum from college. Better to hang out in that safe smoky toilet pondering the meaning of life, his humble existence. He was stoned for the first time in years. Drunken synapse fired awkwardly to drunken synapse. His edges were rounded, his reflexes dulled. The ghosts that lived inside him spiraled around in concentric circles. Hershleder's interior buzzed. His head hung heavy off his neck, rested in the field of daisies. A petal went up his nose; pollen dusted his mouth. He couldn't really think at all; he was full to the brim with nothing.

It was perfect.

"Laaarchmont," cried the conductor. "Laaarchmont," ruining everything.

• • •

Hershleder lit up a cigarette and coughed up a chunk of lung. Larchmont. The station. A mile and a half from Casa Hershleder, a mile and a half from Itty and the kids, a mile and a half from his home and future heart failures. His eyes roved the Park and Ride. Had he driven his car this morning or had Itty dropped him off at the train? Had he called for a cab, hitched a ride with a neighbor? Where was that beat-up Mazda? His most recent history dissolved like a photograph in water, a dream upon awakening, a computer screen when the power suddenly shuts down. It receded from his inner vision. Must have been the weed . . . It really knocked him out.

Good shit, thought Hershleder.

He decided to walk. What was a mile and a half? He was in the prime of his life. Besides, Hershleder couldn't arrive home like this, stoned, in front of his innocent children, his loving wife. A long stroll would sober him; it would be a head-clearing, emotional cup of coffee.

Larchmont. Westchester, New York. One curvy road segueing into another. A dearth of streetlights. The Tudor houses loomed like haunted mansions. They sat so large on their tiny lots, they swelled over their property lines the way a stout man's waist swells above his belt. A yuppie dog, a Dalmatian, nosed his way across a lawn and accompanied Hershleder's shuffling gait. Hershleder would have reached down to pat the dog's spotty head if he could have, but his arms were too full of daisies. He made a mental note to give in to Itty; she'd been begging him to agree to get a pup for the kids. There had been dogs when Hershleder was a child. Three of them. At different times. He had had a mother who couldn't say no to anything. He had had a mother who was completely overwhelmed. The longest a dog had lasted in their home had been about a year; Mrs. Hershleder kept giving those dogs away. Three dogs, three children. Was there some wish fulfillment involved in her casting them aside? His favorite one had been called Snoopy. His sister Mindy, that original thinker, had been the one to name her.

Hershleder remembered coming home from camp one summer to find that Snoopy was missing. His mother had sworn up and down that she had given the dog to a farm, a farm in western Pennsylvania. Much better for the dog, said Mrs. Hershleder, than being cooped up in some tiny apartment. Better for the dog, thought Hershleder now, some twenty-eight years later, better for the dog! What about me, a dogless boy cooped up in some tiny apartment! But his mother was dead, she was dead; there was no use in raging at a dead mother. Hershleder the motherless, the dogless, walked the streets of Larchmont. His buzz was beginning to wear off.

Why neurology? Mrs. Hershleder had asked. How about a little pediatrics? Gynecology? Family practice. Dovidil, don't make the same mistakes I made, a life devoted to half-lives, a life frozen in motion. But Hershleder had been drawn to the chronic ward. Paralysis, coma. He could not stand to watch a patient suffer, the kick and sweat, the scream of life battling stupidly for continuation. If he had to deal with people—and wasn't that what a doctor does, a doctor deals with people—he preferred people in a vegetative state, he preferred them noncognizant. What had attracted him in the first place had been the literature, the questions: What was death? What was life, after all? Did the answers to these lie, as Hershleder believed, not in the heart but in the brain? He liked to deal in inquiries; he didn't like to deal in statements. It was natural, then, that he'd be turned on by research. Books and libraries, the heady smell of ink on paper. He'd been the kind of boy who had always volunteered in school to run off things for the teacher. He'd stand close to the Rexograph machine, getting giddy, greedily inhaling those toxic vapors. He'd walk back slowly to his classroom, his nose buried deep in a pile of freshly printed pages.

Hershleder was not taken with the delivering of babies, the spreading of legs, the searching speculum, the bloody afterbirth like a display of raw ground meat. But the brain, the brain, that fluted, folded mushroom, that lovely, intricate web of thought and tissue and talent and dysfunction, of arteries and order. The delicate weave of neurons, that thrilling spinal cord. All that communication, all those nerves sending and receiving orders. A regular switchboard. Music for his mind.

A jogger passed him on the right, his gait strong and steady. Hershleder's Dalmatian abandoned him for the runner.

Hershleder turned down Fairweather Drive. He stepped over a discarded red tricycle. He noticed that the Fishmans had a blue Jag in their carport. The Fishman boy was his own boy's nemesis. Charlie Fishman could run faster, hit harder. No matter that Hershleder's own boy could speak in numbers—a = 1, b = 2, for example; when Hershleder arrived home at night, the kid said, "8-9 4-1-4" (translation: Hi Dad!)—the kid was practically a savant, a genius! So what, the Fishman boy could kick harder, draw blood faster in a fight. Could Charlie Fishman bring tears to his own father's eyes by saying "9 12-15-22-5 25-15-21" when Fishman's father tucked him in at night? (Even though it had taken

Hershleder five minutes and a pad and pencil to decode the obvious.) Charlie Fishman had just beaten out Hershleder's Jonathan for the lead in the second-grade play. The Fishman father was a famous nephrologist. He commuted to New Haven every morning on the highway, shooting like a star in that blue Jag out of the neighborhood, against the traffic, in the opposite direction. Hershleder admired the Jag from afar. It was a blue blue. It glowed royally against the darkness.

The jogger passed him again, on the right. The Dalmatian loped after the runner, his spotted tongue hanging from his mouth. The jogger must have circled around the long circuitous block in record time. A powerful motherfucker. Bearded. Young. Younger than Hershleder. The jogger had a ponytail. It sailed in the current of his own making. His legs were strong and bare. Ropy, tendoned. From where he stood, Hershleder admired them. Then he moved himself up the block toward his own stone Tudor.

Casa Hershleder. It was written in fake Spanish tile on the front walk, a gift from his sisters. Hershleder walked up the slate steps and hesitated on his own front porch. Sometimes it felt as if only an act of courage could get him to turn the knob and go inside. So much tumult awaited. Various children: on their marks, getting set, ready to run, to hurl themselves into his arms. Itty, in this weather all soft and steamed and plumped—dressed in an undulation of circling Indian *shmatas*—hungry for connection, attention, the conversation of a living, breathing adult. Itty, with tiny clumps of clay still lodged like bird eggs in the curly red nest of her hair. Itty, with the silt on her arms, the gray sliplike slippers on her bare feet. Itty, his wife, the potter.

By this point, the daisies were half-dead. They'd wilted in the heat. Hershleder laid them in a pile on his front shrub, then lowered himself onto a slate-step seat. If he angled his vision past the O'Keefes' mock turret, he would surely see some stars.

The steam of summer nights, the sticky breath of the trees and their exhalation of oxygen, the buzz of the mosquitoes and the cicadas, the sweaty breeze, the rubbing of his suit legs against his thighs. The moon above the O'Keefes' turret was high, high, high.

The jogger came around again. Angled right and headed up the Hershleder walk. His face was flushed with all that good, clean high-octane blood that is the result of honest American exertion. He looked young—far younger than Hershleder, but hadn't Hershleder noted this before? Must be wanting to know the time, or in need of a glass of water, a bathroom, a phone, Hershleder thought. The jogger was jogging right toward him.

In a leap of blind and indiscriminate affection the Dalmatian bounded past the runner and collided with Hershleder's head, his body, his lap. Hershleder was stunned for a second, then revived by the wet slap of the dog's tongue. He was showered with love and saliva. "Hey," said Hershleder. "Hey there, Buster. Watch it." Hershleder fended off the beast by petting him, by bowing under to all that animal emotion. The Dalmatian wagged the bottom half of his spinal column like a dissected worm would; it had a life all its own. His tail beat the air like a wire whisk. His tongue was as soft and moist as an internal organ. "Hey, Buster, down." Hershleder's arms were full of dog.

The jogger jogged right past them. He wiped his feet on Hershleder's welcome mat. He opened Hershleder's door and entered Hershleder's house. He closed Hershleder's door behind him. There was the click of the lock Hershleder had installed himself. That old bolt sliding into that old socket.

What was going on? What was going on around here?

Buster was in love. He took to Hershleder like a bitch in heat, this same fancy mutt that had abandoned him earlier for the runner. A fickle fellow, thought Hershleder. A familiar fickle fellow.

"Hey," said Hershleder. "Hey," he called out. But it was too late. The runner had already disappeared inside his house.

The night was blue. The lawns deep blue-green, the asphalt blue-black, the trees almost purple. Jaundiced yellow light, like flames on an electric menorah, glowed from the Teretskys' leaded windows. At the Coens', from the second-floor family room, a TV flickered like a weak pulse. Most of the neighborhood was dark. Dark, hot, blue, and yellow. Throbbing like a bruise.

A car backfired in the distance. Buster took off like a shot.

Hershleder sat on his front step feeling used. He was like a college girl left in the middle of a one-night stand. The dog's breath was still hot upon his face. His clothes were damp and wrinkled. The smell of faded passion clung to him. His hair—what was left of it—felt matted. He'd been discarded. Thrown over. What could he do?

Stand up, storm into the house, demand: What's the

meaning of this intrusion? Call the cops? Were Itty and the kids safe inside, locked up with that handsome, half-crazed stranger? Was it a local boy, home on vacation from college, an art student perhaps, hanging around to glean some of his wife's infinite and irresistible knowledge? The possibilities were endless. Hershleder contemplated the endless possibilities for a while.

Surely he should right himself, climb his own steps, turn his key in his lock, at least ring his own bell, as it were. Surely, Hershleder should do something to claim what was his: "If I am not for me, who will be for me? If I am not for mine, who will be for mine?" Surely, he should stop quoting, stop questioning, and get on with the messy thrill of homeownership. After all, his wife, his children, were inside.

The jogger was inside.

Hershleder told the truth when it stared him in the face. In the face! Which was almost enough but wasn't enough, right then at that exact and awful moment, to stop him, the truth wasn't, not from taking his old key out of his pocket and jamming it again and again at a lock it could not possibly ever fit. Which wasn't enough, this unyielding frustration, to stop him from ringing the bell, again and again, waking his children, disturbing his neighbors. Which wasn't enough to stop him, the confusion, the shouting that ensued, that led Itty, *his wife,* to say, "Please, sweetheart," to the jogger (Please, Sweetheart!) and usher him aside, that ponytailed, bearded athlete who was far, far younger than Hershleder had ever been.

She sat on the slate steps, Itty, her knees spread, the Indian *shmata* pulled discreetly down between them. She ran her silt-stained hands through her dusty strawberry cloud of hair. There were dark, dirty half-moons beneath her broken fingernails. She was golden eyed and frustrated and terribly pained. She was beautiful, Itty, at her best really when she was most perplexed, her expression forming and re-forming like a kaleidoscope of puzzled and passionate emotion, when she patiently and for the thousandth time explained to him, Dr. David Hershleder, M.D., that this was no longer his home, that the locks had been changed for this very reason. He had to stop coming around here, upsetting her, upsetting the children; it was time, it was time, Dave, to take a good look at himself, when all Hershleder was capable of looking at was her, was Itty, dusty, plump, and sweaty, sexy-sexy Itty, his wife, his wife, sitting with him on the stoop of his house, in his neighborhood, while his children cowered inside.

Until finally, exhausted (Hershleder had exhausted her), Itty threatened to call the police if he did not move, and it was her tiredness, her sheer collapsibility that forced Hershleder to his feet—for wasn't being tired one thing Itty went on and on about that Hershleder could finally relate to?—that pushed him to see the truth, to assess the available data and to head out alone and ashamed and apologetic to his suburban slip of a sidewalk, down the mile and a half back to the station to catch the commuter rail that would take him to the city and the medical student housing he'd wrangled out of the hospital, away from everything he'd built, everything he knew and could count on, out into everything unknown, unreliable, and yet to be invented.

2

It had not always been this way.

Maybe Itty couldn't remember, but *he* remembered, Hershleder remembered that there had been a time when they were young when even Itty had felt fortunate, and when he himself felt blessed. Thinking back on it now at the Larchmont station, on his way back to the city, while waiting out the interval between the departure of the last train and the arrival of some other, it seemed that the Hershleders' life had been sort of enviable; at least Hershleder was envious of it now. They had once had the proverbial everything: the house, the kids, their careers, their health; why, even their initial encounter had seemed fortuitous, although it had been a long time since he'd even thought about any of that—youth and romance and lust.

Why not torture himself with it all, now when it would make him the most miserable?

There was nothing else to do. He was exhausted and it was getting late. This was the suburbs. The station was empty. Even the Dunkin' Donuts was closed up for the night.

Hershleder sat on the edge of the platform and dangled his legs down into the well of the railway, flirting with a danger that wouldn't be arriving, he supposed, for at least another hour. The steam that rose from the scattered clumps of sodden litter that lined the tracks—damp with the spitty dregs of broken beer bottles and spattered arcs of teenage urine—smelled earthy and rank, recycled, like a heady whiff from Jonathan's famously untended aquarium.

• • •

It was a lauded bit of family history, the story of how he and Itty met; it was a story that Itty liked to tell. She'd been a waitress waiting tables. Hershleder had stiffed her once when he was still an aspiring yuppie slumming at some trumped-up dive down on Avenue A.

He'd been double-dating with Kahn that evening, Jodie Fish and another Debbie. Itty's service had been horrible. She'd had her period; Hershleder found this out two mornings later when he stumbled into the bathroom in her apartment punch-drunk on lack of sleep and came upon the eye-opener of a red scratch of blood cut across the cotton crotch of her flesh-toned fishnets, which were lying discarded in a knot on the cracked mess of the ancient linoleum beneath the sink where mushroomy things liked to grow. Itty had had her period—an event he learned later from years of experience could herald any amount of familial or marital turmoil, or nothing, nothing at all—and she was getting evicted from her illegal sublet. Plus, the art professor she'd been wasting the best years of her life on (this said then by her mother, and then again later, hurled by Itty at Hershleder in a fight: "My mother says I wasted my best years on Stefan, and the second best on you!") had just moved on to another wealthier, younger, and, according to the jerk himself, "more gifted and promising" conquest.

It was a rotten night, a rotten time of her life, and Itty was in no mood. She was over the hill. She and Hershleder were both twenty-eight, born eighteen hours apart on the very same birthday, April 30, the day, incidentally, that Hitler died; and she couldn't sell her art for love or money. She'd taken to rereading Sylvia Plath and listening again, at that advanced age, to Joni Mitchell; she was tired of the struggle. All of life, she told Hershleder later, when he still hung on her every word and observation, was just a series of Herculean tasks we set before ourselves in order to avoid the inevitable. Anything to occupy the mind as we wait to die.

She was a girl after his own heart.

But that night, before she was even aware of him, nor he of her in a real sense, she'd waited on him; and the food was cold, late. She'd brought out the wrong orders. Hershleder recalled a fatty slab of pork on the vegetarian plate. She was the worst waitress in the world.

Kahn had thrown a holy fit. After all, there were girls there, girls Kahn wanted to impress. He'd puffed his chest up and threatened to speak to her employer.

"Oh no," said Jodie Fish, Hershleder's date (at least in theory). "Please, Kahn, let it go, it's nothing. Just be glad you don't have to make a living that way. What a hard job. Wow. I know—I did it one summer up at camp."

She and Kahn were playing footsie under the table, right under Hershleder's nose. Years later Kahn confessed that he nailed her the following weekend, in the same damn tenement apartment that he and Hershleder shared, when Hershleder was on Renal call, but at the time Hershleder had been oblivious.

"Why forget about it?" asked Kahn's Debbie. "The bitch spilled wine on my sleeve." Debbie displayed the stain for all to see. Her blouse, a white silk, was ruined. There were even some bloody wine scabs on her knotted strand of pearls.

But Jodie Fish protested. Hershleder recalled now that she kept saying over and over again, "Maybe I'm too sensitive." It was decided by all that there would be no formal complaint lodged, but also that no tipping was in order. They paid the bill—that is, Kahn stuck Hershleder with it by pretending not to know that the restaurant did not take plastic, even though he had been eating there for the last four weeks. It was remotely Caribbean, Kahn's discovery. Froufrou drinks, free-range jerk chicken. At home, back in their tenement apartment, Kahn kept an array of little cocktail umbrellas from this place as souvenirs. Open, the umbrellas signified when Kahn had gotten lucky; so far three blossomed gaily on top of his battered dresser. He'd end up doing Debbie later, that was for sure; tonight's umbrella already sat behind his ear, frondescent, broadcasting his intentions loud and clear.

They all got up to leave.

Itty took one look at the bill and the payment left her—down to the exact change (two pennies)—and her face broke, slipping out some tears. Their check had topped out over a hundred and twenty-five dollars.

"Hey, aren't you forgetting something?" yelled a waiter friend, protectively, after peeking at the bill over Itty's shaking shoulder. But the Kahn-Hershleder party ignored him, the ladies righteous as they slipped their arms into their coats, each extended by a well-trained escort. They were nice boys. Raised well. Davids.

"Oink," said the waiter as the Kahn-Hershleder party took their exit. "Oink, oink, you pigs!" It was embarrassing. The tips of the sensitive Jodie Fish's ears turned pinky-purple. Hershleder could still hear the waiter oinking as they made their way down the sidewalk toward First Avenue.

That night, Hershleder couldn't sleep. Having to go to the bathroom was part of it. Kahn and Debbie were having sex with an Olympian intensity, and he'd have had to slip through their room to get to the toilet. Lying in his bed that way, hand to crotch, legs twisted in a knot, the sound of Kahn's thumping permeating through their border wall, Hershleder decided to not feel sorry for himself, but to feel sorry for that waitress. The guy was right, what they'd done was piggish. He was feeling ashamed of himself.

Hershleder was back at the restaurant the next evening. He came in early, caught Itty as she sailed by, platter high, out a swinging door. And cornered her. Hershleder handed her an envelope full of money, which she wouldn't take—Itty with her principles, Itty with her hands full. Daunted, Hershleder let her wait on her next table, but when he caught her on the flip side as she reapproached the kitchen, he tried again in vain to apologize, although the words simply eluded him.

"Uh, ma'am? Ma'am? Please take this, you deserve this."

He'd pressed the tip envelope into Itty's hand. In those days she wore black fingernail polish, a silver band encircling her thumb, a broken James Dean wristwatch as a bracelet.

Her lovely, nutty arm, the goldy hairs teased by the restaurant's gaily colored lighting; just that one exquisite glimpse had made Hershleder bite hard on his inner lip.

"Ma'am?" said Itty, incredulous. She balled her hand up into a fist. She didn't want Hershleder's money. "Ma'am?" said Itty. "Is my mother in the room?"

It wasn't that Itty wasn't touched, but that she was insulted, and in a hurry. She sat Hershleder at the bar and spoke to him dryly, in between orders, making the snarliest, meanest fun of him. By the end of the evening, Hershleder was smitten, and so that night he'd walked her home. It was late autumn, leaves lined the gutters, leaves that came from some far-off, mythical tree—he'd never noticed anything remotely arboreal in that area before. The streets were lively for two o'clock in the morning. They stopped at a cash machine so that Itty could deposit her earnings. "If I don't do it now," said Itty, "by tomorrow there won't be anything left to feed me."

Hershleder was entranced by this, a girl who could spend all her money in the wee small hours of the morning. Clearly, she led a more exciting life than he did. And so he was jealous, jealous of her joie de vivre, jealous of all the men who accompanied her in costly nighttime sorties. If he saw one at that moment, Hershleder could not have trusted himself; he'd have wanted to take a knife to the bastard's throat.

Itty slipped her bank card into the slot that opened the automated door. There were three other people in the ATM lobby: a punk, what looked like an NYU law student (probably on an all-nighter, out getting coffee), and a bag woman. The bag woman reclined on the wide ledge that lined the plate-glass window like an odalisque. When the punk finished his business at the one operating bank machine—the other two temporarily out of service—the bag woman loudly announced, "Next."

The law student moved obediently forward.

When the law student finished his transactions, Itty politely waited for her turn.

"Next," barked the bag woman from her perch.

On the way out, Itty gave her a dollar.

"Next," shouted the bag woman, after Hershleder, stopping him in his tracks.

He was next in line for something, he could feel it in his bones, but what?

Hershleder shivered in anticipation, digging into his pocket to pull out another bill; he wanted to ensure himself a good omen. He liked this girl. So he gave the money to the bag woman. Then he spilled out of the bank after Itty, and out of some primal need for contact or reassurance, he swept her up in his anxious arms, forcing physical contact. He hugged his unknowing wife-to-be close to him for the first time in the street.

"Poor dear," said Itty, "poor dear," sounding wise and old and sweet.

It was only on recollection, now, some ten years later, that Hershleder wondered which one of them, he or the bag lady, Itty had been referring to.

That night, Hershleder slept in Itty's bed without laying a finger on her; that's not true, he'd held her in his arms. She'd said she wasn't ready for sex—she didn't know him that well, she was exhausted, there was that genius Stefan who had just dumped her—and Hershleder told her that he understood.

Itty said, "Maybe for once, I've actually found myself a nice guy."

Was that the beginning of her undoing? Had she decided that she was old enough and worn out enough now to settle for a nice guy? Wasn't that the problem essentially, that a nice guy, at least on paper, was pretty much all he was?

At the time, back then, when mutual failure and disappointment were still unknown to them, her words sent Hershleder soaring; he'd translated them into "I like you." And then carried away by the headiness of his own simultaneous interpretation, Hershleder carried the translation further, adding his own embellishments: "If you play your cards right, David Hershleder, you might eventually see me naked." So Hershleder was careful to play it cool.

They lay butt to groin, like two links of an s-chain, his knees lined up with her knees, his mouth in the curve of her neck. He wore a borrowed T-shirt and his underwear. Itty slept in Hershleder's striped button-down; they exchanged no bodily fluids, just clothing. He had his arms around her waist, nose to hair, breathing in the essence of her cream rinse; it smelled the way leaves do when you crush them between your fingers. Once in the gray light of dawn, he'd dared to brush some of her curls away from her face. A little runoff of drool puddled on her pillow. He touched his finger to it, brought his finger to his lip, and spread it like a balm. It amazed him that what would have turned him off with any other woman, with Itty turned him on. By the time the garbage trucks rattled down her street in the dusty early morning, Hershleder was in love. Even though it took Itty three more months to catch up—there was still that Stefan to get out of her system, not to mention the one heart-searing episode when it looked like she might go back to him—they celebrated Hershleder's romantic fall by going out to breakfast. Veselka's Ukrainian Restaurant. He turned her on to the kasha and eggs of his youth.

Luck.

Where had his all gone? Hershleder leaned forward. There was no train coming, no train down the rails for miles. Instead, the night encircled the tracks, invoking a ghostly long black tunnel, a tunnel that lacked promise. His shirt stuck to his skin.

On the platform at the Larchmont station, Hershleder hugged his knees to his chest and rocked.

• • •

Later, much later, and somehow back in the city, Hershleder lay on the fold-out couch in the squalid "living space" of his tiny studio apartment, trying to find relief. He was anxious and exhausted, but there was no such thing as sleep, not for him. The night would not wane; all there was was a hot and sticky nowness, a trenchant, miserable infinity, frightening and interminate. Since Itty had thrown him out again earlier that evening, Hershleder had become increasingly incapable of doing much more than twist, in the thick, syrupy suspension of his grief.

When he was a much younger man, when Hershleder was a college student, there had been a night not unlike this one in its endlessness; it was the night that followed the day that his mother died. He had lived in a place known for cold and snow. Ice storms, howling winds, such a constant whirl of slushy precipitation that when venturing outside, Hershleder often imagined himself at the vortex of a frigid funnel cloud, surrounded by 360 degrees of intensity. That night, the worst of his life until this night, Hershleder had stayed out late, quite late, in the bars of the student ghetto that bordered the entrance to his campus; he'd been trying to drink himself to death. Alas and obviously, he was not successful; in fact, Hershleder had not even gotten drunk successfully, rather the opposite, for with every tossed-back shot he was made more steadfastly aware of who he was.

By two, the bars had closed down and Hershleder had found himself out in the snowy streets. As he remembered it now, the traffic had long since stopped; there were a few cars stranded right in the road where they'd stalled out. Hershleder's dormitory had been at the other end of the college from town, over two stone bridges that spanned two frozen gorges, with icy stalactites so mammoth and layered, they looked like giant incandescent white candles working their way against gravity, dripping right side up. Across the gorges were three sprawling academic quadrangles: Ag, Engineering, and Arts & Sciences. So much knowledge separating him from where he needed to go. Perhaps the actual distance from bar to dorm room was about two miles. Not a bad hike in the month-long season that was spring in those parts, or during the bedizened crisp ravishment of fall, but then it was solidly winter and the pathways had vanished, resolute, it seemed, like everything else in their pitiless effort to abandon him.

Hershleder recalled now that it had been snowing *that* night, and he was amazed at how in the heat of *this* night he could so easily recall that unyielding thick white torrent. The ground had been buried in huge drifts, difficult to maneuver, the snow behaving like mud, swallowing each bony Hershleder calf encased in its own faux duck boot and releasing it with a sound that sucked. The wind had pierced all his layers, and his sensitive pale skin had burned red—horripilant and raw in all the worst places, which of course made it even more awkward to move. Hershleder had had to angle his body from the waist as he shuffled his way through all that icy mess, so that he pointed forward with his bowed neck and shoulders as if his crown were a little lantern lighting the way for his legs to follow. He'd been positioned like a ski-jumper, but an amateur, one who was afraid of the increasing arc of his view, so he directed his gaze at his own belt, to keep his face out of the way of a series of hyperborean blasts.

Hershleder remembered now on *this* horrible long night how badly and inadequately drunk he'd been during *that* horrible long night, for with every swig of scotch he'd felt more achingly clear on what misery had driven him to this point.

His mother was dead, she was dead. He was a drunk and frozen young man without a living mother.

He remembered now how hard it had been to lift his boots in that deep snow, how the wind drove the snow so wet and so thick into his face that he couldn't see and that his lungs itched from all that cold air, and then how his cilia began to freeze, making it hard to breathe; how it hurt. Hershleder's eyes had squeezed shut against the wind and he had made his way blindly, and slowly, so slowly it was as if he were sensing his way emotionally through the storm rather than moving physically within its boundaries. Once in a while he'd open his eyes to try and get his bearings, but that simple act proved terrifying; the air had transmogrified into the embodiment of white noise—which frightened his eyes shut again. Tears had leaked out over Hershleder's curvy lashes and one slipped down and froze against his cheek, glassy and hard as a barnacle. The walk home was endless, and the snow was endless, and no matter how many steps Hershleder took, he never got any closer to where he wanted to go.

It was during this interminable stretch of time that it was made clear to him that there really was no such thing as progress, and that the naive theory behind the concept—that he himself had held so dear—was in and of itself erroneous.

He was twenty-one.

At the time, Hershleder thought for sure he'd freeze to death, but he didn't. Maybe he would have liked to, but he didn't. Somehow he had made his way home, and then home again, and now so many homes later to this dank, hot sofa, in this dank, hot studio apartment on yet another ceaseless night, the night that Itty threw him out, again, again, and once and for all perhaps, to face it all alone; the phrase ran through his head from an old song, but he couldn't remember which one.

Characteristically, Hershleder had trouble recalling a lot of things, like how he had managed to make it back from Larchmont, what train he'd ended up taking and so forth, how—heartbroken and mystified—he had somehow swum blindly through the damned heat, out of the moist green of suburbia into the thick, toxic chum of the city. He couldn't remember how he'd gotten from Grand Central to his apartment—did he cab it or did he walk it?—if he had stumbled over the small homeless encampment on his front stoop as per usual, if he'd taken the stairs or the elevator the several flights up to his floor; he couldn't even remember what it felt like to stick his key in a lock and have it turn open, a sensation he would have killed for a few hours ago. Hershleder had no idea when he had undressed himself down to his sweaty T-shirt and shorts, or how finally he had collapsed onto this cruddy sofa bed. No, Hershleder had traveled this night like he'd traveled that awful night long ago in Ithaca, without much room for self-reflection, alone on an interminable march, focusing solely on the image of the woman who had left him.

Now, if a tear were to slide down his cheek, it would probably sizzle. But tears didn't come in Hershleder's small bachelor apartment. A palmetto bug came instead, wedging its way through the gap between the front door and floorboard, then skittering across the room like some small armored rodent, or as Hershleder thought at the moment, a giant date with legs. It scuttled its way under the gentle buckle of the closed wooden portal into the bathroom.

Without thinking, Hershleder climbed atop the sofa the way the movies taught him a certain type of girl would, and from that vantage point he waited for the intruder to reappear. But hot air indeed rises, and after a while, tired and sweat-soaked, he gave up; the very enterprise of being fearful created too much heat. He was boiling, and the whole concept of time and waiting out a palmetto bug seemed as useless and unappealing as he felt, high on his perch, poking out into the hazy atmosphere like that, his white T-shirt soaked clear now to his body, his body covered in slime, his skin giving off a complex and deepening stink as if every pore bloomed wide open; he had ripened, he was runny.

No wonder she had thrown him out.

And thrown him out again; couldn't Hershleder take a hint? It had been months and months since Itty had last requested his presence in their home, months and months and months since she'd expressed a desire for him to return to her. As he remembered it, the last time his wife had asked to see him, he'd received an urgent call from her at work.

"Dave, it's an emergency," Itty said.

Hershleder instantly tallied the number of privates he was treating who were in jeopardy and cursed the ones who would feel free enough to disturb their reluctant physician at his home, instead of contacting him properly through his service.

"Livitsky?" Hershleder asked Itty, dreading the reply. Livitsky suffered from torticolis, a form of dystonia. Hershleder had been treating him with biofeedback; he had also been contemplating a series of experimental injections of botulism and other therapeutic molds.

"I bet it's Livitsky," said Hershleder. "Goddamn that son of a bitch."

"Hershleder," said Itty.

Hershleder was quiet. It had been years since she'd called him by his last name. He rather liked it.

"Jonathan. Jonathan Hershleder. Your goddamn fucking son," said Itty, and she slammed the phone down hard enough to crack the receiver, although Hershleder did not know this until he got home several hours later and Itty threw the same receiver right back at him, with a less-than-deadly aim, but with terrific *heart* in her throwing arm. He'd noticed the crack in the plastic as it flew through the air, missing his nose by inches.

After Itty hung up, Hershleder had sat in his office, trying to amass the courage to return the call—which he did after two long, agonizing minutes.

"Itty," he'd said. "Honey. I'm sorry. Let's try it again, okay?" He'd said this in a rush, before she could hang up again.

It appeared that Jonathan had invented a new game to play at school. During recess. While the other children were running around the schoolyard screaming at the top of their lungs, bouncing off of one another like colliding molecules, Jonathan Hershleder had pulled a classmate, Anna Levine, aside. He was going to hide, Jonathan had told Anna, a weak and compassionate girl known for her kindness to misfits. He wanted Anna to keep track of all the kids who noticed he was missing.

"A born independent pollster," said Itty.

This went on for a week. Jonathan would remove himself, Anna would tally the "Where's Jonathan's?" and "Anybody seen Jono's?" and present Jonathan with the sum total of inquiries on his behalf at the end of each play period. If the teacher herself were to ask, Anna was instructed to rout Jono Hershleder from his secret spot, which was located behind the garbage Dumpsters, and bring him into the dodgeball game or whatever other supervised childhood traumas were taking place in the schoolyard. Together, the two kids conducted this experiment for a week.

"Clearly, the numbers tallied were in the negative," said Itty.

"So did Mrs. What's-her-name ever notice he was missing?" Hershleder asked.

"No," said Itty. "It gets even more painful and pathetic. Anna Levine got tired of trying to eavesdrop on nonexistent conversations; she wanted to play with the rest of the kids, so she complained. Formally. She marched herself into the assistant principal's office and announced that she didn't want to 'baby-sit' Jonathan any longer."

There was silence on both ends of the line.

"Oh, who could blame her?" said Itty. And then, "Come home, Dave."

"Itty, I can't," Hershleder said. He took a breath and waited out her response.

Nothing.

So he went on. "I can't come home now, Itty. I have an afternoon full of patients. Besides, this isn't a real emergency," Hershleder said. "If he were injured, if he were hurt, you know I'd take the next train out." There was silence on the line. He could hear Itty breathing. Disapproving.

But if she'd only listen, she'd realize he made sense. He was a doctor; he knew from emergencies. An emergency was broken bones, a concussion, or God forbid, the prison of paralysis. Jonathan's behavior felt a bit sad, sure, but so what, his son displayed a little harmless creepiness—didn't every kid go through a pitiful loner phase? Hershleder certainly had, that was for sure. For that matter, so had all the then-losers he counted now as friends. Look at those guys today! Look at Kahn, for God's sake!

Hershleder put his head in his hands. The thought of that poor, lonely, friendless kid (his kid) hiding out behind the Dumpsters was more than he could take.

"I can't come home. Not now, at any rate. I'll try and take an earlier train. We'll discuss the whole mess with him at dinner. Make it right. You'll see, Itty. It's really no big deal." And then: "I didn't know anyone called him Jono."

"No one does," said Itty.

Come home, come home. Less than a year before, Itty Hershleder had said the words "Come home" to him, and Hershleder the scared, Hershleder the weak, had squandered them.

"Fuck you, Dave," said Itty. "When are you going to wake up and notice that you're the one who's missing?"

"I notice now," said Hershleder, aloud, sweating atop his couch, frightened by a harmless water bug, in the exile of his bachelor apartment.

"I notice now," he said, out into the empty air.

He felt like an idiot.

So Hershleder decided to do the brave thing for once and descend his perch and pull out the as-yet-unopened care package he'd received two weeks before from Kahn's mother, the hand-me-downs that were to be his bedding. Until now he had slept directly on the thin blue-ticked fold-out mattress with no covering, like a teenage boy would. Night after night he'd wrapped himself in a dirty sleeping bag, one that he'd purposefully neglect to re-roll come morning. It had seemed to him then that just the act of making the bed would be a symbol of giving in, giving up, that it would seal his fate, make his exile permanent; but magical thinking, like all his other lame attempts at bettering his situation, was proving itself useless. Now he needed only to save himself.

Mrs. Kahn's linens were clean and ironed, of course, though musty, folded neatly between sheets of thin brown paper. Hershleder fanned them forward and up over the sloping tablet of his sofa bed, and when they billowed down, he bent over to form as tight a hospital-corner as he could with a mattress that had warped and curled at its edges. It was nice for him, this having something to do, a task at hand here, and coupled with the wary eye he kept out for the palmetto bug—who, appearing to be the smarter of the two, was luxuriating around a dripping faucet in the bathroom—this occupation kept him somewhat apart from his suffering. For a while.

Hershleder entombed himself in Kahn's mother's cousin Emma's old guest sheets, soft and aged and yellowed like paper; he pulled high Kahn's very own vintage camp blanket—the fibers like spun gray and blue steel, hairy filaments, an ancient horsecloth that even had David Kahn's name tag still sewn sturdily in at a corner; and when his body was supine and protectively covered (under the sheets he was naked except for boxers), Hershleder allowed himself to focus. It was still hot, even at this late hour, really hot out, so inside his apartment it was worse. Hershleder wasn't the type to resort to air-conditioning. His own parents, Irv and Adela Hershleder, had believed only in the simplicity of fans. He himself didn't cotton to humidifiers either, for that matter; they and the a.c. were just high-priced petri dishes, a couple of viral incubators. So he baked in that hot place under the yellow sheet and the scratchy blue blanket he did not need nor want, but still pulled higher under his chin in an effort to comfort himself.

Why on earth did he keep bothering to go home? What could he possibly be thinking? It was as if with each ill-timed and unstrategic strike, Hershleder actually believed that Itty just might forget all that had transpired between them.

Was he nuts?

Was Hershleder so deluded as to think that if he pretended everything was okay—if in the privacy of his own mind he assured himself that they were back on track, that the separation was just a little blip, a typical marital episode, a figment of *his* imagination—then everyone else's reality (Itty's, for example) would subsequently be realtered to fit his own? Did he really believe that out of some surreal force of habit, Itty might willingly continue on with him in that same half-baked manner as before?

Yes, yes, and sadly yes again.

Hershleder wasn't sure of his diagnosis, although he felt certain that he was committable. Still, wasn't there something about the doggedness of his devotion that could be found endearing? he wondered now with hope. Sure, he'd sleptwalked through much of their marriage—Itty had made him recognize that much by taking the phrase and pounding him over the head with it—but kindly, Itty, he'd slept-walked kindly, so couldn't she be big enough now to return the favor and do a little sleep-walking of her own? Itty, Itty, there was no brutality to his indifference, just a myopic self-preoccupation; he was a scientist after all. He was supposed to be this way. So what, she felt "overlooked," "untouched," "ignored." They were married. That's what happens to married couples. Every relationship has its bumps.

It had felt unfair, really, at the end of a long day back in February to hear her say that what they had together just wasn't enough for her any longer.

It was enough for him.

Itty had felt (at least this is what she had expressed then) that there was more "out there"—here Itty had gestured with her freckled hand, outward and upward as if she were referring to heaven, or some vast ranch in Big Sky country—than what they had together at home.

Ironically, what was far too much, a cornucopia of tangled-up emotion and attachment, for Hershleder was for Itty a sentimental anorexia.

He'd tried to brush it off when she'd first approached him. He'd been tired. He'd had a long hard week at the hospital.

"Itty, I hear you, I really hear what you're saying, but we're both exhausted, strung out. . . ." Hershleder went on a little. "All we need is a vacation, a trip for two without the kids, Mexico or the Caribbean." He'd been thumbing through the Travel section of last week's Sunday *Times* as they talked. It was splayed out on the coffee table, photos of couples in bathing suits, splashing in the ocean, sunbathing on the sand, locked in a series of erotic embraces. Had Itty left these images out to torment him or were they to function as a less-than-subtle hint as to how to win her over?

He chose to focus on the latter.

"We'll go away, babe. Club Med or San Francisco. The wine country. Maybe the Yucatán?"

He continued thumbing through the paper, hunting for bargains, packages, low fares.

"I'm not sure I still love you, Dave," Itty said. Hershleder turned the page.

Hershleder turned the page on his wife. He thought, Don't *honor* this. It's either hormonally induced hysteria or a figment of your own imagination. Divert her. This, too, will pass.

"Once," Itty said. "I must have loved you once." She said this kind of quizzically, as if she was trying to reassure herself. She wouldn't have married him or had kids with him if she hadn't loved him, that's not the kind of woman that she was, *Dave.* But her voice faltered here, for even that well-documented attachment that led to the birth of their two children was too long-lost an emotion for her then to conjure up.

She began to cry, heartbroken and heartless, until no one alive could stand the sound of her crying any longer; and then, mercifully, she choked. She coughed and sputtered a little. Hershleder resisted the impulse to pound her between the blades. Finally, she caught her breath. She said, "Oh God, why is my life so stupid?"

Then his Itty took her face and hid it behind her hands.

"A vacation, you need a rest, I need a rest, Mexico," Hershleder repeated himself. His eyes frantically scanned the colored advertisements. It would have hurt too much to look at her, Itty all pink and wet and blotchy, pummeled and wounded from all that suffering. If he allowed his gaze to fall upon her, he might feel compelled to touch her, and Hershleder was afraid she might move away.

Hershleder touched the *Times* instead, rustling a sheet of newsprint. The page was thin and gray and smudged inky beneath his hands.

"You're not listening, Dave," said Itty. She was shaking. "Even now, I can't fucking believe it," but of course he was listening, he was listening until his ears bled, she didn't love him, she didn't love him, what was left for him to hear?

Between her tremors and her tears, it leaked out. She had met someone. A guy. A guy who made her feel good about herself. Another artist. Someone who cared for the things she cared for. A man who made her feel smart. Who made her feel sexy.

Sexy.

What had Hershleder made her feel?

"What had her husband made her feel, Kahnny?" Hershleder had asked his friend several nights after the dreadful incident, over a fifth of bourbon.

"You?" Kahn said. "You made her feel like chopped liver, Hersh. You made her feel like nothing."

Now, lying alone in his scratchy bed, amidst the squalor of

his pathetic bachelor apartment, during the hottest, longest, most putrid night on record, there was no more use in denying what everyone else he knew had long ago accepted as given truth. His wife, his Itty, had fallen in love with another man.

In his heart of hearts, Hershleder couldn't blame her.

3

THE NEXT MORNING, IN DAYLIGHT, THINGS SEEMED SOMEwhat less horrible; certainly the surrounding atmosphere itself felt balmier. Hershleder's bedclothes were a twisted tangle kicked to the floor. Somehow he'd fallen asleep, and now he lay grateful and naked across the bottom sheet—what had happened to his boxers? Who cared? A breeze was actually playing across his moist, spent body, and his mind felt vaguely clear. It was time—*it was time, Dave*—to take a good look at himself, but what if all he saw were things he didn't like?

His apartment gave every indication that a tornado had hit it in the middle of the night: Clothing, bedding, a few half-eaten bags of chips, were lying in gnarled heaps along the floor like felled trees and prostrate bodies. A pair of khakis lay inside out and crumpled like the torn-off bumper of a smashed-up car. Hershleder leaned over and balled up a pair of socks.

He could live without her. He'd lived without her before he'd met her, after all. He'd been living fine without her the past six months.

He got up. First things first, a shower and a cup of coffee. A brief attempt at straightening up, and then a frightening glance into the bathroom mirror. Who was that balding, gray-skinned man?

What followed was remedial and vaguely homeopathic: a shave and powder, the sticky, cool application of his roll-on. Pants, shirt, socks, shoes. Everything was going smoothly until that queer, lone moment when, at midpoint, tying his tie, he suddenly felt like calling out for help.

"Help," said David Hershleder, M.D., softly, like a little escape of breath.

But there was no one there to rescue him.

He went to the phone and picked up the receiver. Since he couldn't call Itty, his father was remote and his mother was dead, and both his sisters were useless to him, he called Kahn. At six-thirty A.M., David Hershleder called David Kahn, his best friend in the world, and he whispered, "Help. I need help, Kahnny."

"You're not kidding," Kahn said. Then he ordered up a dial car to meet his pal for breakfast: "What the hell, you're on my way downtown."

• • •

They met at a coffee shop, Three Cousins or Three Brothers. A nice bright neon light. Faux-marble countertops. A series of vivisected cakes on pedestals, protected by translucent bowlers molded from scarred Plexiglas. Cut cantaloupes were displayed open-faced in the refrigerated case, like an array of tissue samplings. Kahn ordered steak and eggs. Hershleder a toasted bran muffin, which he picked at, pulling the stuffing aside, leaving the tumorous hard little dome of the crust to play with. He had just finished confessing to Kahn the various humiliations of the previous night.

Kahn said, "Next thing you know, she's going to want an order of protection."

Hershleder hung his head. "I want," he said, "I want, I want . . ."

"Everyone knows what you want," Kahn said. "What matters now is what she wants."

Hershleder looked at Kahn and suddenly his eyes filled up, which mortified him, so he looked quickly at the table. A fat tear splattered onto his place mat.

"You're gonna win her over, I know it, Hersh," said Kahn, sounding uncomfortable and unconvincing. "As soon as she tires of that boy-toy, she'll be running back to you."

He leaned forward, too close, and at once both invaded Hershleder's personal space and knocked over the saltshaker. The crystals spilled out; the shaker rolled across the table, where Kahn caught it before it toppled and hit the floor.

"The thing is, she's got to think it's her own idea. You know, sucking your cock. Reconciliation."

Kahn drew out those last key words. Then he pinched up some of the wasted salt and threw it over his left shoulder.

"You know what I'm saying," Kahn said. "She's got to *want* you. Period."

He piled the rest of the salt into a little pyramid, using the eggy edge of his fork to shape the form. Then he sat back in his seat, cuff links gleaming.

He's a proud little Buddha, Hershleder thought. Proud and ugly. Clearly, he enjoyed giving Hershleder relationship advice after so many years of vice versa.

Hershleder ran his thumb across the blade of his butter knife. He wanted to stab his best friend in the leg.

"Let's change the subject," said Hershleder.

"Fine by me," Kahn said. "You start."

Hershleder was quiet. There was nothing else on his mind.

"So did you end up reading that article about Josephson?" Kahn asked him.

"Yeah," said Hershleder. "I've got to admit, I kind of found it interesting."

"Really?" Kahn said. "I only told you about it so that we could make fun of it."

"My mother," said Hershleder, by way of explanation.

Kahn sighed. "Your mother." He put his hand to the top of his head, pressed down to the right of his crown, and stretched his neck. There was the sound of a small crack and a subsequent little pop. "Personally, I don't know why the *Times* bothers to aggrandize any of that shit. Do you want to go with me Friday night to see the Yanks–Red Sox?"

"No," said Hershleder.

"Why not?" said Kahn. "You have nothing else to do." He stretched his neck in the other direction.

"You keep doing that and you'll end up a quadriplegic," said Hershleder. He grabbed the check, stood up, brushed the muffin crumbs off his legs. He pulled his jacket from the back of his chair and put it on. It was cold in there. Central air.

"Paralyzed? From cracking my neck? Who are you, my great-aunt Sadie?" Kahn said.

"Yes," said Hershleder. "Yes, I am. I am your great-aunt Sadie. I'm also a board-certified neurologist, and as I've told you before, you can cause permanent nerve damage to yourself that way."

"I'm scared," Kahn said.

Hershleder shook his head and turned away. He was aiming for the cashier.

"No more stalking, pal," Kahn called out loudly after him, but Hershleder continued walking.

• • •

Hershleder headed for the medical school library. It was early, too early to arrive at his office, but already steam was rising up off the sidewalks in waves and hitting him in the chest, making it hard to breathe. He took his jacket off and swung it from his shoulder. Even at this hour the day felt long. But it was the first day of the rest of his life, his life without Itty and the kids. He should do something constructive to keep from throwing his body in front of the nearest subway train.

Hershleder passed through the revolving library doors, each partial revolution lessening the oppressive heat by a series of degrees. Inside the building was blasty cold. He nodded at the security guard, still sleeping on his feet. He flashed his ID at the elderly librarian working the checkout desk, the one with the yellow teeth. There were a couple of disheveled residents passed out at a couple of tables, probably up all night studying for their boards, but basically the library was quiet and deserted, the way he liked it.

Hershleder sat down at his favorite computer terminal, slung his now-crumpled jacket over the back of his chair, and logged on. He needed to conduct searches on several subjects: Prader-Willi disease, a compulsive-eating disorder of which he knew almost nothing, and the *New England Journal of Medicine*'s newest article on dystonia. He typed in his requests. The Nexus search found the dystonia paper and listed about fifty sources for the Prader-Willi information. Hershleder highlighted fifteen of the most promising articles and entered them. In just moments, his printer started printing, veils of snowy white computer paper now properly embossed, unfolding down to the dusty floor. The screen came up empty except for a prompt with a question mark.

Next?

What else did he want to know?

Did the Harvard newsletter publish articles on how to win back a wife?

It was all Hershleder could do to keep himself from running to the nearest pay phone, calling her and groveling. But Kahn was right, better to sit on his hands, give Itty time.

So, instead, he typed in *LeClerc, Jacques.* After a thoughtful moment, in parentheses, *Josephson, David,* and pressed Return.

That will show her, Hershleder thought. I am capable of thinking about something else.

There were six entries authored by LeClerc, five in French, magazine articles, Hershleder deciphered, printed in what appeared to be various revisionist reviews. There was a citing of the *New York Times* article that he was familiar with, and another essay in *Tikkun.* Lastly, an entry for the one-thousand-some-odd-page book itself appeared at the end of the list. Hershleder copied down the book information on a scrap of paper he found in a nearby wastebasket and called the *Tikkun* article up on the screen.

There wasn't a lot more information in this piece than had been given in the *Times,* just a bit of background on the revisionist movement and the American Jewish community's response to LeClerc's study—largely positive—information Hershleder was sure would have fascinated his mother, but which he himself only summarily glanced over. What piqued his curiosity was a short riff on LeClerc's personal journey, LeClerc emerging as a man who had embraced one way of thinking *in extremis* and then, after facing up to a swell of mounting evidence, had found the courage to alter his position and turn himself around. In fact, he'd entirely changed his course, no matter what the probable human cost, which Hershleder assumed was high: friends, colleagues, perhaps an equally rabid wife. How unusual. From where Hershleder stood, middle-aged men, especially middle-aged men who believed blindly, didn't often bother reassessing the ideologic cornerstones of their lives.

Maybe there was something to glean there, Hershleder wondered abstractly. LeClerc had taken a good hard look at himself and in due course he'd learned to accept the truth. In some strange way, wasn't that what his own wife had been begging him to do? LeClerc's study sounded like an exemplary example of self-examination.

A high, resonant beep permeated his thoughts. Hershleder's printer had run out of ink. While he was waiting for the librarian to go into the back storeroom and rustle up a cartridge, he filled out an extra call slip. When she returned,

Hershleder politely requested that if and when she located a copy of LeClerc's limited edition, that she please give him a buzz, scrawling his extension down on a little yellow Post-it, as if the practiced librarian hadn't long ago learned his number by heart.

• • •

Several weeks later, on a Thursday afternoon, while Hershleder was doing his thing—running the EEG lab, actively not calling Itty, burying himself in his work—the phone rang. As always, he hoped that it was Itty, willing to talk, but the voice on the other end of the receiver belonged to one of the attendings, asking him for a consult on a patient. A patient. It was two o'clock, Inge's lunch hour, an inviolate stretch of time, which sent Hershleder into a panic. He hated examining patients by himself. He needed Inge by his side. What to do? Call her in and then listen to her threaten "to no-tee-fie de yoo-nion"? Or be a mensch and attend to the patient all by himself?

When he was a boy, Hershleder's life was frequently intruded upon by patients. His father had seemingly forever been on call. The phone would ring, his father would sigh loudly, make a motion toward making a motion to move toward it, but it was always his mother who picked up the receiver. It was as if Dr. Hershleder had feared an allergic reaction, phone-to-ear = anaphylactic shock. "Hello?" said Mrs. Hershleder, reverent, quiet, as was her way. Then, usually, his mother gave into a sympathetic nod, as if unaware of the fact that the suffering human being on the other end of the line was an obstacle to her marriage. Hand over mouthpiece, in a respectful stage whisper, Mrs. Hershleder would disturb her husband: "Irv, it's a patient."

Time would stand still then, be it dinner, a game of Monopoly, a family conversation. Parent-Teacher Night. The school play. Induction to Arista at the Bronx High School of Science. Patients come first, Dovidil. And in his mind, his six-year-old, ten-year-old, sixteen-year-old, thirty-nine-year-old mind, Hershleder pictured a fat, brown little godhead on the other end of the line. A Patient. A patient person, waiting patiently for one Hershleder or another to forsake himself and save the patient's life. Now Hershleder was blessed with a whole bevy of his own, an entourage big enough to satisfy the Dalai Lama. A ward full. When one bothered to reach out and touch Hershleder at home, when it had been Itty who passed her clay-creased palm over the receiver or Cynthia or Jonathan (16-1-20-9-5-14-20), Hershleder would still picture a plump, half-naked little person in the lotus position, willing to wait, to bide his time.

Inge was needed; he couldn't face the next twenty minutes on his own. Hershleder left his office, moved swiftly down the pale green, fluorescently lit hall. There were dust piles in the corners. Like tiny tumbleweeds, hair balls wafted across the linoleum. Hershleder sidestepped a few dime-sized dollops of blood—fresh, wet, shiny—and a urine puddle. The passageway smelled like a pet store. Hershleder wondered vaguely if all this bodily fluid had sprung from the same source, and he wondered about the why of it. For all he knew, the organism that produced this specific mess was some Chihuahua smuggled in to comfort a mangled child. Hershleder opened the door to the room where Inge usually indulged in her Chinese takeout. It was a storage space for old computers and expensive medical equipment that no one really knew how to make much use of, fully equipped with a sink and a half-fridge stocked with ancient specimens, nail polish, and a bottle of Finlandia.

Behind this closed door Inge and her lunch date Louie were on a spare examination table, naked, a tangle of braided muscle. He in her mouth, she in his, white lab coats draping the scale, the sink, shrouding the storage room like sheets on furniture in a house about to be painted. Lengthwise, Inge was twice his size, but Louie made up for it latitudinally—her boyfriend's shoulders went on for miles. They moved, up and down with his head, his whole body and soul, into what he was into with Inge. Louie loved her.

What's not to love? Hershleder thought when he happened upon this scene. They could easily be sold to the erotic screen: *Inge Does Bellevue; Hot, Wet, and Brainy; The Rocket Scientist and His Seven-Inch Projectile.* Louie's penis was so purple it looked like it might shoot off his body, like a bottle rocket (Hershleder's hands involuntarily rose to ward it off), and Inge's breasts were as circular and yolked as bull's-eyes.

Hershleder closed the door quietly behind him before the lovers noticed him. It was not his intention to catch them in the act, although he'd be lying to himself if he didn't confess to having imagined that same erotic scene many times before.

Because he'd now witnessed a reality that did not pale when juxtaposed with Hershleder's most active and inventive imagination, all he felt was lonely. Sex like that, in a hospital no less, during business hours, sex because there has to be sex, a coupling that cannot be confounded, was so far outside of Hershleder's own experience, it made him feel weak and noodly. Very much alone.

He walked rapidly away from the closed storage-room door, trying to catch his breath.

Alone, alone, one could go on: the studio he rented from the hospital, the meals in the cafeteria, in the coffee shop on Twenty-eighth Street, the Sunday-morning trek down to Veselka's Ukrainian Restaurant. Hershleder was bored by his loneliness; as equations go, there was no mystery to it, $1 \times 1 = 1$, except for every second weekend when he'd have Jonathan and Cynthia in sleeping bags on the studio's gray carpet, with popcorn in the microwave and old *I Love Lucy*s in the VCR. His funny-looking, befuddled, depressed children, over at Hershleder's for what would probably turn into a twelve-year bimonthly slumber party.

Aside from his rights of visitation, his nights and weekends were free, they were free! for Hershleder to do with as he wished—although he had no idea what that was—a little freedom was what he had long longed for. ("When you get what you want, that's when you run into trouble"—Mrs. Hershleder, on Hershleder's election to the presidency of Arista at the Bronx High School of Science.) Let Inge and Louie set all the acrobatic records, let Kahn court favor with the newest round of venereal diseases, let Itty and that bestubbled ponytailed tadpole of a man do their best to break his heart. Hershleder had work to do. Wasn't it Freud, himself a Jew, who divined the mathematical ingredients to human happiness as a combination of love and work? And wasn't it Kahn who said, when posed with this very same theory by Hershleder one early Saturday morning over a bottle of scotch, "You might as well do something with your time; we'll all pretty much be dead soon"? With minds like these on his side, Hershleder did what he could do. He kept on working to keep from drowning.

In the next room, there was the patient an attendant had asked him to observe. A child. Children had no business being sick. Tumors snaking up a strand of tiny vertebrae, choking off the escalation of a spine. Kids with meningitis, cerebral hemorrhages, brain-injured from falling off their bikes. You couldn't blame them for eating too much fat, for driving drunk into a wall, for diving headfirst into a swimming pool without water. You could blame their parents for the latter, but the kids still broke your heart. Hershleder needed her. Inge. He could not face the child alone. There was an Amazonian motherliness to this woman. For example, she could hold the little girl's hand, which Hershleder decidedly could not.

Sex or no sex, fucking or no fucking, romance and all that enviable stuff be damned, Hershleder, freshly awash with sweat, resorted to the hospital intercom. He went to the front desk and had her paged.

"Inge Miel, please report to examination room 801."

It was the easiest way out, so he took it.

Back in his office, Hershleder poured himself another cup of instant coffee. He examined his hairline in the reflection of the glass that protected an ancient poster of the earth—he'd had it since boyhood—with the caption "Love Your Mother." The timing here was of the utmost importance. He counted backward from ten. At one, Hershleder started over again. He called his own phone number back in Larchmont and hung up when he got the answering machine. He imagined the zippers zipping, shirttails tucked, Velcro pressed into its place. The knotting of a faux-paisley tie that was really a pattern of animals fornicating. Hershleder dressed Inge and Louie in his mind. There was time for a peck on the cheek, even a bite of sesame noodles. When the imaginary sip of Diet Coke was sipped, when Inge was examining her teeth in a compact for stray bits of scallion, only then did Hershleder emerge from his office into the hall. He bustled down the corridor, past a group of anxious interns (one young lady practically saluting him) and into the examining room.

When he arrived, Inge was already there applying lubrication for the electrodes to the child's head, just as he had hoped.

The little girl giggled: "It's icky," she said. Her hair was plastered to her skull. The goop was cool and sticky; it went on like liquid Jell-O.

Inge's expression was smooth. One sculptured, ringless hand slipped under the little girl's arm and poked her. The little girl laughed out loud. "She tickled me," she said to no one in particular.

In the corner of the room sat a young woman, a bit too young to be the child's mother. Except what was too young these days, and in a city hospital? The young woman had big hair. Brown hair, sprayed and teased into wings. She had a dark mole beneath her pink lips on the left-hand side of her face. It looked like the period that marks a dotted quarter in musical notation.

"Shush, be good, Mommy," the older girl said to the little girl patient. The little girl patient stuck her tongue out, and Ms. Big Hair chewed her gum.

Hershleder read the chart. Inge applied the electrodes, laid the child down. There was solemnity in the act and the girl's eyes went deep and wide. Brown. Her skin the color milk chocolate should prove to be: creamy, dusty white. Inge leaned over and whispered something to the kid, to reassure her. Thank God for Inge. Her white-blond hair was twisted in a knot. At the base of her neck, three beads of sweat glittered hard like diamonds. Aside from those telltale jewels, Inge looked like any other six-foot-tall, gorgeous lab technician: a bit ruffled from a hard day's work, but nothing to note the volcanic emissions of love and God knows what else that had occurred on the planet of her body just minutes before. Nothing but a slight rise in color blushing across the high rise of her cheekbones, the pinky-rose of a postcard sunset.

The little girl lay still. Inge operated the EEG machine. Evoked Potentials. Lights on, lights off, at first a little twitch, that's all, maybe something, maybe nothing. Then Hershleder went after it, casting out, ready to reel that maybe-something, maybe-nothing in. The diagnosis. A goal worth attaining, something to spur him on. He fed a flashlight into the little girl's eyes.

Off and on; the seizures began. First a little burble, then an interior bubble, the bubbling agitating into a series of random pops. An escape of saliva glistened like a *filo de aglio* against her chin, as frail and shiny as a bit of spiderwebbing.

The child began to vibrate.

As he'd been trained, Dr. Hershleder flashed his light.

She twitched. A tiny jump resonated out from her center like a swift blow to the belly. She twitched again, her arms and legs now livelier and spasmodic. She was responding directly to the bright and dark, the flickering of the light. The faster the flash, the more the girl bounced. Off and on, twitch and jump, the EEG tracing out needles and spikes. The reading was beginning to look like a stock market chart.

The child was sweating. It was tough work, seizing. Drool was running down her neck. It puddled into a dark stain on the crew of her hospital gown.

Ms. Big Hair stood up. Took two steps toward stopping him. Hovered near the examination table for a second, weaved forward and back anxiously as if she were drunk. When Inge waved her off—"Please let the doctor do his work," she said—the older girl went back to her corner and sat down again, like a boxer after the bell signals the end of a round.

As if a prolonged bolt of electricity were threading through her body, Hershleder's patient jitterbugged on her back across the examination table.

While the situation was now clear to him, Hershleder was unable to stop the examination and console the child; that is, he was thinking he should stop, knowing he should stop, he kept saying "Stop it! Stop it!" in his head over and over again, as he continued flashing that light off and on, mesmerized, horrified, watching the child jerk.

How many moments like this had passed? One? Two? That's all, and no more. But they were moments that stretched into intervals of frozen time. Finally it was Inge, with the big strong arms and the human heart, Inge, whom he had planted there just for this purpose, who rescued him.

"Basta pasta, Doc?" said Inge.

Hershleder mumbled, "Basta," in response. Relieved and trembly, he turned the flashlight off.

The young woman was instantly at the child's side.

"You okay, honey?" Ms. Big Hair asked. She petted the kid's head between the electrodes with one fingertip, but the child did not respond, doe-eyed and hollow, worn out, she was empty of anger or fear.

Hershleder exited the examining room.

Myoclonic seizures. Flashing lights. One could say she was allergic to them. It didn't exactly take a genius to figure that out.

• • •

Back in his office, Hershleder phoned the attending to confirm the original diagnosis, then put his head between his knees. He hated himself.

The phone rang. The review board? How fast could word travel? He deserved scorn and retribution. He deserved to have his license revoked. Why did he have to work with patients? Books and papers, the safety of charts and graphs—why not confine him to something he was good at? He reached up, pulled the receiver down to where he was hiding between his knees.

"Hello? Hello?" Hershleder was ready for punishment.

It was the medical school librarian. The blood rushed to Hershleder's head. He had forgotten what his original inquiry had pertained to.

The librarian was almost giddy. She had gone on quite a wild-goose chase—that's what she said, "quite a wild-goose chase"—there were only three hundred copies of LeClerc's book in this country, but she said, with a little laugh, she'd do anything for Hershleder, he was such a good customer. Sure, it could be ordered and bought, but shipping alone could take four weeks. However, they had two copies on reserve at the library of the YIVO Institute for Jewish Studies and she gave him the address, which Hershleder promptly wrote down and placed inside the pocket of his suit pants. He thanked her, hung up, and immediately checked his calendar. There was nothing scheduled that afternoon to keep him from running away from the hospital and heading out to the familiar refuge of a library. The last thing he wanted right then was to sit around his office thinking about how he'd managed to frighten a poor, sick kid.

• • •

Hershleder spent the rest of that afternoon and evening in the library of the YIVO Institute and then, like a bewildered young man smitten with an unattractive and uninteresting woman, he somehow found himself returning. He was drawn back to those fine onionskin pages—the drawings etched in blue, like thin veins on the back of a papery old hand—for reasons that seemed inexplicable to him. First he returned the following day, and then the following week, when he spent some of his lunch hours plus a few stolen-away afternoons and one entire Sunday studying all the 1,032 pages of LeClerc's magnum opus. Hershleder had no real experience in reading architectural drawings, so this new language alone provided a challenge—that is, it gave him something to do—and soon he found himself in the Mid-Manhattan Library checking out some elementary texts. Once he learned how to read the plans, albeit in a primitive way, Hershleder realized that a lot of the science in the project had eluded him. It was back to the medical school library, to physics, and his beloved chemistry. Because the effort to find his way *into* the work alone required work, the whole project initially proved diverting, research being the one thing left in his life that he was any good at.

After the first few weeks of this particular endeavor, Hershleder finally had to stop and ask himself: Why? Why this attraction to such dull and obvious material? The inquiry itself seemed rather useless. Not especially a thing of inspiration. While the actual study, with its neurotic attention to minutiae, to detail, was somewhat of a methodological work of genius, it only served to prove what he had already accepted as given truth: that the Nazis committed mass cremations of human beings in the camps, and that these cremations were conducted in buildings designed solely for this purpose. Gruesome, sure, but not something a thinking person could dispute. *There was nothing new here.*

What was it, then, that he found so riveting? It was certainly intriguing to think about why such a meticulous mind would become so passionate about this garbage to begin with. LeClerc didn't appear to be your average, racist kook. And LeClerc *had* to have felt passionately about this material, as his investment here was obvious, but even after all his reading, Hershleder was still clueless as to why revisionism had captivated LeClerc in the first place. LeClerc's personal experience remained elusive, try as Hershleder might to wring it from the page.

Perhaps, thought Hershleder, if it wasn't the data itself, then it was the process of collecting said data that turned LeClerc around. Certainly, it had always worked this way for him; the day-in, day-out immersion in a subject was what allowed Hershleder to really understand it. This had been true with the death studies. And dystonia. More recently brain birth. Hershleder needed to be married to his subject, to give himself completely over, become obsessed with the material before anything about it much made sense to him. There was a similarity in their methodologies, both men possessing a profound need to spell things out.

Hershleder decided to contact Josephson. Guys like LeClerc, steeped in controversy, guys with enemies, former Fascists—even in the clear light of day, guys like that hid out. He would want an introduction if he cared to go that far, but perhaps in the meanwhile Josephson could answer some of his more basic questions for him. There were the White Pages if Josephson were living in New York, which he wasn't. The author's bio read that "David Josephson divides his time between the

West Coast and Europe," which didn't exactly trace a path to his door.

Hershleder could write to Josephson's publisher, and he did this a bit reflexively; a polite, informal note from a renowned physician (Hershleder used hospital letterhead) in search of a long-lost chum. When that failed—the publisher wrote back in a loose European scrawl on plain, unlined bond paper that the translator requested he remain the literary equivalent of unlisted—Hershleder, a Cornellian himself, contacted the Dartmouth alumni association, requesting an updated registry in the name of David Kahn. Their long-lost *mutual* friend Jodie Fish had been in the Dartmouth Class of '79. He'd tell Kahn that now that he was sort of single, he was thinking about looking her up.

Meanwhile, he was still actively not calling Itty, not writing her letters, not sending her flowers, not throwing himself in an anxious, hungry heap at her feet. Instead, he was praying that she missed him. Every evening at the same time, either from his office, the cafeteria, or the coffee shop on the corner, Hershleder steeled himself and made his prearranged if awkward phone call to the children, hoping to hear Itty's voice. Every evening it was Jonathan's high, thin squeak that greeted him: "8-5-12-12-15, Daddy, hello."

What would a stranger think if they should happen to call? That something was clearly wrong with the boy? That Itty fed him helium?

About twice a week, Kahn would drag Hershleder out of the apartment for a couple of hours, usually to drink, one awful memorable evening he took him to a porn show. After that Hershleder tried his best to avoid the guy.

But after work one day—at the elevator bank in the Bellevue lobby, where the main corridor branched off into several subsidiary hallways, one of which could take a person through half a mile of subterranean twists and turns and land him at the medical school library—the stealthy Kahn was waiting for him.

It had been a week or two since he'd returned Kahn's calls.

"C'mon," Kahn said, collaring Hershleder from behind as soon as he tripped off the elevator. "Don't you think it's about time you bought your best pal a drink?"

It was a lonely, bleak existence for both of them, so Hershleder acquiesced, out of a sense of loyalty and inertia.

Another powwow followed at the former Southwestern roadstop. After a plate of fried calamari and a couple of rounds of beer, Kahn regaled him with a very graphic report of his latest sexual exploit. Something to do with clamps and ropes. Embarrassingly enough, this went on for about half an hour. When he finally ran out of steam, Kahn asked Hershleder about *his* sex life; that is, Kahn said, "Are you still dating your own left hand?"

Of course, Hershleder had nothing to say. Which caused the victorious Kahn to smirk. Finally, he was getting plenty, and Hershleder was getting nothing.

"Us single guys do better," Kahn said. "You'll see when you loosen up."

"I'm loosening," said Hershleder.

The Kahn-man rolled his eyes.

"I am," said Hershleder, grasping at straws. "In fact, I need your help. I requested the next edition of the Dartmouth alumni magazine in your name, so please don't throw it out."

"Why?" said Kahn.

"Remember Jodie Fish?" said Hershleder. "I wanted to look her up."

Kahn stared at him faux-blankly.

"Give me a break, Kahnny. You must remember her—thick thighs, leg warmers on the outside of her jeans?"

There was a flicker of recognition in Kahn's eyes, but he tried to hide it.

Hershleder continued wearily. "I went to camp with her. We double-dated in the eighties. You stole her out from under me."

"Literally," Kahn said, lighting up with a grin. Finally Hershleder had hit on a memory he liked.

"Well, wasn't she the Class of '79?"

"So?"

"So I was thinking about asking her out."

Kahn wasn't stupid. "You date? Forget about it. Jodie Fish? Come on."

"Do you think she ever got married?"

"The Fish? Nah. The last time I saw her she was totally desperado." And then he thought for a moment. "I amend that," Kahn said. "The best she could have hoped for was to live with some loser who won't commit. You can't possibly be serious."

So Hershleder came clean.

"Actually," he said, "I'm looking for David Josephson."

"I hate this place," Kahn said, trying to flag a waiter down. He didn't understand why Hershleder wanted to speak to the guy again. They were friends, hardly. Josephson was just another roadside attraction on Hershleder's tour of Dartmouth—an eccentric egghead starving himself to death amidst a feast of books; more startling, a twenty-two-year-old virgin; finally, a specimen smarter than Kahn was. All of it shocking, especially at the time when they were young, but who cared about any of that now?

"It's not Josephson I'm interested in, per se," said Hershleder. "It's his collaborator."

"Huh?" said Kahn.

"There's something about this guy, I don't know, Kahnny," Hershleder said. "He interests me. He goes on this wild, elaborate journey for pretty much no reason and still he manages to face up to the truth, to change. I mean, you'd think a guy like that, nothing could turn a guy like that around."

Kahn looked at him skeptically.

"He's a Nazi, Hersh."

"No, he's not," said Hershleder. "That's the point. He once was a Nazi—well, not exactly a Nazi, a revisionist historian—"

"A Nazi," Kahn said, definitively. "What are we really talking about here?"

Hershleder felt his face go hot.

"What's going on, Hersh?" Kahn kept pressing him.

Hershleder's voice quavered. "I don't know. My mom? My mom would have . . . I mean, I think she might have liked this guy." For a moment his voice trailed off.

"Liked him?" Kahn said. "Hershey, are you nuts?"

Hershleder was quiet for a moment, contemplating the validity of the question.

"The truth is," he confessed, "I'm trying to keep busy."

"Good," said Kahn.

"You keep saying 'Keep busy, keep busy, keep busy.'" Even to his own ear Hershleder sounded a bit defensive.

"I sure do," said Kahn. "I do say that. And what else, what else do I keep saying?"

"That I've got to give Itty time."

"I'm a smart man," Kahn said.

Hershleder could tell that Kahn found his little speech ultimately pathetic, but loyal Kahn, friendless Kahn, thirsty Kahn—Hershleder was picking up the tab again—was willing to lend a hand. "I'd do anything for you, Hersh," Kahn said, "poor bastard." He then ordered an $8.50 cognac to test Hershleder's brand of loyalty.

There was a lead: Mrs. Kahn had called up Kahn just the week prior and read off an announcement of Josephson's book that Mrs. Josephson had placed in the local Hadassah newsletter. "It consisted of a lot of motherly kvelling," Kahn said. In light of this fact, the route to take was obvious. The road to Josephson was most easily navigated by Josephson's mother. Mrs. Kahn was enlisted into action. Kahn himself did not want to get involved, something about the fact that during senior year he had seduced away the only girl who had ever deigned to like Josephson, impregnated her, and paid for half her abortion. The two Davids had never spoken since. So he induced Mrs. Kahn into calling Mrs. Josephson brimming with congratulations, asking for Josephson's address so that she could write to the boy herself. A practiced detective, Mrs. Kahn said she'd call Hershleder when she got the "dope." Here Kahn was quoting her.

"What can I say," said Kahn, "Mom's seen too many movies."

Call she did, at the hospital, ten days later. "I've got something for you," said Mrs. Kahn. "But you're going to have to get it in person, and sweetheart, it's going to cost."

No wonder Kahn was such a drama queen.

So the date was set; she would give him the information, in person, on her turf (Co-op City, Section Three, Building 25-A, Apartment 29-F), in a week's time.

In the meanwhile, Hershleder was on his own.

• • •

Outside, the gray September rain of early morning was washing down the gray predawn skyline in sheets of gray. The wind tumbled the rain like dirty linen. All the colors of the city, of the day and the night—the lights in the apartments across the way, the blood on the sidewalk where the latest mugging victim had been pushed and had fractured her skull, the garbage from the upscale deli across the street, a piece of artichoke pâté sitting in the gutter still delicately placed on its lacy paper doily—were merging into that one same hue. Gray. The enduring murky shade of truth.

Inside, Hershleder was in his underwear, a stack of computer printouts by his fold-out bed, Leni Yahil's eight-hundred-page history of the Holocaust, like two cinder blocks, open across his naked, hairy chest. Since a brief period in the tenth grade when he had read every piece of Holocaust material he could get his hands on, Hershleder had thought about this wretched period in history only in the fleeting, skittery way in which he thought about all the things that frightened him. That is, he'd tried to push it out of his mind. Sure, there had been social studies. Hebrew school. Hushed discussions with his mother at the kitchen table. Perhaps that had been the problem. Those little private dialogues that had been so alarmingly quiet. He'd steel up, venture forth with a tentative question, and Mrs. Hershleder would look up from whatever she was doing—slicing cucumbers and radishes for a salad, sponging down the plastic place mats, opening a can of spaghetti sauce—and her eyebrows would knit tight.

"Not now, Dovidil. Let's think happier thoughts."

Or "Don't we have enough troubles?"

And then "I was a lucky one, all right?"

Often after an exchange like that, she would retreat into her bedroom with a headache and his father would resort to Chinese takeout.

It was only later, when she was older, in the final years of her life, that Mrs. Hershleder had wanted to talk about such things. By then, her son had not wanted to hear it. He'd been trained too well, and he'd avoided the subject at all costs.

What did he honestly know, besides the obvious, about the horrors of his century? He decided to bone up, in his downtime, while he waited out his date with the mysterious Mrs. Kahn. He read. Underlined. During one of their rare, awkward phone calls, Hershleder had convinced his sister Mindy to rummage through the storage space in the basement of her apartment building and unearth some of his mother's old cardboard boxes. Once he'd gotten them home, it had taken a day and a half for Hershleder just to get up the nerve to open them, but when he did, his anxiety swept away with the first slight breeze from his open window. They smelled of *her,* those boxes, of Noxzema and lipstick and coffee; and at once he experienced this scent as both painful and reassuring. After he inhaled her, in and out, in and out, lost in thought for fifteen minutes, Hershleder had gone through his mother's books and papers, impressed by the sheer volume of her materials. He perused some of the notes she had taken in her own fine hand, that lovely, careful European script that had won her first prize in Gymnasium. And while he was often horrified by the contents, Hershleder felt his mother's presence permeated those pages—there was a recipe in the margin of her notes about the Wannsee Conference, a to-do list, a reminder to call his sister—which was both bizarre and somewhat comforting.

Now a notebook full of her notes and a notebook full of his notes lay conveniently on either side of him, holding Hershleder together like a pair of bookends. Yahil's study was open on his chest. Facts and figures. The relief of charts and graphs. For example, the spare, elegant beauty of Table 7 (page 474): "Manifestations of Resistance by Small Jewish Communities in Poland During Their Liquidation by the Nazis (in Chronological Order)." This table listed the names of the ghettos in question, the numbers of their residents, and the dates of their liquidations. Unfazed by that chilling term (*liquidation*), the table went on, spreading evenly across the page and then spilling onto the next. Forms of resistance were noted (the ignition of houses, hand-to-hand combat, flight) and the initiators of the resistance studied, their biographical data cited. This is exactly what Hershleder had attempted to do with his own presentation of the death studies, offer his information cleanly, sure, but with signature and grace. However, Yahil's charts put Hershleder's charts to shame. For triumphantly, and surprisingly, she had a section that presented the estimated count of escapees in meager but noble numbers, while of course his had had no room for survivors. Finally, "Comments," the loveliest and most inventive of columns, brushed the closing margins of her second page, in an airy, free-form manner.

Still, the Yahil study was slow going for Hershleder. He could not read more than forty pages at a time. She'd bogged it down with first-person testimonies that invariably tore one's heart out. He'd kept opening and closing those painful chapters rather quickly, the way his mother might have spit-tested her hot iron. Last night, Hershleder had come across an incident where the commandant of a death camp had gathered his wife and young children on the porch of his home on the outskirts of the grounds. He had a guard throw a Jewish toddler in the air so that he could shoot the baby down like a duck, like a clay pigeon. How his wife and children clapped when the father was successful. Yahil's witness recounted that the commandant's little girl shouted, "Daddy, do it again!"

Hershleder had a little girl, Cynthia. When he still lived at home, before she'd seemed so sadly scared of him, she'd often shout, "Daddy, do it again!" His daughter referred to a pony-back ride, to the reading out loud of her favorite book, to the funny face Hershleder made when he rolled his eyes back so that all she could see was a crease of white. In another time, another space, would his Cynthia be capable of such a heinous demand? Could he, Hershleder, be certain that under any circumstance he would not have given in to a daughter's wiles?

That's when Hershleder shut the book. He picked up a stack of computer printouts. Unfolded, they would probably have covered about a quarter-mile. Thank God he'd always been on the hospital librarian's good side. For that matter, he'd always been on every librarian he'd ever met's good side. Even in elementary school, it was Hershleder at lunch hour, studiously avoiding dodgeball, in the reading room, in a beanbag chair, curled up with a science book. Last night, the magazine article that Hershleder picked up had been about the African-American soldiers who had liberated the camps, and their forty-some-odd-year reunion with the survivors. A nice story, a reunion. Hershleder could think of one, two, three people he wouldn't mind being reunited with himself.

He scanned the lines for information. One of the former soldiers attested to what he'd found. An S.S. lounge, decorated with Jewish skin and organs. The infamous lamp shades, but also ashtrays of bone and a paperweight made from a human vagina. Hershleder had blinked repeatedly at that. The old soldier then went on. He'd opened a door, found a naked man, a Jew crucified to a wall. Nailed to it. His gut was cut open and his intestines looped out of his body and around a series of protruding posts. It was as if the man were plugged into something, as if his colon were an electrical cord. He was a living display of the digestive system. Hershleder's hand moved instinctively to his own gut.

Did the experimenters mount the man before or after the primary incision? Did they employ local anesthetics? Were there attempts toward sterile conditions? How long could the subject continue in that state, especially with those dusty liberators marching in and out of the room, tracking a host of bacteria and infectious agents? And what had the Allied medics done, after the liberators had alerted them, to try and save that man? Could they have carefully cleansed and treated the intestine and then just as carefully coiled it back in again?

Unfortunately, none of these issues were explored by the article, but then again, this was the Metro, not the Science section of the *Times,* so what could one expect. Hershleder went into the bathroom, splashed his face with water, then returned to the article splayed across his bed.

The victim's larynx had been cut from his throat. Why? thought Hershleder, always on the lookout for some semblance of a scientific method. It was only when he read further that he realized that the larynx had been removed to quell the voice that could accuse his tormentors. But the man was alive. Alive. His eyes. The ex-soldier remembered those eyes, now some forty-odd years later; he told the newspaper reporter he was haunted by them.

It occurred now to Hershleder that these were some of the very same atrocities LeClerc had once steadfastly denied. What kind of a person was this LeClerc? Why on earth was Hershleder wasting so much time on him?

That's when Hershleder turned out the lights, called it a night. Lay in his bed, shivering, frightened by his own chilly curiosity.

• • •

The next night Hershleder spent reviewing his mother's statistics on typhus outbreaks. His studio was cleaner than usual. A new fold-out couch—a tweedy brown plaid, nubby pillows, another hand-me-down from Mrs. Kahn—was folded up. There were drawings by the kids on the refrigerator: a cityscape and a turtle with its head cut off—the head itself sketched leaky red and neckless off to the composition's far right. Cynthia and Jonathan's toys were huddled together in a corner. The carpet was as gray as the sky. When he got bleary-eyed, there was a video in the VCR, a made-for-TV movie, rewound and ready for his viewing. It was about some camp survivor in L.A. who had stood up to the Institute for Historical Review in Costa Mesa, California, the gathering place for American revisionists. They had offered a fifty-thousand-dollar reward to anyone who could prove that the gassings and cremations had actually occurred. This camp survivor took them up on their offer.

Hershleder put down his mother's notes and picked up her revisionist file. Was it possible that revisionist theory was nothing but a human response to a tidal force of evil that felt decidedly inhuman? None of this stuff—the notes on his chest, the articles by his side, the Primo Levi paperbacks that he had been inhaling on the subway—seemed believable. Had LeClerc once found the Nazis' actions unbelievable as well? There was clearly something appealing about this theory: It was all a mistake, guys, some gross miscalculation. He, Hershleder the neurologist, Hershleder of Bellevue, Mr. Triage!—a nickname from his residency, his weak stomach, and all those rotations in Emergency—couldn't wrap his mind around the nature and scope of those atrocities. Why, he was ready to cry out alone in his little apartment, like a teenager for God's sake, or some righteous college sophomore: How could people do these things to other people? Why couldn't that commandant equate the value of the child in the air to that of the child by his side? Wasn't he really just a loving parent, eager to impress, delight?

Hershleder read on.

The deniers argued that there *were* still Jews in Europe. The artifacts, they said, the found objects, the photos and the physical proof (those lamp shades, that paperweight, the binding of certain books), were planted or doctored. The personal testimonies they dismissed as political fabrications. The mass graves were written off as the results of disease and epidemics. The black-and-white stills—of corpses, piles of skeletons, bones, hair, skulls, false teeth, glasses, shoes—were tampered with, perhaps even produced.

"Exterminationist" theory, they said, was a plot cooked up by Zionists in order to gain sympathy and support for the state of Israel. The Germans who acknowledged Nazi war crimes were just a bunch of the falsely accused confessing to deeds uncommitted in the hopes of lighter sentencing.

Finally, and most important for Hershleder: The deniers insisted that the death camps were not physically designed to facilitate such atrocities, that committing these atrocities in those buildings was, from an engineering standpoint, pretty much impossible. The guards themselves would have fallen prey to all that poison. No gas chambers. Zyklon-B used simply for delousing. Ergo LeClerc and the insanity of his study. No wonder this trash had driven Hershleder's mother mad.

He put down his files and his books. It was too late for all this reading; his mind was racing but it was also growing tired. A perfect time for watching his TV movie. It was about that camp survivor, these days living in Orange County, his whole family wiped out. He stood up to the Institute for Historical Review, took the challenge, and demanded the money in return. The California courts backed the guy up, eventually. But for a while there it had really been tough going. Hershleder was looking forward to screening this real-life docudrama. Leonard Nimoy played the lead. As a boy, Hershleder loved *Star Trek.* As an almost-divorced man of thirty-nine, he still watched the reruns. He wondered vaguely what Nimoy would do about his ears. By the time the tape was done, Hershleder could get up, get out, go a few blocks downtown for an early breakfast, read all three morning papers, and be in the library by seven-thirty. He didn't sleep much these days if he could help it.

Bad dreams.

4

CO-OP CITY. HERSHLEDER TOOK THE EXPRESS BUS. FROM Twenty-third and Madison Square Park. It had been a long time since he'd last made the trip. The fare had gone up to $3.75. It took two minutes of swinging through the aisle and thirty seconds of downright begging to get some nice fellow traveler to break a five. The change box sucked in his bills, one by one, like a snake, paper tongues. By chance, Hershleder sat down next to Debbie Schwartz's mother. Debbie Schwartz had been on the debate team in high school; in the city all-arounds, Jodie Fish and the Stuyvesant team had whipped Debbie Schwartz's Bronx butt. As he remembered it, the two were best friends *and* bitter rivals, Jodie Fish the smarter, Debbie Schwartz the cuter of the two. Now Debbie Schwartz was a retired assistant district attorney. She'd married a fifty-five-year-old widower two years before and was living somewhere in the shadow of the Tappan Zee Bridge, baking bread and being a mother. Her kid's name was Sophie. Sophie Emma.

Hershleder sent Debbie Schwartz and Sophie Emma his regards. He pulled out his wallet and flashed some photos of his own. Jonathan with his arm around Cynthia's neck, the boy grinning as he choked the life out of his little sister. A solo portrait of Cynthia drowning in a pair of ripped-off hospital scrubs, a stethoscope plugged into her ears like a giant Walkman. Mrs. Schwartz oohed and aahed. She didn't ask about Itty. He didn't volunteer.

Perhaps by this point Mrs. Schwartz knew better than to pry. Hershleder's wasn't the only marriage of his generation to have already begun to flounder. He'd been told the rate was about three in five. He'd also been told—truth: he'd looked it up—that the number of divorced people who remarry their original spouse is a ratio of 17:100. Still, when it happens to you it's one hundred percent, which was said long ago by Mrs. Hershleder when Hershleder, then in high school, had argued the odds of his contracting lung cancer from the five cigarettes a day he bummed. "One hundred percent," said Mrs. Hershleder, "if it's my son."

"Two children, a boy and a girl, that's nice," Mrs. Schwartz said when the conversation lagged and Hershleder, open-mouthed, found himself staring into space. "That's nice, a boy and a girl." Mrs. Schwartz had a tendency to repeat herself. Hershleder nodded, to be polite. Two kids, two, well, really 2.2, Itty and David Hershleder exactly abreast of the national average, for Itty had had a miscarriage, two years before, in her second month.

Now that Hershleder thought about it, that's when their troubles began, or, perhaps more precisely, when their troubles became self-evident. The pregnancy had not been planned; in fact it was seemingly miraculous, coming from an exhausted, halfhearted coupling, in the middle of the darkest and most stressful stretch of months; Hershleder had a paper due.

They'd been vacuuming out Itty's van, and when Hershleder and the Dustbuster had reached over Itty in the backseat, his cheek had grazed her breast. One thing led to another and all that, Itty's skirt up, panties off, Hershleder's tangled between his legs. The whole episode couldn't have taken longer than seven minutes. When Itty moved next, it was to get up and take out the accumulated trash.

The pregnancy had probably gone wrong from the start, Hershleder hypothesized. A blighted ovum. There must have been a chromosomal abnormality of some sort. If there were an elderly aunt around, or Mrs. Schwartz herself, she might have termed it "for the best." After all, who in their right mind wants a damaged child? Especially when the Hershleders were already overwhelmed, saddled as they were by two perfect ones?

Itty.

Itty wanted that baby, damaged or not. At first she'd been asymptomatic, none of her usual nausea. Then her breasts had swelled, huge and veined, swinging low. They hurt her to walk, so she'd taken to cupping each in a hand when she was unclothed, braless. One day she said coming out of the shower: "Check it out, Dave, I look like a Barbie Twin." And it was true, she did. Her breasts were long and swollen, her waist and hips were fairly thin. They had both stared into the mirror, chronicling her ripening.

The next morning Itty was off to the doctor on Hershleder's "doctor's orders." The possibility of pregnancy, which numbed Hershleder, somehow renewed Itty, made her brighter, younger. And then the good news: The rabbit died, all the dots came up pink and blue like they were advertised to, the blood and the urine tests were positive. That night they toasted with sparkling cider, just like Itty's artist friends in the twelve-step programs. It occurred to Hershleder, somewhere in mid-toast, that he had not bothered to figure out if he even wanted this kid. That was Itty's department; in the past, Hershleder had left the existential crises up to her. However, two weeks later, when she had her first sonogram—Itty reported back to him—the gynecologist could not find a hint of the developing fetus, search as he might on the screen with that condom-covered, lubricant-slicked, dildolike joystick.

"You're not pregnant," the gynecologist told her, not even bothering to first remove that dreaded probe.

"Not pregnant?" Itty queried, looking down at her chest. "But get a load of these."

The doctor was admiring (he gave her the creeps) but insistent. He told her that *said* pregnancy was just a delayed period, intimating later to Hershleder (on the phone, because Hershleder was far too deeply ensconced in his own research to accompany his wife to a routine examination) that perhaps her symptoms were hysterical.

That night, for the first time in years, Itty sobbed in her husband's arms. "I'm not crazy, I'm not," she insisted, sounding crazier by the second.

The next morning the doctor called back; he'd gotten two new test results indicating an ectopic, a pregnancy in the tubes.

Four sonograms later, and just as many physicians, Itty said she'd felt like she'd *done* the entire ball club. Then a technician stumbled upon a small black dot in the nether tip of her uterus. Within forty-eight hours, the bathroom looked like a scene out of a Peckinpah movie. Whatever was left to link them, those muddy clots of blood, the gossamer membrane that floated like an apparition in the toilet, was soon mopped up and whirled around, shooting out to sea.

By the next morning, when the cramping had subsided, Itty and Hershleder ceased all talk about this spontaneous abortion. In fact they'd long since ceased to talk about a lot of things.

Hershleder had managed to forget the entire episode, some willed if not voluntary lapse of memory until that very moment. If the lapse were "all in his head," as he'd ventured to reason, he wondered why now, on an express bus heading for the Bronx—a slightly insulted Mrs. Schwartz waiting patiently for him to resume their conversation—the incident crept back into his consciousness. Some memories were better left buried.

"Sophie Emma," said Hershleder to Mrs. Schwartz, suddenly panicked, striking stupidly out of nowhere with nothing to say. "What a riot."

• • •

Co-op City was built on the grounds of an old amusement park that was built on top of a swamp. In theory, it wasn't so different from the Stuyvesant Town of his youth, another middle-income housing project. In practice, this one sunk the Bronx. Moved most of the borough's working class to one spot and stranded them there. It was a bus ride away from the nearest subway line, an hour-and-a-half trek by public transportation into the city. The project had been in decline from the moment the first ribbon was cut. Still, Hershleder was surprised when he got off the bus to see the deterioration firsthand. The buildings all looked the same—that is, the same as one another, tall institutional boxes—so that Hershleder had to turn around in his spot three times before figuring out which direction to head off in. The curbs were lined with the same amalgamation of spit and garbage. Nothing too out of the ordinary. It was the lobby of the Kahn building that first shocked him. Broken windows. Crack vials on the floor, a scattering of chicken bones. The essence of urine, which he was used to—downtown, on the stairs leading to the subway, passing a vacant alley, even in the elevators at the hospital, the city's most persistent perfume—but not in his best friend's mother's apartment building. How could Kahn let Mrs. Kahn continue to stay on here? Surely, he was rich enough by now to help her out with some safe suburban retirement community. Florida. Long Island, even. Why, if his own mother were still alive . . . Hershleder dared not finish the thought.

Instead, he buzzed Mrs. Kahn, with five short beeps—da da-da-da da—as if she were his own mother, and then as he waited for her response, he cried a little. That is, his eyes washed over, spilling tear water down his cheeks.

Mrs. Kahn, not his mother, did not respond with a flourish, no dah-dah from Mrs. Kahn, but rather a long, uninterrupted, shrill buzz, which did not let up as he made his way through the door down the hall, nor as he waited for the elevator. It continued even as the electric door shuddered open: Hershleder entered and the electric door shuddered shut. He could still hear her buzzing him in as he ascended past the third floor; perhaps the buzzer was stuck. The elevator was green, graffitied, the button flat and coated with some human-produced scum. Hershleder had pressed it with a pencil.

In 1971 Kahn's father had been mugged and beaten in this elevator, by a gang of Kahn's old classmates, local thugs. Kahn himself had broken up the attack. He'd come home after an afternoon of hitting the books, rung for the elevator, and watched as the door opened like a curtain on a tableau: boys he knew kicking the shit out of his own father.

"Dad!" Kahn said, he'd shouted out, and the boys had stopped, surprised by this intriguing bit of news. One gave Kahn's father a few extra halfhearted kicks, probably out of embarrassment.

"Sorry, man," the leader mumbled, raising his arm in front of the kicker to desist him, as if he were a driver protecting a passenger from the forward motion of a sudden stop. The boys slunk off, leaving the older man beaten and crumpled in the corner.

Kahn had rushed to his father then, helped him to his feet and brushed him off. It was possible that Kahn was even crying.

"Dad," he'd said, "Daddy, are you all right?"

At the sound of his son's sobs, Mr. Kahn pulled away from him in disgust. Still breathing hard, Mr. Kahn managed: "I'm on my way to the store. Do you want something?"

"No," said Kahn, wordlessly. "No," he said, through the nodding of his head.

What could he possibly want from his father, besides everything?

Mr. Kahn, a little shaky, continued on his exit out the building and Kahn rode this same elevator up to their apartment. They never spoke about the robbery and Kahn's coming to the rescue. Five years later, Mr. Kahn died in his sleep from congestive heart failure. Kahn doubted that his father had even confided the incident to Kahn's mother.

Hershleder remembered this now, the story Kahn related to him one snowy night when they were living together in the tenement apartment that never seemed to get any heat. They were sitting in the kitchen in front of the open stove with four burners blazing, drinking Jack Daniel's out of the bottle. Hershleder felt close to Kahn that night, but he did not remember reacting out loud to his best friend's anguish. Even in those days, most of Hershleder's responses had occurred inside his head. Those lively conversations were real to him. It was as if he had spoken to Kahn about humiliation and aging, about pride and grief, about silent acknowledgment, about one generation's unwillingness to relinquish power to the other, about the other's unwillingness to bother growing up. About the humanity in all of it. It was as if Hershleder had truly been able to comfort Kahn. He'd thought these thoughts so loudly, he'd almost believed he'd said them. Instead, he'd just continued to pass the bottle. Eventually Kahn moved from Hershleder to the phone, where he managed to convince some girl to come over and help him warm the sheets, while Hershleder braved out the night alone in the kitchen, worrying about the inhalation of all that gas and its effect on the cerebral cortex.

Now Hershleder sat in Kahn's kitchen, drinking a cup of Kahn's mother's tea, eating some of her nice homemade *rugelach,* admiring her view. If he craned his neck, he could see the spires of the city. They jutted against the sky like surgical implements. Mrs. Kahn could small-talk for hours. But for some reason Hershleder didn't care. It was nice to be around a mother, any mother, having her fuss, telling him he looked thin, having her force-feed him. Freshly sponged, a rubber tree plant glistened in the window. A framed reproduction of a Ben Shahn hung over her head. Cookbooks lined the counters; a stack of newspapers sat like a veined marble column in the corner. Mrs. Kahn's cat, a giant, fur-balled tabby, slept in the middle of the table on the plastic cloth where the printed horn of plenty spilled over and out tumbled the fruit and vegetables.

"The place looks great, Mrs. K," said Hershleder, "but I can't believe what's happened to the neighborhood."

"You. You're just like my David. Mr. Fancy," said Mrs. Kahn. "I've lived here for a quarter of a century. Do you know how long that is?"

Hershleder nodded. He knew.

"I've got my friends, you know," Mrs. Kahn continued. "And David's sister is only twenty minutes away. As for my fancy son, so once in a blue moon he has to get on the express bus to see his mother. That cheapskate, you and I both know he can afford to take a taxi," Mrs. Kahn said proudly. She gave Hershleder a knowing wink.

Hershleder winked back, reflexively. Then he winked again unwittingly; he wondered if he was getting a twitch. He put his palm against his lid to calm it.

"What's the matter, you got a headache?" asked Mrs. Kahn. She moved in closer. "You look thin, darling." Mrs. Kahn was worrying over him.

Hershleder nodded gratefully. He felt thin. He was glad somebody noticed.

She cut him a nice thick slice of cake. Pushed it forward, and then just when Hershleder reached out, she pulled the plate away. Hurt, Hershleder searched her face. Was she just teasing him or was this her own twisted attempt at torment? Was she withholding what he wanted, until he gave her something she wanted in return? Was this beautiful slice of babka—golden yellow, swirled with chocolate, dusted with drifts of powdered sugar and tiny pecan clusters—being reduced to an irresistible implement of barter?

"I suppose you vunder vhy I called you here today," Mrs. Kahn said, kittenish, her voice suddenly low, throaty, an aging Marlene Dietrich.

No, thought Hershleder, I was wondering why you are torturing me with this cake. He said nothing. He was too busy staring at Mrs. Kahn. He'd known her for half his life. She was American born, so it was miraculous that she now sported an accent. But the accent was a good choice, he thought, she wore it well; vaguely exotic, it added mystery to her. And she smelled good. Chanel No. 5. Mothballs. Talcum powder. Mrs. Kahn reeked of motherhood.

Hershleder forgot about the cake.

Mrs. Kahn angled her head; she gazed up at him dramatically from beneath a veil of flirtatious lashes. Her gray hair was swept up like a cone of something airy, something that could pop. For a moment, she looked oddly beautiful and Hershleder felt something stir inside of him, something he hadn't felt in months. How perverse, to get a chubby over Kahn's mother. He choked on his tea.

"Cough it up, darling," Mrs. Kahn said, back to herself. "Get it out."

Like an infant, Hershleder spit up into his napkin.

She nodded encouragingly at him. "Here's the deal," Mrs. Kahn said. "I give you the dish, and you do whatever I want."

Hershleder nodded numbly, his eyes still watery, stifling a cough. He was hard up enough to be interested.

"Good," Mrs. Kahn purred. "Ve understand each other."

Hershleder suddenly wondered if he was having an acid flashback, except that he'd always been too timid to try acid. He wondered if having an acid flashback without ever having actually dropped acid could clinically be termed a psychotic episode.

Mrs. Kahn reached one hand down the front of her dress, a vintage Diane Von Furstenberg silky blue wraparound, and pulled out a folded piece of paper from her brassiere. She slid it across the table under a nail polished the color of calamine lotion. Her fingers were long, but her knuckles were swollen and bent in opposing directions, and what looked like three or four stacked wedding and engagement rings clangled loosely under the joint on her bony right ring finger.

Hershleder reached for the piece of paper, but Mrs. Kahn pressed down firm.

"There are two addresses and two phone numbers, David. David Josephson's, which his mother says might not be working, and Jodie Fish's. You're not to call one without calling the other. My David told me you might still be carrying a torch? The poor thing's living with a good-for-nothing, a comedy writer or something. Her aunt and I belong to the same shul." Mrs. Kahn sighed loudly. "Dartmouth. A Ph.D. in Literature. What good is it if her eggs are rotting in her tubes?" She paused here, letting this sink in. Then, with her hand shading her mouth, she continued on in a loud stage whisper: "My David told me *everything.* Some Romeo. As his mother, it's my duty to give you kids a second chance. Who knows, maybe it was meant to be?"

Maybe indeed. Jodie Fish. He'd kissed her when he was fourteen behind bunk number nine at Camp Trywoodie. In high school he'd seen her at a couple of parties and he'd kissed her again and again on the back and side of her neck, leaving a path of hickeys up to her ear. In college on some Jewish ski weekend he'd dry-humped her in the back room of a corny faux-Swiss chalet that was doubling as a boys' dorm. And on the night that he'd met Itty, on the cusp of turning thirty, lonely and desperate, before Kahn stepped in, they'd given each other another shot. Jodie Fish with the dark brown hair and the thickening thighs, such a long, long time ago.

She talked a lot, Jodie. But she was easy.

Hershleder reached for the bait and took it.

• • •

September. Afternoon. A low hot light. Co-op City. The Bronx. Across the street the world seemed sleepy in the playground. A teenage boy lounged against the wire fence blowing a joint, his girlfriend lazing in his arms. The sun bleached the gray cement bone white. A couple of kids were hanging out in the basketball courts behind them, listening to music, flirting, getting high. Backboards but no hoops. No ball. No game. No nothing, but drug deals, beepers, and camaraderie.

Hershleder was watching all this from across the street at the shopping center, planted at the pay phone. The pair of phone numbers were crumpled in his fist. The last time he'd dated Jodie Fish was on the night he met his wife. Would it be of any help karmically to try dating Jodie Fish again?

She was a nice girl, Jodie.

She'd played footsie with Kahn under the table.

Worse, Jodie Fish did more than that with Kahn, in Hershleder's own tenement apartment, the very next weekend while Hershleder was away on Renal call.

He tore off her number now and scattered it to the wind.

Hershleder picked up the phone and dialed long distance, charging the bicoastal phone call to his calling card, but Josephson's number had been disconnected. Hershleder had Josephson's address in his pocket, so he supposed he could just go home and write the guy a letter. Would Josephson even remember who he was?

Outside the cage of the basketball courts, the buildings melted in the haze, tall gray hills surrounded by a rising watery air. Below, the cars were as dull and dusty as rocks. Hershleder felt high from the heat, as if he was dreaming.

He looked at the teenage couple. The girl was leaning back against the boy in the chair of his arms. The boy looked out at the world over the top of her silky head. He rested his chin upon her hair.

Hershleder could just go home and write the guy a letter. He had the express-bus schedule in his pocket. The express-bus bus stop itself was around the corner. But Hershleder stayed where he was.

The couple across the way shifted their weight; the boy's arms were up under her breasts now. Her T-shirt lifted and Hershleder could see the little tan band of her stomach. The girl leaned her head back and whispered something in her boyfriend's ear. He looked at her in mock surprise, and then one of his hands lifted directly to her breast. The squeal that emanated from her throat traveled across the street. She turned and flew her fists at the boy, who pressed both her arms back and down to her sides and kissed her, again and again, until she gave in, wrapping herself around him, kissing the boyfriend back.

Larchmont. Larchmont was just twenty minutes away by cab. He was closer now to Larchmont than he was to his studio apartment. He was closer now to Larchmont than he had been in weeks, in months.

He looked at the kissing teenagers.

Once again, Hershleder picked up the pay phone. He dialed 411, got a 1-800 number, hung up and dialed again. An airline. When a pleasant enough young male voice answered his call, Hershleder quickly booked two round-trip tickets to Los Angeles. Supersavers and nonrefundable.

He was going to ask his wife to run away with him.

He was going to do his best to sweep her off her feet.

There was a travel agent in the shopping mall around the corner. He could just walk over and pick the two tickets up. One for her and one for him.

Itty loved California.

• • •

Hershleder had the cab drop him off in front of the Fishmans', and circled around back, cutting across his neighbors' yards. Then he gently knocked on his own back door, which was slightly ajar—for the breeze, perhaps, or from forgetfulness—and entered quietly so Itty would have no warning. Fresh from a full day in her studio in the basement, she was in the kitchen, trying to will herself into straightening up the house. She was listening to Mozart.

She was a sitting duck, Itty.

And so it was Hershleder and Mrs. Hershleder around the kitchen table. The kids at their various after-school programs. Michael, her boyfriend, holed up in his studio all the way out in Brooklyn. As far as Hershleder could tell, Michael had yet to take up permanent residence in the home that he himself had bought and paid for, which was both a good sign and further postponed any need for legal action.

The late-afternoon sun poured in through the leaded windows. The sink was full of breakfast dishes. An army of ants ate the crumbs that fell on the floor. Buster, the dotty dog, slept in a cardboard box lined with two of the old flowered towels Hershleder had sleazed off of his own mother while she was alive and still could have made good use of them. The radio was tuned in to a classical station with an announcer with a deep, hollow voice that sounded half-British, a voice that sounded like footsteps walking away down a long, empty hall.

It was Itty and Hershleder alone.

She made him coffee—that is, she warmed some up on the stove. He took it black, out of one of her own raku mugs, and drank her in. Itty in sweatpants and an old SILENCE = DEATH T-shirt, sitting in her requisite cloud of dust.

It was nice like that, quiet between them. She even ventured a smile. As long as they did not speak, husband and wife seemed to do all right.

Hershleder luxuriated in the moment, as if he were stretched out in one long, oily bath. He even waggled his toes inside his loafers.

He was home.

"You look good, Dave—I mean, better," Itty ventured forth.

A miracle.

"The kids, they'll be sorry that they missed you."

A miracle every moment.

She was silent then, her hand raking through the tangle of her hair. It looked like it was tied up on top of her head with a sock. His sock. Black and, at the top, ribbed with a yellow thread.

"Itty," Hershleder croaked. He took another sip of coffee. Hershleder would do anything. He willed this promise to her, but his lips barely moved. For a moment, he looked like someone she might slide away from on the subway.

Itty saw the twitching mouth, the pantomime of a mumble, waited, then looked down. There was a crayon on the floor. Raw Umber. An heirloom. She picked it up, scratched absently with it at the back of her hand. It was as if she were a local mall rat out testing makeup, Itty seemed that innocent and young.

Eyes down, she spoke into her chest. Hershleder looked at the weave of her hair, red, yellow, gold, and white; some strands, he knew from greater moments of intimacy, were colorless. The hair beneath her arms was the color of shaved carrots, and between her legs that precious copper wire always faintly glowed.

"Kahn called me, Dave," said Itty. When she looked up, Hershleder's focus skittered away in fright. "He's concerned. I mean, he's worried."

There was *concern* and *worry* in her voice, which thrilled him. Kahn, Hershleder was sure, couldn't give a shit. Hershleder gathered strength and returned her gaze. When they met eye to eye, Itty's couldn't possibly have been larger. One contact lens floated against her iris like a small contraceptive device. Domed and circular. The other was not visible to Hershleder's naked eye; perhaps it had sailed around to the other side. Whimsically, Hershleder wondered if, like a searchlight, it combed the velvet insides of her head. This would perhaps account for the fact that, unlike Hershleder, Itty "knew herself" so well.

Itty went on. "I don't get it. I mean, Kahn told me about the Nazi-hunting—"

"Revisionist," cracked Hershleder. Then he corrected himself. "Denier." For some reason, he spat this out at her.

Itty was taken aback. "Are you saying that I'm denying you?" asked Itty.

"No," said Hershleder. "No, denier is the preferable term."

She took a deep breath; she was trying. "So you're saying that you're denier-hunting?" Itty queried. She played with some old forgotten jelly that had hardened on the table. She scraped it up with the crayon, then rolled it with her thumb. It coiled thin and fine, like the dirty sloughed-off skin a person can sometimes find himself, in the privacy of his own bedroom, rolling off an ankle.

"Yes," said Hershleder, staring at her moving hand, fascinated, repulsed. "No." And then, "He's an ex-denier, Itty. That is, he's reformed."

A long pause followed between the two of them.

"Dave," Itty ventured carefully now, testing, as if with the light press of a single finger she were measuring the intensity of a child's sunburn. "Forgive me, but . . . is this about your mother?"

Hershleder nodded, yes. He nodded, no. There was more to it than this. He didn't trust his voice.

"Is it about me, then?" asked Itty, gently, gently. "I always knew you resented that I'm not Jewish."

Not true. Hershleder wanted to cry out here. He loved her because she was not Jewish. He loved her because she was not like him. This is what he was ashamed of, himself, not her, he was ashamed of his own self-loathing. That had to be part of the reason, it had to be one of the things these days that made him tick. Self-loathing. Surely this was part of it.

Itty twirled an errant curl of hair around the crayon. The colors were an even match. Itty was waiting for an answer.

Hershleder took out the two airplane tickets. Full fare and nonrefundable.

"I'm going to L.A. to catch up with this guy, this David Josephson," he said. "Did Kahn tell you about him, too?"

"He told me, Dave," said Itty, "but I don't pretend to understand yet."

Hershleder nodded. Of course she didn't understand; no one could understand yet. He didn't understand it yet himself. That was a natural obstacle they could surely overcome.

"I, ah, I want you, Itty, to go along."

Hershleder felt dizzy; his upper lip began to sweat. The kitchen was getting hazy, so Hershleder closed his eyes.

"It could be like a second honeymoon."

Itty laughed out loud.

"Only you, Dave, would think that hunting Nazis in L.A. would be like a second honeymoon."

She laughed and laughed, and in a few seconds Hershleder was joining her. They smiled at each other across the table.

"That's not what I meant," Hershleder ventured.

Itty nodded reassuringly.

Which gave him strength, her belief in his intent. So he grew cocky, stupid, reckless.

"That kid, Itty," Hershleder said.

"He's not a kid, Dave," Itty snapped back at him. "He's my friend." The good mood vanished.

"Friend," said Hershleder. "Friend?" His voice searched out a higher pitch.

"Don't start with me now, Dave," said Itty.

Instead, he said, "I'm lonely."

At that very moment, a small bird flew right into the window over the sink, and plummeted down, out of sight, to the ground. A winged kamikaze. This had happened before. Something to do with the placement of their eaves, the trees, the way the leaves on the trees hung down. Itty had decorated the windows with brightly colored daisy decals, what she'd hoped would be signs of warning, but the decals seemed to serve more as bull's-eyes. One summer there had been three fatalities, two robins and a redwing.

Itty jumped up, startled.

Hershleder grabbed her wrist.

She pulled it away from him.

"I'd rather be lonely alone," said Itty, "than lonely with you again."

The words hung on their own in the air, a long, painful vibrato. Then Itty walked to the back door. Buster yawned, stretched, got up on all four legs and followed her. Together, they disappeared into the yard.

"You're not alone, Itty," Hershleder muttered after her.

He sat still, for a moment wondering if his wife had actually spoken the words he'd just heard, or if he'd imagined them in order to further torment himself. Why didn't she miss him? Hershleder, who was growing more and more lonely all the time, would have eagerly adopted an imaginary friend these days if it would have provided any element of comfort; perhaps that's what this interest in LeClerc was: company. A golem.

With Itty gone, out of the room, out of the house, Hershleder was suddenly wondering if he had not only imagined the entire conversation, but the encounter as a whole. The totality of his marriage. The shock of his adulthood. The dream that was his wife. These days he did not trust himself.

Hershleder pushed some crumbs together with his right forefinger. When there was a pile, he wet his thumb with his tongue. Then he pressed his thumb to the crumbs. They stuck to his fingerprint. He raised the lace to his mouth and sucked them off. The crumbs felt grainy on his palate, like sand, before they melted from paste to glue, then wet dust.

Itty came back inside. She had a sparrow, stunned or dead, borne before her in a trowel. "He's hurt," said Itty. She placed the trowel on the table, in front of Hershleder the healer, the doctor. Was it a challenge or an offering? Excited, Buster tried to nose the bird, but Itty used her knee as a bumper to fend him off.

Hershleder shuddered. The bird was not a thing he wanted to touch. There appeared to be no breath left inside it. The airplane tickets were sitting on the table. One was weighted by a coffee cup. Itty must have placed it down in her haste. Hershleder moved the mug. A ring of wet marred the ticket. He picked it up and, as if to dry it, waved it in her face.

Itty pushed away his hand. She was looking at the bird. Buster's tail was thumping at the table. It jiggled the bird into little winged shudders of apparent life. Itty pressed down on the small of Buster's back with the heel of her palm, and the Dalmatian sat dutifully, but alert, on his haunches.

"It's dead, Itty," Hershleder said.

Itty looked away.

"I know it's dead," Hershleder said. "It probably broke its neck."

They stared down at the little thing, all brown and gray. The neck, indeed, bent at an odd angle. Hershleder ventured forth a finger, touched the feathered breast. It felt like fur.

"I don't understand," said Itty. And now her voice was rising. "I'd hoped . . ."

Hershleder had hoped, too, hoped long and hard, so he hoped now, ignoring the sound in her voice, and his own warning symptoms, the proverbial butterflies in the belly, the acid in his throat, the pull of blood surging through his body, which made him feel jumpy and slightly nauseous, as he was after any major caffeine jolt. He ignored these and all other diagnostic signals confirming that he was lying to himself.

"I'd hoped you'd take this time to take a good, hard look at yourself, not spend it hunting Nazis. . . ."

"Revisionists," Hershleder corrected her. "Deniers! Ex-deniers!" Correcting himself. "I am, I am taking a good, hard look at myself."

"Not hard enough," muttered Itty.

• • •

Hershleder dug awkwardly in the dirt at the far corner of the yard. Somewhere nearby, Buster's predecessors had been laid to rest, an ark's worth of goldfish, turtles, and hamsters. The three or four other birds who had made the same regrettable mistake as this fallen comrade. Itty believed in teaching the children about death; this was their "learning" graveyard. Last winter when the white hamster Snowflake was found stiff in the corner of his cage, the ground outside had been too hard, too frozen to dig up. Snowflake waited out the winter in their freezer in a Dixie cup. Hershleder wondered if they had bothered to give him a proper burial after the spring thaw. Spring at home was something he had missed out on this year. Buster, locked up in the house, was scratching at the screen door and mewing like a cat. The sound was pitiful. Humiliating. It embarrassed Hershleder just to hear it.

Itty had laid out the body of the sparrow on some pretty light-blue tissue paper inside a cardboard shoe box. Without the lid, the makeshift casket looked like an open gift box. Out in the sun, the bird's feathers glinted silver. Hershleder covered the box, placed it carefully in the open earth, troweled dirt on top and all around it, then patted the dirt into place.

Itty rocked on her heels nearby.

"Poor bird," said Itty.

"I'm giving all I've got," Hershleder whispered.

"Now you're lying," said his wife, but gently and she smiled. She rose to her feet, shook out her legs, and stretched for the sky. Her T-shirt lifted with her arms. Beneath her belly button a little path of downy hairs sewed a seam that ran into her sweatpants.

Hershleder stayed crouched graveside, admiring her.

"Call me when you get back," said Itty. "And tell me what you've learned."

As if there were any point in taking the trip without her by his side. Still, Hershleder grasped on to whatever he could find. "Does that mean there's hope?" asked Hershleder hopefully.

"Hope," echoed Itty. "You're alive, right, Dave? While you're alive there's always going to be some hope for you."

"You know what I mean," said Hershleder.

Itty shrugged her shoulders. "I would say this is something that you need to do for yourself."

"Itty," said Hershleder.

Itty shot him a warning look.

"Don't push me."

Don't push her? For one moment, Hershleder felt like leaning back, extending his leg, and kicking her up, up, up into the sky. He wanted to punish her, but not too harshly. He wanted her to miss him, to adore him. He wanted to shake her by the throat.

They stayed that way for a moment, Itty still, Hershleder, as always, paralyzed by his own shifting emotions.

Itty walked back into the house.

• • •

It was late when Hershleder got back to the city. He'd forced Itty into inviting him to dinner, by staying on and on and babbling in front of the children about how incredibly hungry he was, how he'd been losing weight; it was shameless. The kids tiptoed around uneasily, no longer used to having their father in their home. Even when he had lived there, Hershleder most often returned from work too late to sit down with Cynthia and Jonathan for supper. So the entire family silently slurped their spaghetti, stealing sidelong glances at one another like a collection of wary strangers dining separately in a coffee shop.

After dinner, out in the living room, Cynthia demonstrated the new toe-steps she had learned at ballet class. She practically tap-danced across the wooden floor, bunching up the old Mexican rug in the corner. Jonathan shyly sat on the arm of his father's chair, playing with Hershleder's hand. He'd lift each finger, release and watch as gravity took its course. *Plunk.*

Hershleder began putting the kids to bed, Cynthia first because she was the younger and it was only fair. He started by carrying her upstairs on his shoulders as if it was her birthday. Then he read to her out of some rhymey book, truly amazed at the schoolteacher lilt that slid into his voice. He even rested the book on his extended forearm, turning the pages from the bottom corner in a poor imitation of his own beloved kindergarten instructor, Miss Antonucci, so that he and his daughter—her blond locks radiating like a sunflower on her pillow—could both see the pictures at the same time. But this theatrical presentation was wasted, because somewhere during the growing tenure of Hershleder's absence, the text to this particular story had been imprinted inside his little one's head. He was reminded of the study on baby ducks he had encountered in an elementary psych course at Cornell that his mother had coerced him into taking.

"Go learn about yourself, darling," Mrs. Hershleder begged him. She'd rifle through his lecture notes whenever he was home on vacation, trying to educate herself through some familial osmosis.

The duck study observed how those little downy balls of fluff would attach to the first entity they laid eyes on after birth, usually their mother. Oh, those witty researchers. They replaced the mama ducks with a series of balloons. Now, sitting next to his little duckling daughter, her yellow head reminiscent of those crowns of downy fluff, Hershleder remembered how the baby ducks had trailed after the helium-filled balloon, trusting in their biology that the red latex was a parent, one who would always have their best interests safe at heart. What about his Cynthia? How had they all, the adults in her life, those witty researchers, managed to confound her? Clearly, *someone else* had been reading to her from this very book, a book that Hershleder had never before encountered. By the time he got to the middle, Cynthia was seizing control from her father, by reciting the verse from memory.

"To the tiger in the zoo, Madeleine said: 'Pooh-pooh.'"

Her voice hit notes like wind chimes do. Hershleder sat on the side of the bed, as auxiliary as a page-turner at a concert.

It wasn't until he finally came back downstairs—Cynthia had nodded out mid-verse—that Hershleder realized that he'd never spent much time reading to his daughter anyway. For all he knew, this *Madeleine* book could be some old favorite. Was it true that he'd been a lousy father? He didn't know most of his kids' friends' names, what their parents did for a living, how his own offspring occupied themselves at all those various lessons after school that Itty spent the bulk of her time schlepping them to. He'd missed out on a lot of parent-teacher nights. He couldn't remember the last time he'd been shown or signed a report card. It wasn't until the separation that he'd bothered taking either of the kids to a ball game, the movies, or that hell on earth, the circus. Who could stand the sticky cotton candy, the children bewildered and frightened by all that three-ringed activity, those swinging flashlights that seemed designed for the sole purpose of knocking out the swinger's eye? Was the entertainment itself designed as a fitting punishment for all those divorced, non-custodial fathers?

But would a lousy father be so undone by the sight of his child's tears? Would a lousy father lose himself in the sweaty musk of his son's neck when the boy cried onto said father's shoulder, "Don't go, 4-1-4, don't go," on the day Hershleder finally packed his few white button-downs and moved out? Would a lousy father not care about the wet spot on his own shirt, the string of saliva that connected this shirt to his boy's lip, when the kid finally exhausted himself and pulled away his head in anger? The same precious boy who shouted, "I hate you, I hate you, I hope you die," to the man who was abandoning him?

Yes. Sure. Why not?

Hershleder was a lousy father, he was a lousy husband, there was no denying it. He needed to be better at both, but how?

• • •

Itty and Jonathan were in the kitchen when Hershleder came downstairs. Already dressed for bed, Jonathan was filling up the blank spaces in his mathematics workbook. Itty tossed various-colored beans and green and yellow splits into a pot for some type of veggie soup or stew. His kids would be eating that glop for a week.

When Hershleder harrumphed from the doorway, and quietly guessed that it might be time for him to head on back to his apartment, Jonathan looked up from his homework. "23-8-25, Dad? 23-8-25?" he asked.

"Because," said Hershleder, sounding as hollow and old as his own father had while giving this same weak answer. Then, with an awkward pat to Jonathan's head—"4-1-4," he wailed, "4-1-4"—and a child's wave to Itty, Hershleder backed out of the house, leaving all of them.

On the train heading to the city, Hershleder took a break from wondering about himself and instead thought about Jonathan's behavior. What did all this numbers business ultimately add up to? 4 + 1 + 4 = 9. And in Jonathanese nine would equal "I." Numerologically speaking, could this mean that Jonathan might end up just like his dad? An exile from his own house? Replaced by another man?

Michael.

Where was the motherfucker?

Itty had said "friend." She'd let Hershleder stay for supper. She'd told him to call her when he got back from California and tell her what he'd learned. Would it be completely stupid now to try and hope?

When he got off the train he headed for the movie theater on automatic pilot. It had been a long, long day. His whole head throbbed like a pair of very hot, swollen feet that he needed to ease into a tub of cool and soothing water.

• • •

The eleven o'clock showing. He arrived with minutes to spare. Some sci-fi adventure comedy—furry monsters, a boy who would befriend them—just his speed. He bought two tickets from the beautiful big-haired girl with the lyrical smile, who was not smiling at him. In fact she glared at him as the machine coughed up his strip of tickets. Two. One for Hershleder, one for his mythical companion. One for Itty. As soon as she pushed the tickets forward, as soon as she counted out the change, Hershleder realized his mistake.

"I did it again," said Hershleder, out loud.

The girl behind the counter chewed her gum.

"I'm alone," he said exhaustedly, by way of explanation. He pushed one ticket back through the Plexiglas tunnel.

She replied, "You get what your ass deserves."

Hello? Was this the voice of God? An angelic judge sent down from another faith, calling out to him through the body of a new, ethnic Madonna?

"You call yourself a doctor." Ms. Big Hair snapped her gum.

Hershleder was in shock. How did she know this about him? What was going on?

"You know, a little kid like that . . . you know, maybe a little kid was scared. What's the matter with you? I understand you gotta run some tests, but couldn't you at least have asked a kid her name?"

Hershleder felt increasingly baffled by the outburst. He even looked over his shoulder to see if she was addressing someone else.

"You don't even know who I am, do you?" she said. "Don't you ever look up?"

At the sound of her voice, Hershleder looked up at her. The young girl before him was one of the loveliest young girls he ever saw.

She looked at him with hate.

She was too beautiful to hate him so; how had he disappointed her? Was this the same expression Itty herself had when she gazed upon his face? How had it come to pass that he'd failed almost everyone he'd ever come in contact with, even the world's loveliest ticket-taker? It had never been Hershleder's intention to cause pain.

He had to make it up to her. Hershleder pushed the movie ticket farther back through the Plexiglas window.

"For you," he said.

She glared at him. Shook her head like he was hopeless.

What could Hershleder do? The last thing in the whole world he could afford to be consigned to was hopelessness. The movie ticket was as useless to this beautiful young girl as the airline ticket had been to his wife. He felt desperate. Suddenly, winning her over seemed to be more than a side step out of an unpleasant situation. It was as if his future now depended on it.

Hershleder had to give her something.

He patted his suit jacket pockets. He reached for the inside lining. There were two. Two. One for her and one for him.

Supersavers and nonrefundable. There was no one else left on the planet for Hershleder to give it to. He removed the envelope, pulled out Itty's airline ticket.

"For you," he said, and pushed the ticket through the Plexiglas. "I want to make it up." And it was true, Hershleder wanted to make up for everything. Why not start here, with this beautiful girl who hated him? He nodded at the ticket; he urged her on. She picked up the envelope; she weighed it in her hand. She extracted the various layers of paper—schedule, receipt, boarding pass—and laid them out before her in a fan. She studied the information. Then, without a word, she put the ticket back in the envelope, put the envelope in her pocketbook, opened the back door, and disappeared into the theater.

In Hershleder's world this amounted to a "yes," his first in quite some time.

It was with some relief, then, that he hurried into the theater. He gave the usher his ticket and entered as the lights were getting dimmer and the music was starting up. As Hershleder scrambled inward, he was suddenly filled with a response as learned as those of Pavlov's dogs. A burgeoning excitement. He thrilled to the thought of the world he might next enter, of the story that—perhaps, if it was done well—might unfold its long arms and extend an invitation, cajoling him along in a form of narrative peristalsis. For the next hundred minutes or so Hershleder would exist out of his world, out of his time; totally passive, thank God.

Only four other customers peopled the theater. A young couple were making out in the back row; Hershleder resigned himself to the fact that they would probably make out the entire show. No need at all to think about sitting in their vicinity. Dead center sat a middle-aged man in glasses; nothing of potential interest there. In the corner was an old stinker; why do they always smell like cheese? As a physician, Hershleder knew the chemistry behind this answer, but squeamish as he was about living organisms, especially living organisms in a state of chronic decomposition, he couldn't bear to ruminate. This was the type of fat guy who seemingly spends his days going from screening to screening. They're a font of information, those cinema rats, Hershleder thought. One of these days he would have to offer to buy one of those guys a cup of coffee and really learn something. But now was not the time. No, now was the time to choose from the hundreds of available seats the particular seat that most suited him.

The lights dimmed to black, the music began to chime. Hershleder hurried down the center aisle, squeezed left, and sunk down just in time. The screen lit up with the beginning stages of the credits, without a preview as a grace note or warning. Still, Hershleder was hopeful that something significant was about to commence. Call him psychic, call the phase prodromal, but whatever it was, Hershleder could sense that *it* was coming. He could feel a tiny buzz percolating in the soles of his feet, lightly bubbling up his spine, for his own private curtain had just begun to rise.

5

AT THE AIRPORT, HERSHLEDER SEARCHED OUT A STAND OF pay phones. Kahn. He needed human contact. Maybe not specifically with Kahn himself, but he needed it with somebody. So he called his best friend in the world, first at work and then at home, where Kahn was kicked back and wrapped up, nursing a hangover with a round of bullshots: beef bouillon, tomato juice, horseradish, Tabasco, and a finger or two of vodka.

"Took a snow day, Hersh," Kahn said, and then he sipped and swallowed audibly.

Hershleder shuddered at the sound. Kahn had whipped up a batch of these concoctions for both of them on more than one regrettable occasion. For Hershleder they had always been a purgative. But not for the Kahn-man. His stomach was made of steel.

Hershleder leaned into his little metallic cubby and yearned for the days of the privacy of the old-fashioned phone booth. A fat lady, with eight pieces of luggage, standing next to him coughed in his direction. He huddled over, informing Kahn of his plans. Then he made a confession: "You know, I don't exactly know what it is I'm doing."

"Eeess alive, Igor," Kahn said, in some weird Germanic accent. "Eeess brain eess vorking."

Hershleder didn't say a thing. It wasn't like he had that many friends. "You know this trip was just an excuse for Itty and me to get together. But without her there, Kahnny . . . I mean, I'm interested in this stuff, but it's not like I'm *that* interested."

"Look," said Kahn, "you don't have to go, there's no law that says you have to. Just eat the ticket, that's all. Eat it and forget about it."

This was a rational thought. It appealed to Hershleder. He could just go home and lie down in his underwear on the pull-out couch.

Then what? What would happen next for him?

He'd put on another pair of underwear and lie down on the pull-out couch again?

"I don't know, I've already bought the tickets," Hershleder contradicted himself. "And I've already taken the time off. Plus, Itty told me I should go. She told me to call her when I got back to tell her what I learned. So I have to go, then, don't I? If I want an excuse to call her?"

"Listen," Kahn said. "I just got a fucking brainstorm. You give me Itty's ticket. We take a long weekend, drive up the coast or catch a flight to Vegas. It'd be like old times, Hersh." He paused, to let the lure of this sink in. "I know I could use a little vacation."

Kahn sounded a bit overeager, like a lonely bachelor.

He sounded the way Hershleder felt.

"That's a great idea, Kahnny," said Hershleder. "The weekend part, I mean. Too bad Itty's ticket is nontransferable and nonrefundable. I mean, I know it is because I tried to cash it in."

A little fibbing was in order.

"Bummer," Kahn said, "'cause I hate to admit it, but I'm a little short this month."

Hershleder held his breath. He'd already given away one plane fare. There was no way he was going to find himself getting stuck with this cheapskate's ticket, too. He waited another beat.

"Well, I guess I *could* cash in a few frequent-flier points," the Kahn-man said.

"Great," said Hershleder, audibly relieved. "I'll call you when I check in."

• • •

On the airplane the in-flight movie was *Shining Through.* Hershleder read this in the in-flight magazine. Melanie Griffith as a Jew. It was one of the first films he'd taken in after Itty threw him out, so many months and months ago. There was no point now in forking over the four bucks for the headset. Instead, he sat back in his seat and did what his people do: He expected the worst. Hershleder had been raised this way, having not earned, but inherited, a perpetual state of fear. So he waited for disaster: for the pilot to announce a mechanical malfeasance, for gun-blazing terrorists to come on board, or for that girl from the movie theater to shamelessly take him up on his most bizarre and generous offer.

And there she was.

From his mind to God's ears. Filling the mouth of the entrance to coach like some heavenly apparition. She floated down the aisle of his airplane. He could only hope that his eyes were playing tricks. Who would really have the audacity to accept an airline ticket from a stranger, and then summon up the temerity to use it?

This girl.

She was real all right, real enough to sit down next to Hershleder—without so much as a "How are you?" or a "Thank you for your generosity"—real enough to close his throat off with her perfume. Or was it anxiety? The mere proximity of such a glorious female creature, one he had recklessly given three hundred dollars away to, was probably enough to make his tongue swell and keep him from breathing.

Hershleder began to sweat. It was warm, too warm, seated next to her seat. Outside, it was almost October, time for pumpkins and falling leaves, kids freezing in their costumes, candy corn stuck between their teeth, anything orange. But inside, Hershleder was steaming as the plane vibrated down the runway.

The young woman didn't speak to Hershleder for the first hour and a half of their journey. Once Hershleder began breathing normally, he glanced over, gleaning that her name was Maria from the gold-scripted necklace that bridged her clavicle. On a slightly longer chain, a simple cross dangled in the dark down that carpeted her cleavage; she was wearing a pink scooped-neck tee and a pair of stone-washed denims, and she looked terrific. Hershleder, daring to use only his peripheral vision, marveled at her. Since the separation, he'd practically lived at the Kips Bay theater. Why hadn't he ever noticed how exquisite she was before?

Stare as he might, Maria wouldn't give him the time of day.

So for the first hour and a half, it was Hershleder alone again, with his forehead sticking against the plastic of the window, watching the country recede, every once in a while straining his eyeballs to their right corners to give Maria a peek. Beneath him, the world was a wonder of geometry: circles and squares, oblongs, rivers snaking like sign curves, highway octopi knotted up in a series of infinities. As he watched the earth spin (Hershleder imagining that the plane stood still on some magical current of wind while the planet itself turned steadily on its axis), he thought about all the people living down below. He wondered if anywhere within his field of vision was someone who he knew, driving to work, shopping or going to the bathroom, suturing a wound perhaps, maybe making love; and he blessed them. Which was out of character, but Hershleder blessed them just the same.

Finally, a female flight attendant woke him from his reveries, proffering soft drinks or spirits, those honey-crusted beer nuts. He was on the brink of an out-and-out adventure, the first in his previously predictable, just-add-water life. Why not celebrate a little? Here was the break he'd been looking for. Hershleder proposed to buy Maria a drink.

"Excuse me, Miss," said Hershleder, and then he stopped, cotton-mouthed; he'd forgotten what else to say. It had been so long since he had been in the position to offer a woman anything.

Maria looked at him expectantly, and his jaw was still agape, so he ventured to push on. "What's your poison?"

How cheesy could he get? How ancient was that line?

To make up for this new faux pas, Hershleder hastily added, "Of course, it's on me."

Of course it was on him. Wasn't Maria's whole trip on him? This pink-shirted ticket-taker with the surprisingly attractive hairy chest who had somehow, like the rest of his world, become his fiscal charge.

Maria ignored Hershleder and his private existential crises. She spoke pointedly to the flight attendant, saying politely, "I'll take a vodka tonic, please."

"Ditto," said Hershleder, reentering his time warp. "I second that emotion."

Horrified, he realized that he sounded an awful lot like Kahn did on the make. Was Kahn his only model? Had he himself gotten so rusty in the girl department that he'd forgotten how to behave? Or truth be told, had he never really known how to act around girls in the first place?

The edges of his ears were burning. He turned his face to the window, in order to best hide his glowing shame. Behind him, he could hear the flight attendant small-talking with Maria as she poured two on the rocks with a twist. She leaned over and tapped Hershleder on the shoulder, passing him his cocktail. She handed Maria an extra silver-and-blue packet of beer nuts. They were alone again, in seats fourteen A and B, sipping their cocktails slowly, staring into the back of row twelve. No number thirteen, just like in an elevator. An amazing idea, really, that one could fool bad luck just by the simple act of renumbering. A magical theory, sure, but a theory Hershleder was drawn to just the same.

Twelve A pushed back rapidly in his seat. This sent Hershleder's tray table into his knees and his knees into his teeth. Twelve A's upholstery was some coarse blue weave. Hershleder had no choice but to examine it. Blue and yellow and hints of orange, pilling like a sweater. The yellow stood out like a highlighted strand of fuzz. He was afraid to turn his gaze to Maria, although Hershleder deciphered a buzz proliferating in the tract between their seats, his thigh aware of her thigh. Energy fields. The blurring of personal space. It was like a first date. Neither of them could think of a thing to say.

Finally Maria snorted. It was a strange sound, and Hershleder wasn't sure of its origination; was it calculated to capture his attention, or was it a snort of censure? Was she just clearing her nose? He turned to her.

"Back at the movie theater, how did you know that I was a doctor?"

She snorted again, now a censorious snort. Laid out that way, side by side like that, it was clear that the first such sound had involved something nasal. There are people, Hershleder knew, who have trouble with cabin pressure.

"My niece, at the hospital, don't you even remember?"

The myoclonic seizures, the dusty cream of the child's skin. Suddenly Hershleder felt like he was going to be sick.

Maria looked concerned. She handed him a breath mint.

"Yes, thank you," said Hershleder, taking the mint and dissolving it on his tongue. It was peppery and sweet, and the flavors released him, his muscles untensed and his skin cooled;

Hershleder felt moist and pale and loose. He said, "I'm sorry that I didn't recognize you. I'm sorry I wasn't gentler with your daughter."

"Niece," said Maria.

"Niece," said Hershleder.

For a while it was quiet.

And then again, Hershleder said, "You know, I'm really, really sorry."

Maria nodded. She looked like she believed him. She asked him shyly, "Why did you give me this ticket? None of my friends could believe it." She looked down at the floor. "They were afraid you wanted something."

Hershleder thought for a moment. Did he indeed want something? Maria's implication was obviously sexual. More obviously, Hershleder was in a position to want something sexual; he'd been on his own with his own left hand for what was beginning to feel like years. Before that, well, he and Itty weren't exactly breaking any records, the kids and all, work-related exhaustion, that misfortunate blighted embryo. Truth be told, he wasn't above using an airplane ticket as a tool of coercion; he'd like to think he was, but he wasn't. Maria was a good-looking girl.

Then again, if her attractiveness had initially registered, he'd have to admit it registered subliminally. While he wasn't past fantasizing, Hershleder just wasn't the type.

He was married.

Hershleder said, "I had an extra ticket. You looked like you could use it."

Bewildered, Maria said, "Thanks."

They each took a sip from the remainder of their drinks.

"Why did you take it?" queried Hershleder.

Maria spoke with conviction, her voice lifting, her eyes alight. "I want to be an actress," she said. "That's why I work at the theater."

"To make money." Hershleder nodded.

"To see movies," countered Maria. "Also to make money. To save up to go to Hollywood."

"You're going to Hollywood now," said Hershleder.

Maria nodded. "Thanks, Dr. Hershleder."

"Sure," said Dr. Hershleder. "Sure."

• • •

Maria slept through most of the flight. Hershleder woke her gently when her meal tray rolled on by. She ate the stuffed manicotti and rice and peas, her roll, two bites of her pineapple upside-down cake, and then she went back to sleep. A brave girl, Hershleder thought; he could learn from a girl like that. To pick up and take off, a girl who threw caution to the wind. Just like in the movies.

Hershleder sat back in his seat and thought about the rising balance on his credit cards.

When they landed at LAX, Hershleder helped Maria retrieve her bags from the overhead compartment. He carried them out of the plane. Maria had a cousin, Lucy, who was waiting for her at the gate. Which relieved him, this news did, that someone else would be helping with her luggage, that she—thank God—had a place to stay. After she exchanged kisses and hugs with her cousin, Maria shook Hershleder's hand.

"Good luck, Doc," said Maria.

"A tú también," said Hershleder. He'd been first in the city in high-school Spanish, in the non–native speaker category.

"I'm Italian," said Maria.

She disappeared into the airport with her cousin, the two young women dragging the heaviest suitcase between them like some joint, vestigial limb. Hershleder was sorry to see her go.

Now the moment of truth. He was in Los Angeles. Palm trees and convertibles, Arnold Schwarzenegger and Michael Jackson. Swimming pools. Big, black water beetles. Beaches, canyons, freeways, mud slides and earthquakes, riots and drive-by shootings. Josephson. "The Legion for the Survival of Freedom"—The Institute for Historical Review.

He'd been here once before with Itty. They'd stayed with her roommate from art school in a little dilapidated bungalow somewhere out by the beach. It was so long ago, back in time even before they were married, that all Hershleder remembered was the bitter down-on-her-heels ex-roommate and a boardwalk akin to the honky-tonk carnival that was Eighth Street in New York City. Kids in wild clothing, the pithy smell of marijuana, nuts and winos, a plethora of dogs. He would go to the beach. Josephson lived near the beach. The beach was the primary reason anyone ever went to Southern California.

That, and to get their dreams smashed.

• • •

Hershleder took two steps forward. He stopped. He had no idea what to do next. It took a while before a security guard asked him if he could move along now, "step lively" (the guard must have gotten his training in the NYC subways), and it took thirty seconds or so for Hershleder to respond. His reasoning had gotten him to LAX and then abandoned him. What lay ahead for him here? Hollywood and Vine? Disneyland? He had a couple of days on his own before Kahn would arrive and become his private tour guide. Venice Beach? The observatory at Griffith Park? He had Josephson's address in his breast pocket, but he couldn't just show up at his door. The Davids hadn't laid eyes on each other in twenty years. Hershleder looked at the guard. "Help me," he said.

"Say what?" said the guard.

"Help me find the rental cars," said Hershleder.

"Follow the signs," said the guard, rolling his eyes and stalking off.

Hershleder followed the signs, the signs leading him out into the world. Down escalators, down corridors. He ended up at Hertz. Riding the Hertz bus to the Hertz parking lot, Hershleder contemplated his immediate future. First things first; find his hotel. Shower, change, maybe a little dinner. If he was lucky, a couple of laps around a pool before ordering up a nightcap, playing with the remote control, and taking in an array of late-night talk shows. Ultimately, hitting the hay. A wake-up call nice and early. Then he could begin his day.

Tomorrow, before Kahn arrived, he'd see if Josephson had some time for him.

Hershleder stepped off the shuttle bus into a field of shiny cars.

• • •

Shangri-la. Hershleder was awakened by a shaft of sunlight shining in his eyes. The room was art deco, detailed down to the doorknobs and the hinges, the glass-enclosed shower stall. Across the street and through the wafting curtains, Hershleder could see the Pacific extend its wide blue arms. A complimentary newspaper sat at his door. Hershleder picked it up, shook off some imaginary canyon dust, and headed through the hall and down the stairs to the hotel's breakfast nook.

What other room could give Hershleder the same amount of comfort? A nursery perhaps. The yellow kitchen in the downtown apartment Hershleder had grown up in. The slant-ceilinged single dorm room with the iced-over windows in Ithaca *before* Hershleder received the phone call from his father (via his father's second wife) informing him of the death of his beloved mother. Any bedroom strewn with Itty's underwear and tights, her Anaïs Nin notebooks, her volumes of Woolf and Plath and Faulkner, her clay dust dusting the furniture so that hearts could be drawn with a finger pad on any surface, a chest of drawers, a TV, a mirror on her dresser. But at this point in his life could any of these rooms—rooms that he had no access to but could conjure up only from memory—hold a candle to the breakfast nook of the Hotel Shangri-la?

It was clean, light; the underskirts of the ocean's waves paraded prettily outside the curtained windows. The tables were tiny, practically patio furniture, set up for one (thank God, something in this culture set up for one!) or two. On every table lay a toaster. Hershleder popped in a couple of slices of wheatberry bread at his seat tucked away in a sun spot in the corner, before returning to the buffet for hard-cooked eggs, half a grapefruit, orange juice, and cold cereal. He carried the various dishes layered across an outstretched forearm. Itty had taught him this balancing act during her waitressing days.

The toast popped up. Sunny, California tan. Hershleder spread both slices with butter and then again with jelly. Out the window, the bright-colored flash of Rollerbladers trailed by like a series of bows on a kite's tail. Inside, at the table on his left, were two movie execs; young white males. From back East. Hershleder did his best to eavesdrop.

"So we hire her, right? She wrote the book. So, take a guess, she punts. I don't know, who knows?"

"Maybe she couldn't connect to the material."

"If I had the time, I'd whip off the damn thing myself."

Hershleder turned back to his meal. He cracked open an egg by rolling it across the table, removing the shell carefully so that it stayed together, a mosaic connected by the sheerest pellicle. It unfolded all in one piece. Then he sliced off the top of white, revealed a bit of greenish-yellow. He cut down deeper, sliced that egg into suns, then laid them out on another piece of toast. A field of daisies. *Daisy, Daisy, give me your answer true. She loves me, she loves me not.* The golden yolk, the pinky white of Itty's eyes when she'd been crying.

If he proceeded to eat the rest of his breakfast at this same painful pace, he could further delay the inevitable.

"Here's the deal," said the first studio exec. "This girl, she's a real number—Sharon Stone or Ellen Barkin, but in a bun. You know, glasses. She's alone with her cat— Did I tell you the babe lives for music? A piano, a harp or something, a harpsichord, maybe." He pauses. Reaches into his pocket for a pen, writes this down on his napkin. "But even the music's not going so hot. This bun-babe can't get arrested. So one day she puts the cat out, seals up the windows and the doors in her kitchen, and this gorgeous but dried-up musician turns on the gas. Hanks or Beatty or whatever, driving by, practically runs over the cat. Irate, he picks it up, reads the dog tags and pounds on her door, smells the gas, gets concerned the way only Hanks can . . ."

Hershleder stood. He wiped his mouth hastily on his napkin and walked out into the lobby. By a long, low pink couch sat a courtesy phone. Hershleder picked up the receiver and dialed on automatic pilot—something just propelled him—but Josephson's number was still disconnected.

Thank God.

Hershleder had no idea what he would say to him.

• • •

Josephson's building looked like an old motel. A faded, cornflower blue. It smelled like one, too, like chlorine and disinfectant, like mold growing on pretreated shower curtains, like post-cleaning time at Bellevue. A hesitant Hershleder opened the gate and entered a dark, shaded cement corridor, where the mailboxes were. He'd been walking the beach for hours when he'd hit upon Rose Street, Josephson's street, seemingly by accident. He'd circled around Josephson's building, then walked back down the promenade again. He bought some lunch. Browsed a bit in a café-bookstore. Tried on sunglasses at a sidewalk stand. And then he'd headed back down to Rose. Why not stop by and say hi, when he'd already come so far?

The bright Santa Monica sunlight had so seduced his vision that now, in the inner courtyard of Josephson's building, under the overhang of interior walkways, Hershleder's world went temporarily dark. He felt his way along the damp cement walls, passed the buzz of a vending machine and the *clunk clunk clunk* of an ice maker. When he got to the stairwell, he was hit by another shaft of light. He blinked and closed his eyes; it was too bright, far too much variegation to adjust to. Blinded, Hershleder ascended the stairs as if he were being transported by a celestial beam.

By the time he reached the top landing, Hershleder's eyes finally adjusted. In the center of the complex, there was naturally a pool. The apartments radiated around it as though it was one of the air shafts of his youth. Hershleder leaned over the side rail and stared down into the dead, green water. What would it be like, he wondered, if I were to jump?

It would hurt, thought Hershleder, I would hit hard.

He stood up then and reassessed his position. Mrs. Kahn's note said that Josephson lived in apartment 205. Apartment

205 was catercorner from where Hershleder stood, so he walked there. On this new wing, the exterior walls were painted the palest, sickly yellow, the extension appearing even more ticky-tacky than the original.

Josephson's front door was slightly ajar. Which was funny, considering the fact that it was outfitted with half a dozen different locks, including two chains that dangled limply like long earrings, and one rusted dead bolt. Hershleder politely knocked on the armored door. He knocked again. He knocked louder. He called out "Hello!" but Josephson did not respond to this salutation. Hershleder searched the doorjamb for a doorbell, but Josephson didn't appear to have one. So what could he do? He pressed the door lightly with his thumb.

It creaked open.

Hershleder entered Josephson's abode. Closed the door behind him, exactly the same crack-width wide that he'd found it open. "Hello!" he called out again, but there was no response, so he proceeded cautiously down Josephson's damp, dark hall. There appeared to be wall-to-wall carpeting, the floor was covered with something gray and industrial, something fermenting, probably teeming with microscopic life; he could, unfortunately, imagine what was living there. The end of this long, skinny hallway promised a kitchen/living-room area, not unlike the tenement apartment that he and Kahn shared in their youth. A "stomach" apartment, he had termed it then. A long esophagus leading to a paunch.

In the dark, dank light of Josephson's hall, the walls seemed to be water-stained, shadowed, and they appeared, too, to be painted gray. Who could really tell, coming in from the bright to the dark that way? As he made his way down that skinny hall, Hershleder sidestepped an old rusted bicycle and a couple of loose sheets of paper, pamphlets, half a disembodied book. A paper trail, as it were. Although Hershleder followed the trail, he tiptoed carefully, in order not to disturb the evidence.

When Hershleder reached the empty doorframe, the heart of Josephson's apartment, he had to sidle past a screen that appeared to have been lifted from an old suburban Chinese restaurant. It was black faux-lacquer, with tiny gold embossed rickshaws pulled by gnomelike Chinamen sporting peaked bamboo hats and pointy Fu Manchus. That screen looked MSG-inspired and served as a door from the darkened hallway into the darkened studio; Hershleder slipped around it, afraid of what he might find there. The place was a wreck, the door was open—had Josephson been robbed, injured, murdered?

Next, next! Josephson's place was covered floor to ceiling with Nazi memorabilia. Flags and posters; wherever one turned, that frightening pinwheel of the swastika. The red, the white, the black bones, fanning out against a bloody target. A ton of books—books on shelves, in piles, books that had been in piles and were now toppled and dominoed onto more of that gray industrial carpeting. Hershleder's eyes roved onward, for there was so much more to see. Posters on the walls. Nazis in the *Sieg Heil* position, Atlanta Braves fans doing the Tomahawk. Hitler in salute. Charlie Chaplin as the Great Dictator balancing the globe on his arabesqued foot. A yin-yang environment. For every third artifact of horror, there was a balancing totem of horrific comedy. Here was a satirical mind at work.

Josephson's.

He was sitting up on a futon couch, at the back of the room, where the light was dimmest. He seemed to be eating a croissant.

Josephson!

Josephson, bald as a cueball, except for a tiny, graying ponytail curled against his neck like a salamander.

Josephson, ancient and ageless, looking far older than his thirty-nine years, and far, far older than Hershleder.

(Ha.)

Josephson, in a pair of old silk Chinese lounging pajamas.

(He must have made a clean sweep of some sale in Chinatown, Hershleder thought.)

His old pal Josephson lifted his left hand out of his lap—which had a gun in it, Josephson's left hand had a gun in it. Josephson pointed the gun at Hershleder and shot him.

Josephson shot him.

Hershleder collapsed, skinning his cheek on that rancid, rough-edged carpet.

Hershleder was down.

6

SHANGRI-LA. HERSHLEDER WAS AWAKENED BY A SHAFT OF sunlight shining in his eyes. The breeze played with the white curtains that separated Hershleder from his view of the ocean. Still, every other waft or so, he could glimpse a band of silvery water. Silver, so it was early in the morning. He lifted his head—that is, he tried to lift his head to take a look at the clock radio that sat astride the night table by his bed, but someone had tied a two-hundred-pound weight to his ears, and he didn't have the neck strength to hoist it; that, or he was paralyzed. So much for his choices. Not something he wanted to think about, so he closed his eyes and mercifully fell back to sleep.

When Hershleder awoke the next time, he woke to the sound of voices. Men's voices, voices that he knew. Gingerly, he tried to move his head, and thank God he found he could, so he flipped over onto his right shoulder. At least he'd proved himself to be mobile, which in and of itself was a relief. Not that he wasn't still replete with anxiety. He'd been shot. Josephson had shot him.

The hotel room was dark. Perhaps it was night, or better yet early evening; in the kitchenette stripes of gray light fell through the slatted wooden shades. The nocturnal world seemed brighter on the outside than it was on the inside. A topsy-turvy temporal purgatory.

Two men sat at the table in Hershleder's kitchenette, those same stripes of evening falling lightly across them in bars, so that they looked like they were inmates in a penitentiary. They each sat huddled over a cup of something steaming. Tea?

What had happened to him? The raw skin on his cheek had begun to sting. Hershleder tried to think. Here he was back in his hotel room. Had the episode with Josephson all been part of a dream? He felt for his gut, for the gunshot wound, for blood and gore; he sniffed for intestinal stink. But his stomach was as smooth as it could be for a guy his age who didn't take the time he should have to work out. It rippled, not with muscular cuts, but lightly, lightly, so that a layer of something (flab) slid softly between his skin and skeleton. His love handles swelled over his undershorts on the side that touched the sheets. In fact, all of him puddled over. So far he was intact, bodily, which both relieved and puzzled him. Was he so crazy these days, so willing to invent and reinvent, that Hershleder made up the entire shooting thing? Or had enough time passed that the enter-exit wounds had already begun to heal? There were two men in his room, one of whom was standing now and pouring his tea water down the sink. Perhaps one of them held the answers to his questions.

Kahn. Kahnny. It was the Kahn-man. David II. At the table, and at the sink David number three. Josephson. Josephson, the guy who shot him. Out of his lounging pajamas, into a pair of cutoff jeans, a thin, oily ponytail made up of his remaining fringe, a little greasy wick that rested on his collar.

Hershleder shut his eyes and passed out in an effort to escape this image.

• • •

"Enough's enough, Hersh," Kahn said. "I can't hang out forever watching you sleep."

Hershleder opened his eyes and sat up. He had a hell of a hangover. His head was pounding. His chest was bare, so he yanked up the sheets out of some primitive sense of modesty.

"Do you feel all right? I mean can you hear, smell, taste, see? How many fingers do I have up?" Kahn said, his fingers folded into a fist in front of his crotch. He sat down on the bed.

Hershleder was surprised at how concerned Kahn seemed.

Josephson hovered nervously in the distance. "Thank God he's okay," said Josephson.

"You shot me," said Hershleder, incredulous, in a scared and tiny whisper. As the reality of his statement began to dawn on him, he spoke a little louder: "I can't believe you shot me." Again, his fingers searched his belly for some semblance of a wound.

"You fucking broke into my apartment," said Josephson.

"What are you talking about, I knocked first," said Hershleder, his voice rising. "The goddamn door was open."

"It was?" asked Josephson in surprise. He sat down in a chair near the TV.

"It goddamn fucking was," said Hershleder.

Josephson gazed out the window; his skin glowed a pasty gray. In profile, his bald head looked like an armadillo; his pate appeared plated, that sickening wick a spiny tail. In fact, he seemed less like a man than a man's body with an armadillo sitting atop its neck. This head business had happened to Hershleder before, so he didn't let it scare him. Wasn't he already scared enough? Often, when Hershleder gazed at Kahn when Kahn was really, really excited, Hershleder imagined that Kahn's head might whirl around, emit some steam, then pinwheel off his shoulders.

"Sorry, man," said Josephson quietly. "I didn't know."

The three Davids sat in silence.

Hershleder was not ready to let the issue drop yet. "You still didn't have to shoot me."

"I already said I was sorry," said Josephson. "And I didn't really shoot you. I mean I shot you, but not with a bullet, I shot you with an animal tranquilizer gun," said Josephson, explaining a lot of things. Here he turned to Kahn again. "I've got a buddy who trains grizzlies for the movies; he's the one who turned me on."

"Cool," said Kahn.

"A tranquilizer?" queried Hershleder, quite a bit relieved. And then, "A tranquilizer for a grizzly? Do you know how much those things weigh? You could have killed me!" Hershleder fairly shouted. Anger gave him energy. It felt good. "Are you crazy?"

"Uh-huh." Kahn nodded. "You got that right."

Josephson looked agitated. He ran his fingers through what had once been his hair. He started pacing. "Look, I'm surrounded by fucking Fascists. I've got a lot of enemies. You gotta understand, Hershleder, I need to protect myself. I found something that would fuck a guy up, but that wouldn't fuck him permanently."

"Wouldn't want anyone fucked permanently," Kahn said dryly.

Hershleder looked from Josephson to Kahn and then back again.

Josephson said, "Don't look at me like that. I'm a pacifist. I'm a pacifist!" He glared hard at Hershleder.

Josephson's glaring scared him.

"You are." Hershleder was suddenly eager to agree with him.

Josephson moved forward, pushing past Kahn, and pointed his fleshy finger in Hershleder's face.

"You," Josephson accused him. "You just wouldn't wake up. Every once in a while you'd open your eyes, I could roll you around a little, but you were only supposed to be out for a couple of hours. Not two mother-humping days. Good thing Kahnny tracked you down at my place. I'm really sorry if I scared you, but a guy's got to protect himself. Am I right or am I right?"

"You're right," Kahn said, from his vantage point down on the bed. He shifted his weight and almost dislocated Hershleder's kneecap.

"When you're right, you're right," Kahn said again, reassuringly. Then he rolled his eyes at Hershleder, indicating that Josephson was a nut job.

As if Hershleder couldn't figure that much out for himself. He watched quietly from the bed as Josephson walked over to the bathroom and shut the door. Immediately there was the sound of a Josephson waterfall; the guy pissed for what seemed like hours.

"You tracked me down at his place?" Hershleder asked Kahn. He wanted to rehear this small good piece of news.

"Sure," said Kahn, bragging. "What a filth pit. I couldn't let you stay there all unconscious."

"Thank you," said Hershleder. "Thank God for you."

Kahn smirked happily. "You should have seen the look on the concierge's face when Josephson and I dragged you through the lobby. I highly doubt they'd ever let you stay in this hotel again." Then, bragging a little more, "And that's not all, I called Itty."

For this Hershleder straightened out his spine. "You called Itty?" Hershleder asked, turning on his side, hoisting himself back up on one elbow.

"Relax, Hersh, I didn't tell her you got shot, just kept her up to date about the pathetic quest you're on. Oh, and I told her that she'd never find another guy who loved her as much as you do. I even made her cry, Hersh."

"You made her cry?"

"You think I'd waste a golden opportunity to get Itty to feel sorry for you?" Kahn said with disgust. "Whose side do you think I'm on?"

• • •

The Davids went out to breakfast. Cafe Casino. Kahn had bacon and eggs; Hershleder, still a little dopey from his massive course of sedatives, had a doughnut and a coffee;

Josephson downed a cocktail of royal jelly, wheat grass, and ginseng juice, and then he ordered a double latte and a croissant. They sat outside, under a striped umbrella, and watched the stalled traffic on the Pacific Coast Highway: a lemon-yellow Caddy, a couple of foreign silver sports jobs, a light-green Karmann-Ghia swollen and curved as a giant lima bean. The brightly colored cars idled like a school of anesthetized tropical fish while the boys caught up on old times, sharing the details of their lives, Kahn and Hershleder in short order. Kahn told Josephson about B-school and Bear Stearns, dropping some heavy hints about his net worth and about the hundreds of starlets and models and secretaries he'd jammed in the intervening years. He neglected to mention the brief interlude of his marriage, perhaps because it was or wasn't important to him. Hershleder spoke about his wife, his separation, the two children, his thirty-year mortgage. He gave some vague examples of his research. All in all, it took the two of them twenty minutes to sum up the past two decades.

"Frightening, huh?" Kahn said, looking at his watch. Then it was Josephson's turn.

It was hard for Hershleder to eat while Josephson was talking. Perhaps it was the tranquilizer, that or the sugar doughnut, a taste treat he hadn't had since he was a boy. On weekends, his mother would schlep all three kids downtown to Washington Square Park and its better-than-average playground. In the summer, Hershleder and Mindy and Lori would swim in the scummy fountain; in winter they would play on the hard dirt of the worn-out lawn. Mrs. Hershleder would stop at the Chock full o'Nuts on the corner and get coffee for herself, whole-wheat sugar doughnuts for her children. For years, Hershleder associated Greenwich Village with having a powder mustache. He and his sisters would chase one another, trying to lick them off.

Now he was dizzy from the sugar buzz. Josephson was going on and on. For Hershleder's benefit. Kahn had heard a whole bunch of this stuff before, when Hershleder was out cold. After college he'd received a Marshall grant, a free ride to the doctoral program of his choice. He'd chosen Princeton and philosophy. But they were all a bunch of assholes there, said Josephson. He could take it only a semester and a quarter, so he dropped out and did a lot of acid.

"No shit, Sherlock?" Kahn said in a snotty, sarcastic voice. "You?"

Josephson nodded for verification. He *did* do a lot of acid and saw a vision, saw lots of visions. One vision in particular told him to go fight for his people, but who were his people? White American males, residents of the Bronx, the prematurely bald, the preternaturally brilliant? He was clueless. He called his mother.

He said, "Ma, what am I?"

Mrs. Josephson said, "What do you mean what are you? Darling. You're a Jew."

"A Jew," said Josephson.

"Sure, a Jew," said Mrs. Josephson. "You and Kirk Douglas and Charlton Heston. Didn't I send you to Hebrew school?"

Yes, and he'd been bar mitzvahed, too, but Josephson had never really seen himself as a Jew before. Not in a profound sense.

Hershleder listened to him closely, wondering how his own beloved mother would have responded if queried with this same exacting catechism. So while Josephson continued talking, Hershleder posed it to her privately.

"A sweet boy, a smart boy, a good boy," his dead mother gently soothed, but this time the familiar platitudes did not satisfy.

"Ma, Ma, what am I?" Hershleder pressed her once again.

"My life, my life," Mrs. Hershleder faintly crooned from the dark, rotted mouth of her grave.

Josephson was loudly telling Kahn how he had decided to get back to his roots. He'd joined the Israeli army. Served a year; shot at a couple of Arabs. But was "damn glad I never hit anybody."

Unfortunately, Josephson himself had been clocked on the head with a rock, a rather large rock, thrown by a teenage Palestinian. He was lucky it was not a grenade; many people told him so, but Josephson didn't feel lucky lying in his hospital bed in Galilee. He didn't feel lucky when he pondered the part he played in this young man's anger. He didn't feel lucky when he discovered that he was now permanently distracted, restless, and more than just a little paranoid.

"I'm fucking brain-injured," said Josephson. "I'm mother-humping organic."

When Kahn brightened infinitesimally at this confession, Josephson said, "Don't get cocky, Kahnny. I'm still smarter than you. "

Kahn had to nod in affirmation. In business, in racquetball, in school, Kahn always gave the devil his due. It was his way.

After several weeks in rehab, Josephson spent the next few months studying the Intifada, interviewing the inhabitants of East Jerusalem, even venturing into Gaza, but everything about it—the breeding brutality, the pain and degradation, his fear, prejudices, his own chauvinism—made his soul sick and his head hurt. It made his heart hurt. And what do the heartsick in Israel do besides come to the States and move furniture? He joined a kibbutz, became a farmer, went back to the land and communed with it. For a while Josephson was even a shepherd, but an irritable, restless shepherd, prone to kicking at the sheep and goats for entertainment. So he was transferred to the orange groves. Once, on a day off, he ran into a couple of hyper-religious Jews, guys from Aish-Hatorah, one of those Brooklyn Orthodox yeshivas sponsored by American Jews. They offered to send him to religious school.

"What the hell," said Josephson. "I like to study. And ever since that rock hit me on my head, I do a lot better when I have structure. So I spent sixteen hours a day learning the Talmud. Like everything you wanted to know about Torah Judaism but didn't know how to ask, you could fucking ask me. They put me in a boys' dorm; I barely saw any women after that. Which at the time was kind of a relief, you know what I'm saying?"

They knew. Hershleder and Kahn both nodded in agreement.

"If I'd wanted, they would've scared somebody up for me to marry." It was clear that the concept really did appeal to him.

"For a while there, I thought about being a rabbi. You know, finding my way to God." Josephson ran his fingers over his scalp. "I don't know, man," he said. "Maybe that's my next chapter. Shit."

He stared out across the paralyzed Pacific Coast Highway, above the shimmer of the rising exhaust, all the way out to sea.

"So what happened next?" asked the Kahn-man.

"My mother died," said Josephson.

Hershleder picked up the check.

• • •

It wasn't until later, when the three men were walking barefoot near the water, their shoes and socks dangling from their fingers, that Hershleder realized that Josephson was lying. After all, wasn't Mrs. Josephson his Josephson connection? The Hadassah newsletter, Kahn's mother and his chubby—Oh God, how could he ever look Kahn in the eye again? Hershleder shuddered, digging his toes into the sand.

But Josephson was worse. How could anyone lie about a thing like that?

"Your mother's alive," said Hershleder.

"Huh?" said Kahn.

"Josephson," said Hershleder, nodding in Josephson's direction. "He said his mother died but she didn't. She's alive and well and living in the Bronx."

"Oh, her," said Josephson, wading out into the water. "I meant my spiritual mother." His calves were getting wet. "It was the death of my spiritual mother that kept me from going *rebbe.* It shook my faith in God."

"Who's that?" Kahn asked, skipping a stone one, two, three times before it dive-bombed into a wave.

"God?" asked Hershleder.

"Yeah, right," said Kahn. "I meant, who's his mother-humping spiritual mother?"

"Language," said Josephson. And then, "You know, I think I'll take a little dip." He threw his moccasins at the shoreline and plunged into the water.

• • •

Kahn and Hershleder sat on the strand waiting for Josephson, like a message in a bottle, to return to them. The chances seemed that slim. Still, they could chart his course from the swell of sand where they were perched. He appeared to be doing laps to and from the Santa Monica pier.

"Was he always like this?" Hershleder asked Kahn.

"He was always a nerd and a brainiac," Kahn said, "but I don't remember him being a paranoid psychotic. Must have been that rock, huh, Hershey?"

Hershleder said, "It sounds to me like a combination of a number of things. Drug abuse, head trauma, loss . . ."

"What about that spiritual mother business?" Kahn said.

Hershleder wondered, too. He reached between his legs and began to sculpt and shape the sand. The beach smelled beachy, exciting: salt and tanning oil and surfing wax, that familiar odor of fish and gasoline—a pungent industrial bouillabaisse of the soul. Hershleder's nose began to run. He wiped at it with a sandy paw.

"Here," Kahn said, producing a silken paisley hankie.

Hershleder reached for it and blew. Silence echoed loudly after this trumpeting, and Kahn availed himself of the opportunity.

"So, uh, Hershey, what the hell are we doing here?" Kahn said.

Hershleder looked at Kahn, but Kahn was looking at the water.

"You almost got yourself killed. What the hell are we doing here?" Kahn repeated himself.

"I don't know, Kahnny," said Hershleder. "Maybe I had no other place to go."

Kahn kicked at the sand. He sounded angry. "You can do better than that, Hersh, you can do a whole hell of a lot better than that. I mean, sixteen hours ago, you were practically in a coma, all you could do was drool." And here he did turn his face around, so that his eyes blazed into Hershleder's, forcing Hershleder to hold the connection with the same horrific intensity with which his hand might meld to a live wire.

"I'm sorry," said Hershleder. "I didn't think."

"That's the problem," said Kahn. "You don't think. You're oblivious. Like with Itty . . ."

"What about Itty?"

"Did it ever occur to you that if you continued to ignore her she might just get accustomed to your absence?"

"You told me to leave her alone."

"Now, I told you, leave her alone now, but before, n–o, Hersh. Before, you should have paid a little attention to her. It wasn't preordained, your divorce, you know. She didn't have to end up happier without you."

"Do you really think she's happier without me?" Hershleder asked Kahn in a quiet voice.

Kahn broke their gaze and stared back out to sea. "Honestly," he said, "I don't know."

Hershleder looked down at his hands; they were hiding in the sand.

"She needed a break, Hersh. You were making her crazy. You know that's true, in your heart you know it. But maybe all's not lost, you know? I mean I probably shouldn't say this, but deep down I think it's possible that Itty might still like you. "

Hershleder looked up at his friend, his friend who refused now to look him in the eye.

"Might," said Kahn. "The operative word is *might* here."

A cloud passed over their heads, veiling the sun, hushing both men into silence.

"What do I do now?" Hershleder asked.

Kahn leaned back in the sand and sighed. He said, "I think you and I should go on a little vacation, take the rest of the week, take the weekend. Head out to Joshua Tree, maybe do a little camping . . . Or we could catch one of those shuttle flights to Vegas and pick up a couple of girls. You need to have some fun. Relax a little. Then I think you've got to go back home and get your shit together. You're traveling blind, pal. You're stewing in some big pathetic losery morass, and if there's any way I can help you, well, you're the only real friend I've got. . . ."

Kahn spit into the sand. Kicked over the spit with his foot and buried it.

"Except for that jerk Bledsoe, and the truth is, I can't fucking stand him."

Hershleder stared at Kahn. Itty had once said Kahn was an asshole-in-recovery. Now Hershleder finally understood what she'd meant.

"Dave," said Hershleder, wanting to thank him, but although he was full of heart, although inside Hershleder pretty much was brimming, his voice shook out thin and scattery, tripping on the heels of the wind.

Hershleder had no clue as to what to say. That he was truly grateful not to be all alone? That he didn't deserve his friend?

Hershleder tried to speak again, but his words came out in a frequency only a dog could hear. There was just a little warble, a trembly, webby, high squeak at the back of his throat, and Kahn seemed determined not to help him out; he just glared furiously at the sand. It looked like Hershleder's sputtering was beginning to annoy him.

What if Kahn felt like taking it all back?

Hershleder began to panic. He still had Kahn's hankie in his hand. He'd been wringing it, twisting it in and out of a little knot. Hershleder passed the lustrous fabric along his lip line and his chin. It snagged against his stubble. He held it in his hand. It was a moist, wadded blossom, limp and dying. He stared at it for a while and then he handed it back to Kahn as if he were presenting him with a sacrifice, an offering.

"It's yours," said Kahn, with a flick of his wrist in Hershleder's direction. "I certainly don't want it."

Hershleder balled up the hankie and stuffed it in his

pocket. "Let's go to Vegas. Okay? I think it's a great idea, Kahnny. I really do."

Another awkward silence.

Hershleder changed the subject.

"What's he doing in L.A.?" Hershleder indicated with his head at the surf; Josephson was no longer in eye range.

"Go ahead, ask me," said Kahn, back to himself again. "I know the nut job's whole life story." And then with some resentment: "You were out for a long time."

Hershleder shaped the first level of a castle; he used his hands to dig out a little moat.

"I'm asking you," said Hershleder.

Hershleder asked, so Kahn told, while Josephson did his laps. Hershleder kept on building his castle in the sand. Josephson came to Southern California because it was home to the Institute for Historical Review. Josephson had more information on those deniers than any other Holocaust scholar in the world.

"Is he writing a book?" Hershleder was curious.

"Nah, as far as I could tell, he's just watching them," Kahn said. "Which, if you ask me, is pretty weird, not to at least try to get something out of it."

Seems Josephson was watching Them, and They were watching Josephson. That was the situation according to Josephson. Hence the animal tranquilizer gun.

"Zolatil," said Kahn. "Or something—Zovirax?"

Zolatil. Josephson could have killed him.

"The bastard," Hershleder said, contemplating all that could have happened to him. He lay back in the sand and looked up. Over the ocean the sky was blue, but hovering around the shore, it took on a yellow cast, smudging oily and fingerprinty into a diluted bloody brown. Charcoals. Downtown. His neck arched back as far as it could so that his eyes could see, and a little ridge of sand crusted around his forehead.

"What led him to LeClerc?" Hershleder asked, upside down.

"Huh?" asked Kahn. He had trouble hearing him. He was looking at his watch again.

"Stop looking at your watch, Kahnny," Hershleder said, sitting up. "The guy who wrote the book."

"It was a job," Kahn said. "He needed the bucks." Kahn stood up, dusted off the large bow tie of sand that was imprinted on his backside. Josephson, on two legs, was coming to them by way of the water, his clothes swaddled to his body. It was possible that he sported a nipple ring; something glinted through his T-shirt. Kahn started walking forward.

"How many historians are there in the world who are fluent in French, German, Hebrew, and English, who have an expert knowledge of mechanical and chemical engineering and a working knowledge of architecture?"

Hershleder trotted after him.

"Hebrew?" queried Hershleder.

"Some Israeli was the one who hired him." Kahn shot this over his shoulder.

"Engineering?" called out Hershleder.

"He was like some quadruple major in undergraduate school." Kahn stopped at the shore. Josephson was doing a back float in the shallowest part of the water.

"Architecture?" said Hershleder, now that he'd caught up.

"Self-taught," said Kahn, not even bothering to turn his head and aim the words toward Hershleder, so the sound trailed to him on the wings of the breeze.

"Was he ever married?" whispered Hershleder, wondering if Josephson was even marriageable; he was "thisclose" to the Kahn-man's ear. Then, remembering that not everyone on the planet was heterosexual: "A lover?"

Hershleder needed to know.

"Alone. Alone." That ocean breeze tossed Josephson's secrets around like sea spray.

"Come on," said Kahn. He threw a shell that landed on Josephson's stomach. "Enough already. I mean, Jesus."

At the sound of his voice, Josephson rose to his feet and shook, shedding water like a puppy. Then he stretched his arms, his shoulders, his back, in an arc, his chest smiling at the sky.

"God, that felt good," said Josephson.

The sun broke through the smog. And for one corny, fleeting moment, it seemed to Hershleder that the sky smiled back at Josephson.

The three men trudged across the sand.

• • •

It wasn't until they were back in Hershleder's hotel room, and he'd already started packing, that Josephson got around to asking him: "Why did you come to see me in the first place?"

Hershleder paced the kitchenette. Josephson hung out by the table. Kahn was busying himself at the sink; his hands had gotten tar-stained at the beach and he was trying to scrub them clean. He used a glass brush and some lemony liquid soap. The hotel air smelled like a lollipop—sweet and sticky and artificial.

"I was curious about LeClerc," said Hershleder.

"Why?" asked Josephson.

Hershleder tried. "My mother was a survivor. LeClerc, he denied what happened to her. I guess the truth is he denied what happened to me. Which is ludicrous, when you think about it. . . ." Hershleder was surprised by his own heat.

Josephson nodded. He was listening.

"Then somewhere along the line he switches his position. I guess I wanted to know why. Why did he believe these lies in the first place, and how did he find the courage to face the truth?"

Josephson said, "You should talk to him."

"You think so?" said Hershleder.

"Sure," said Josephson. "Why not? I could ring him up in France for you. But I've got to warn you, he's a cold fish, Hershleder. Personally, I can't stand the bastard. Plus, he doesn't speak much English."

"I don't speak any French," said Hershleder.

"Maybe," said Kahn, a figurative lightbulb lighting atop his head, "maybe instead of Vegas we should all go to Paris, have a little fun before we die."

"Go to Paris," said Hershleder. "Now?"

"Yeah, go to Paris now," said Kahn, getting all excited. "Then you could meet face-to-face with the guy. A little Q&A, get him out of your system."

"I can't go to Paris now," said Hershleder. "That's ridiculous."

"You did just come all the way to California," said Kahn. "And we were going to take a few days away together anyway. Go on a little vacation. That's why I came out here in the first place."

"I know, but Paris? I'm running out of money," said Hershleder. "Remember the mortgage, the kids, the wife?"

"The ex-wife and *her lover,"* said Kahn. "You want them to get your dough?"

He had a point.

"Besides," said Hershleder, "what in the world would I say to him?"

Kahn went on. "You know, who cares? I mean, I don't care. I don't care what you say, and I don't care if you see the guy or not." His eyes were getting crazy. He stood up. "I love Paris. Now I just want to go."

"I love Paris, too," said Josephson.

"There's a girl I know in Paris," Kahn said. He was practically dancing in place then.

"This is crazy," said Hershleder. "You're acting crazy, Kahnny."

"Any crazier than you?"

"No," said Hershleder.

"Look," said Kahn. "This whole revisionist thing, it's boring me already. You're boring me already. I mean, between the divorce and this Nazi stuff, I'm tired of spending so much time on you. I earned this trip. I deserve it. I don't even care if you decide to come along. For me, you're already beside the point."

• • •

It was decided that they would all travel to Paris together on the weekend. After a quick series of phone calls, Kahn closed his big deal on the phone. He was a wizard, a mastermind. He was entitled to a little vacation. This was said by Kahn's immediate supervisor. All of it.

Hershleder phoned in to Inge and she said, "I'll cover for you, Jack. I'll say your uncle kicked the bucket."

"Thank you, Inge," said Hershleder, relieved. "I'd like to have a job to come home to."

"Sure," said Inge. "We'll be waiting with open arms."

Josephson had no job, had no one to clear time off with, no one who might miss him, plus Josephson had no money. He'd been living off, what—a couple of book reviews, scant royalties, the Israeli army's version of disability. Once in a while a rent check arrived from his living mother. He was busted broke. During the first round of negotiations it looked as though Hershleder would get stuck with paying the bill.

But then out of the shadows it was tightwad Kahn who offered to carry the three of them on his frequent-flier points just to shut them up. Corporate travel and all that. It would be like an egghead reunion. Kahn loved French food. There was that Musée d'Orsay that he'd want to look into. Plus, a certain novelist whom Kahn had met at Canyon Ranch was now living in the 16th arrondissement and he was hoping to check out her novella.

So it was done.

"Road trip!" bellowed Kahn, raising his hand for a high five, in Hershleder's room. "Road trip," whispered Hershleder, slipping Kahn some skin. "Road fucking trip," said Josephson, who was lying on the bed with a pair of Hershleder's shoes on. "My first fucking road trip."

• • •

Paris, France. Josephson knew this town, or so Josephson claimed. He found them a cozy little hotel in the Latin Quarter, three to a room to cut on costs, two double beds, a private bath and a bidet, a little wrought-iron balcony. Hershleder got the cot. After several showers and shaves (although Hershleder was avoiding the razor, the rug burn on his cheek not healed yet) and an oiling of a wick (Hershleder peeked in Josephson's backpack and found a tube of Brylcreem), the Davids hit the streets. There had been a light afternoon rain, so the cobblestones shone a slippery dark gray, the muck holes all aglow as if the curved surface of the earth were embedded with puddled stars. Hershleder looked down at his feet. He followed Josephson and Kahn from a few paces behind, led onward like a mule by a yoke of clamorous voices. Josephson was their guide to the Parisian night. And Kahn clearly had veto power as Josephson listed their choices and Kahn ix-nayed almost all of them. Hershleder silently trailed behind.

Josephson led them down a side street. They paused at

several doorways, entering one lined with blue-black tiles. It was a Moroccan nightclub, Hershleder noted when he bothered looking up.

This is where they all stopped to dine, downing a couple of bottles of wine and eating their way through a couscous mountain. The dish was steeped in a light tomato essence, fragrant with nuts and herbs and anchored by a giant shank bone. It was one of Josephson's old haunts.

The Davids sat there for hours, eating and drinking, Josephson chain-smoking his Gauloises. The smoke whirled around them so thickly that Hershleder felt like he was living in the center of a grape. The light was aqua, which added to the feeling of being suspended in some pale, shadowy opacity.

Selena, the belly-dancing maven, was rolling her bejeweled abdominals just inches from Hershleder's nose when he started to feel faint. Josephson had done the ordering in the proprietor's native tongue, so Hershleder wasn't exactly sure what he had been imbibing, including the after-dinner drinks he'd downed one after another, without bothering to keep tally. The drinks glowed purple and more purple, which somehow made them easier to slide down. Hershleder felt soaked, as if alcohol might ooze out his open pores if you were to press him lightly with a finger.

He drank another round.

Kahn had gotten up—Hershleder had assumed to take a leak—about forty-five minutes before, but he didn't appear to be returning. Perhaps he had been accosted in the bathroom and sold into the white slave trade. Josephson had excused himself to the backroom to do a little gambling; Hershleder was welcome to accompany him, but Hershleder cordially declined, too mesmerized by Selena to move much.

He found himself there hours later, slumped at the table, silly drunk, mouth agape and cottony. He looked like an easy mark, so Hershleder decided to pay off his own bill and accompany himself home, stopping to hold his head on the way when all that liquor rebelled and he vomited. What a great date he was, gentlemanly and honorable, Hershleder the perfect escort, even though he got himself lost on the twisty cobblestoned streets a few times and, during one practically hallucinogenic moment, found himself poised on a bank about to jump into the Seine. Thank God he arrived (that is, his consciousness made its way back to him) in enough time to rescue himself, talk himself down as it were, Hershleder reminding Hershleder of the various dangerous parasites that lurked beneath the black patent-leather surface of the water.

• • •

In the morning, Hershleder awoke on the cot, alone in their hotel room, to the smell of bitter coffee. Both double beds were still turned down, unslept in, unfolded at the corner. A gold-foiled chocolate sat on each downy, plumped-up pillow.

He rose to his feet, on impulse ballooning his bedding up in a cloud around him. Standing, Hershleder was surprised by how light he felt. Sunbeams danced their way into the room from out on the balcony and warmed the worn wood mantle and the dull, rich burgundy carpet. The hotel room really was a study in faded splendor, and Hershleder stood in the middle of it practically weightless, suspended by the inflated bedclothes as if he were sailing down to earth, slowed by a giant bubble, a fine white linen umbrella. The sensation felt divine.

The fact of the matter was that Hershleder wasn't a bit hungover; rather, he felt buoyant and empty and very, very bright. After an unearthly amount of time, the sheet finally festooned down, enfolding Hershleder in cool cotton. He marched himself into the bathroom and scrubbed his mouth and tongue with his toothbrush. He ran a bath. He eased himself gently into a pool of just-warmed water. He floated there.

It had been years since Hershleder had been in Paris, actually since the summer between college and med school, six months after his mother died. All he remembered was subsisting on Nutella-filled crepes that he bought on street corners and lighting a candle for her at Notre-Dame. A dead Jewish woman. Now the act itself felt vaguely sacrilegious, although at the time he hadn't known what else to do—he'd never known how to properly mourn her—and lighting the candle had felt right. It had felt right to come in out of the hot, bright sun, into that cool, dark, holy arena, to look up at the stained-glass visions of another people's God, another people's Son, and commune with her.

His mother. She'd been dead now for so many years. Sixteen? Seventeen? How many years since she'd last held his face between her hands? Hershleder tried to conjure up her image, but every time a feature came into focus, another slipped away from him; she was as blurry and as fluid as if he had tried to develop a photograph of her on the surface of the warm water of his bath.

He looked down at his knees. Two pinkish hairy globes rising like twin mountains out of the glassine encasement of his bathwater. When he straightened them out below, he could see himself ripple across one and then the other. He closed his eyes, his own visage still clearly imprinted in his memory.

He knew what he looked like. Why, then, couldn't he fully recollect his mother's image?

Her voice. That he could reconstruct; it was high and thin and sweet, it was layered with a rasp of gravel, ballasted by the scattery weight of her German accent. But her face, her face, that radiant, suffering smile—even as a child, he'd been forced to shut his eyes.

Hershleder splashed these thoughts away. The day was unfolding before him, the bright new Parisian day. There was so much for him to do and see—he couldn't quite believe in the good fortune that had brought him here. He should take advantage of feeling this way, concentrating on the various pleasures that lay before him. He could connect the dots between patisseries and then rest up at some café. He could delight in the luxuriousness of the city's shops—the windows laid out like jewelry boxes—and the bright, wet, ripe palette of the open vegetable markets. He could turn his gaze from gorgeous woman to gorgeous woman, perhaps gleaning a little therapeutic knowledge just by following their hedonistic lead: wine, cigarettes, runny cheese—and most of them svelte and cancer-free. Certainly, he could watch their chic little children run and scream in the Luxembourg Gardens. Who could guess what he'd do next? Next. Next. Next. The city of Paris would unfold before him like an aesthetic dream.

Why in the world did he feel this way? Reprieved. Hopeful. Content. Nothing had changed yet. Why is it that the very same set of circumstances can seem unbearable on some days, and on others, a veritable delight? He was still lost and on his own (probably) in Paris; he hadn't yet learned what he needed to learn. All over his body, his skin was beginning to pucker, and the bathwater had taken on a chill. His wife and his children were on the other side of the ocean being corrupted by a minor. His work was as far away as the sun was; for all he knew, Inge, *his* chief lab technician, had summoned the authorities together to fire him. And yet for this brief hour or so, before Josephson came ranting in, four more before they heard from Kahn (who had spent the night with his novelist), Hershleder was feeling good. His demons had taken this time off from haunting him. He'd been stripped of his history, his inheritance, whittled back down to nothing. Zero. He purified himself in his morning tub.

Refreshed and inexplicably rejuvenated, Hershleder decided that the time had come to do what he'd set out to do in the first place.

Hershleder got up, dried off, and dressed carefully, respectfully, a button-down shirt and a tie. When Josephson arrived, all upset and nutty, Hershleder was patient and firm. He was clear. He settled Josephson down (something about being ripped off by some Africans in some goddamn poker game) and made him make the call.

Josephson ranted a little as he dialed, telling Hershleder how much he despised the guy, but he sounded a bit calmer somehow in French: "Jacques?" he said when the call was put through, then he rattled on melodically.

LeClerc agreed to meet with them that afternoon. And on such short notice. "He doesn't have a fucking friend in the world," said Josephson, who didn't appear to have any either. "He's probably just jumping at the thought of showing off for you."

They were to arrive at LeClerc's apartment at six. Hershleder set Josephson loose until then, and they both agreed to meet outside LeClerc's building at a quarter to.

For now Hershleder was on his own. On his own in Paris. What more could a person want?

Hershleder gathered up his few things and waited for the elevator. The hotel hallway was lit by a timer and he didn't feel like leaning over and turning on the switch, so he stood there in the dark. When the tiny, triangular-shaped elevator arrived, he squooshed in beside the two other passengers and below a single bulb. On the ground floor he stood aside, holding the door as the older men got off. The lobby, too, was dimly lit. Light suffused in from the front glass doors, through some hidden backroom window, but no artificial illumination appeared to grace the premises. He nodded politely to the concierge behind the desk, not really quite able to see through all that gloom whether the concierge bothered nodding back at him. He exited the hotel.

Whoa.

It was so goddamned bright out. The world seemed such a shocking place.

Hershleder had to lean up against the nearest tree and press his forehead against the bark to steady himself. One minute, two minutes, three, until a pattern from the bark imprinted on his forehead, until it began to itch; and then Hershleder blindly flung himself away from that itch and out into the world with his eyes shut. Away from the tree and down the street, away from the tree and down the street, and then opening his eyes, breathing, breathing, it was David Hershleder, M.D., eyes open, mind going, walking the streets of Paris, eager, finally, to meet the bright and shocking world.

7

Here is where she fits in.

Several weeks *after* Hershleder returned from Europe, after saying good-bye to LeClerc and pressing for the final time those cool dry fingers, after saying good-bye and good luck to Josephson, after letting Kahn know that, exemplary best friend for life that he was, Hershleder needed a little time off ("You're from hunger, you know that, right?" said Kahn, hurt and for once not trying to hide it); several weeks after Hershleder returned to work, to gorgeous, brilliant Inge and the dusty EEG lab, to the demands of the hospital and his research; several weeks after Hershleder set foot back on American terra firma and did not call his children, did not call his estranged wife, Hershleder headed out to Long Island and the cemetery where his mother was interred. He went for the first time since they'd buried her eighteen years before. It was a wet, cold, raw day and not much of what he wanted to have happen to him happened to him there. He found no peace, no solace, no spiritual connection. Still, he stood out in all that weather for half an hour, hoping for something, feeling nothing, but open.

It was raining—isn't it always raining when one goes out to the cemetery?—or rather it was doing what Mrs. Kahn would call "spitting." Hershleder was wet, but not from raindrops; the air itself was sodden and soaked him from the inside out. In all the years since his mother's death, he had never bothered to make this trip; why, he wondered, now? Now after the long and bizarre journey that had given him far too much of what he hadn't wanted and nothing of what he'd sought.

Hershleder was standing, stooped, over the grassy, flat patch of her grave. Tall and rawboned, almost gaunt, but bearded, his thinning hair plastered by the wet against his head; his nose, long, thin, Jewish. His face so sensitive, even his Itty might have wanted to take it in her hands. The dead leaves of late autumn were decaying into winter mulch around him. He looked down at the ground. Soon he would walk back to the caretaker's house, call a cab and ride out to the LIRR, take the train hopelessly back to town.

"David? David Hershleder," a woman's voice sang out.

Could it be the ghost of his beloved mother? Was he being called to by a miraculously forgiving ex-wife?

Hershleder's heart beat inside his throat.

He looked up.

"David. David."

The high, thin voice rode a swell of the wind.

Hershleder turned his gaze up the pebbly path and across a stand of gravestones.

A woman, not his mother, not his wife, was skittering across the wet lawn, obviously distraught. She was around his age, her hair was brown and her nose was red, and although she was thin, her thighs were thicker than they should be.

She was heading straight toward him.

Hershleder's palms rose automatically, as if to ward her off.

Did she notice? For she sort of stopped, she wavered for a moment, before sliding on some slithery leaves and falling cruelly to her knees.

As Hershleder approached her, she dissolved into sobbing tears, a quiet, racking grief that startled him. He helped her to her feet, the stockings torn, the knee skinned, the eyes and nose both running. There was even a dewdrop of drool in the right corner of her lips, a kiss of wetness, a moistening. Or maybe it was only a bit of collected mist. Whatever it was, this detail, it almost broke his heart. So for reasons not then very clear to him, Hershleder drew her up against him, pressing her to his chest, and the woman melted gratefully in this embrace. For a moment their bodies held no boundaries. He imagined he could feel his own heart beating in her back as he patted her reassuringly.

"It's all right, darling," said Hershleder.

Darling? He hadn't known the word was in his vocabulary.

Hershleder continued to hold her then, patting her between the shoulder blades in circles with the flat palm of his hand.

He said it again. "It's all right, *darling,*" to a sobbing, sniffling stranger; a term of endearment he'd never used, even with his wife. Did this woman think him crazy? What was going on?

Hershleder the inarticulate, the man who often spoke solely and silently inside his head, suddenly found himself fluent in solace, as if the language of comfort and consolation were his mother tongue. He surprised himself. And then he surprised himself further by reaching into his pocket and tending to her tears so delicately with Kahn's balled-up silken hankie that the woman didn't even blink when he handed her that same crusty paisley blossom and said, "That's a girl, darling, blow."

She obeyed him.

"God," she said, "what a dramatic entrance." She stepped back and smiled. "This isn't how I imagined it would be."

"What?" said Hershleder.

Her eyes were brown, and her hair was braided, long, thick, and chestnutty in its hue, and while she was around his age, her gestures were fluttery and girlish and light, they were the gestures of a lovelier, younger woman.

"This isn't how you imagined *what* would be?" Hershleder asked her again, politely.

The woman said, "You know, you and me. If I'd have known, I would have put on a little makeup." And she smiled, laugh lines pleating, the fan of her fingers playing against her bottom lip.

Hershleder looked at her inquiringly, and when that glance registered, all the flirty hope began to leak from her face. In a thin, watery voice, she said, "C'mon, David, don't you remember me?

"Jodie," she said. "Jodie Fish." One winged hand flew upward, where it tremulously tucked an errant lock of hair behind her ear. "Have I aged that much?"

His old girlfriend from summer camp.

A slow smile spread across Hershleder's face and then he burst out laughing.

"Jodie Fish," said Hershleder, shaking his head. "All roads lead back to you."

She smiled, too, eyes slanting, her face screwing up into one corner, as if he'd pulled too hard on a single string of a window shade. Light flooded out, as if something inside turned on. She looked pretty to him then, glowing in the gloom, her hair curling gracefully out of her long braid, her mouth twisted in the twistiest of grins.

"You remember," said Jodie.

"Of course," said Hershleder. "Of course I do." And as soon as he said it, it was true, he remembered it all, the kissing behind the bunk, the impassioned teenage speech she had given him at some dumb party back in high school; he'd had his way with her then—whatever his way was at the time—he'd kissed her; he'd kissed her again, later in college, he'd rolled around with her, grinding hipbones against hipbones as he lay atop her on some moldy couch, during a faraway ski weekend. And on the night he'd met his wife, Jodie Fish had kissed him tenderly on the lips on the downtown side of the platform as they waited for the subway.

That is, before Kahn stole her out from under him.

Jodie Fish. In the flesh.

"What the hell are you doing here?" said Hershleder.

"What the hell do you think I'm doing here?" Jodie said. "I'm paying my respects to my mother." She pointed several headstones over.

"Me, too," said Hershleder. "I mean, I came to see my mother. Your mother . . ." said Hershleder. "Hey, wow, I'm sorry. I mean, it's been a long time now, but I still feel sorry about it."

"Yeah," said Jodie, "I know. I remember when your mom died. Mrs. Kahn kept us all informed."

"Mrs. Kahn?" said Hershleder, suspiciously. "Does Mrs. Kahn have anything to do with this?" He motioned with his hand across the burial field.

"With what?" she said, looking down the endless line of tombstones. "With their dying, you mean?"

"No, no," said Hershleder.

"My mother died in a car," said Jodie. "Mrs. Kahn had nothing to do with it."

"I'm sure that's true," said Hershleder.

"It was an accident," she said. "We had no warning. My parents were divorced, my mother had no family of her own, there was no plot, so we got this one on the spur of the moment."

"Us, too," said Hershleder. "No warning, divorce, dead relatives, plotless."

Hence the two women occupied the same last-minute corner of the boneyard.

They shared an awkward silence, Hershleder and Jodie Fish, a contemplation of indignities.

Perhaps, if it were possible to recollect the funeral of a mother in all its detail (which for Hershleder seemed impossible, funerals like weddings, a series of mental snapshots—a kiss here, a sob there—all he could invariably recall was some uncle picking his nose, the whole business a blur), he might have remembered passing Jodie Fish's mother's grave site. Still, he found it somehow comforting that they each stood on that same freshly tilled Long Island earth—red and wounded from all that copper—on different days, during different years, but at the same awful moment when they both buried their mothers. It struck him as significant that they'd crossed paths, perhaps at a time and in a manner that was useless to each of them, but that they had crossed paths just the same.

"You know, in all the years since her death, I never bothered to make the trip to my mother's grave site," said Jodie. "A funeral a daughter can't skip out on, but the rest, what can I say? It wasn't my way."

This was a shame they shared.

Although Jodie Fish's knee wasn't badly bleeding, Hershleder kneeled down to examine it anyway, basically because he didn't know what else to do.

"I'm a doctor," Hershleder offered as explanation.

"I know," she said. "I'm a writer," in way of an answer. "A teacher slash writer. I'm a professor. I mean, I teach and write in college. Oh God," she said, "I'm a babbler. I mean, I'm babbling, David, I'm sorry. Do you think it's related to the trauma from my wound?"

Was she serious? Hershleder stood. "You should be just fine."

Grateful, Jodie Fish thanked him for the prognosis. As she spoke Hershleder noted that she wasn't exactly pretty—not as pretty as she should be, for she had been pretty as a girl—still she had some nice internal something; and also that he wasn't really listening, but Jodie Fish kept going on anyway, apologizing for her behavior. She was thanking him for his many kindnesses, so here he tuned back in again. She said "many kindnesses" like a foreign friend who spoke in melody.

Her mother was dead. She was lost and floundering somewhere out in East Jesus, Long Island. And Hershleder *had* been kind to her, he realized, he'd actually been kind to somebody. Perhaps some of Itty had finally worn off.

Jodie Fish wasn't about to let a guy like that fade away into all that weather.

"Look," she said, "this is a little embarrassing. We haven't seen each other in years . . . but it's cold out. Why don't we go for coffee, on me, to catch up, so I can thank you properly? My boyfriend's working late, and well, no one's exactly waiting up."

"Coffee would be nice," said Hershleder.

• • •

To get to the Shady Rest or whatever the cemetery's name translated to from the Hebrew, Jodie Fish had borrowed her father's car, and she a skittish driver. The ex-suburbanite, Hershleder had schlepped out on the train. So he was grateful for the ride, and was happy to get back behind the wheel, which allowed Jodie Fish to sink with relief into the leather passenger seat. They drove around in the well-tended but aging Volvo for about half an hour, looking for a diner, both agreeing that they wanted the kind of place where the cakes were six inches high and revolved in a tall glass case, displayed as if they were made up of lemony sapphires and diamonds. There had been such a diner near their camp. One of the big treats of the summer had been hiking to it. Hershleder had been the kind of boy to order rice pudding. Just like an old man. This time around, he decided to be more age appropriate, especially after she teased him with the memory. They slid into a booth of torn red Naugahyde, drank cup after cup of bad coffee—thin and stained as melted brown crayon water—and shared a dish of lime-green Jell-O. Jodie Fish was watching her weight and Hershleder, halfheartedly, his cholesterol.

Inside the diner the air was scented with warm, kitcheny scents, like bacon and coffee and beef stew—foods that smell better than they taste. Outside the rain turned to mist, then fog, and then the window steamed completely over. The whole world faded away. It was heavenly, Hershleder and Jodie Fish, wrapped up in that gray cotton batting, nothing to distract them from each other. Although Jodie Fish swore she had never done anything like this before—"I live with somebody," said Jodie—she asked him to meet with her again.

And he agreed. He agreed! At that time, several weeks after his crazy trip to Paris and his self-exile in New York City, Hershleder guessed he needed a friend as much as she did. The following week they met again at the cemetery and ended up back at the same booth in the diner. Jodie Fish told Hershleder that after she'd dropped him off the previous week, she'd returned the car to her father's garage in the East Nineties. Her boyfriend and she lived on the Upper West Side, not far from Hershleder's sister Mindy—"In fact," she said, "I think I saw her recently: Did she grow up to be a brown-haired tallish woman in sweats? But then again, didn't everybody?" So after she'd dropped off the car, Jodie Fish took the crosstown bus. A bunch of schoolchildren got on at Madison Avenue. Two boys, twelve years old or so, one white, the other black, and a large older black girl boarded together. The white kid was reading aloud from a pamphlet he'd probably received in health class.

"Urethra!" he crowed. "Vas deferens!"

The three of them screamed with laughter.

"You circumcised?" he asked the black kid, a beautiful kid, one of those boys with eyelashes so long they curled back and tickled his lids.

The kid smiled shyly, not sure of the right response, then shook his head no.

The first boy shouted gleefully, "It says here that your dick is dirty! Smegma! Smegma!" Then he danced the booklet just outside of the other kid's grappling reach.

"Shut up, shut up!" the other kid shouted, lunging at the taunting tract.

"An oozy, cheesy substance!" the first boy positively shrieked. He couldn't get enough of this.

"I have never heard a voice sound more joyful," said Jodie.

"God," said Hershleder. "It could have been me and Kahnny when we were kids."

"It could have been you and Kahnny when you were thirty," said Jodie wryly.

The whole time the bus lumbered and lurched forward, the two boys wrestled over that precious pamphlet, knocking into as many old ladies as they could find, and Jodie Fish sat in her seat not being a good citizen, not stopping them, but wondering about what she had done.

"So I had coffee with an old friend," said Jodie. "What was the big deal? So we made a date to go back out to the cemetery. Misery loves company. It's that innocent."

"Sure," said Hershleder, "sure. It's totally innocent," said Hershleder.

"But you know, Jack wouldn't take it like that. He's a jealous guy, Jack. He wouldn't understand, so I thought about calling you up and canceling. But I kept hearing my mother's voice saying, 'He doesn't have the right.'"

Her boyfriend refused to marry her; he said he was happy with the way things were.

Jodie Fish was not so happy. "What do I owe the guy?"

What did she owe him, Hershleder thought.

Hershleder had said, *"It's all right, darling,"* to Jodie Fish. He had said, *"That's a girl, darling, blow."*

Now, a week later, his stomach dropped at the thought.

• • •

That evening, at home alone in the tiny bachelor apartment he had wrangled out of the hospital, Hershleder wondered if now, after their discussion, Jodie Fish would tell her boyfriend about her visit to the cemetery, her encounters with her old pal Hershleder. Or would she tell him she had gone downtown to check out the fall line at Barneys? To make that falsehood seem realistic, would she also tell him about the kids on the bus?

"The trick is in the details," Itty used to say. "With details, we'll buy anything."

As they continued to meet in the weeks that followed, Hershleder wondered if Jodie Fish was telling Jack that she was spending more and more time at her studio. He wondered if she was recounting to Jack in great detail how she'd taken the train into town to check out the new Bryant Park, the Winter Garden in Battery Park City, the flea market on Twenty-eighth Street, the Big Apple Circus, or about the fat lady she saw methodically wadding Kleenex after Kleenex up her sleeve while the salesgirl rang up her purchases at the local drugstore, the mother of dancing triplets who stood behind her on line at the post office, or a sculpture that she saw on some campus somewhere that looked a whole lot like scaffolding and some scaffolding that looked like a wild and skeletal work of art.

These were all anecdotes Itty had tried to entertain him with—probably when she'd first begun seeing Michael—although at the time Hershleder hadn't paid her or her stories any mind.

He asked Jodie Fish one day when they were sitting at their booth, "How do you explain to Jack the time you spend with me?"

"I don't," said Jodie softly. "He's a great guy, Jack. He's secure and unselfish and emotive. But he's a jealous guy, too. He just wouldn't understand."

"What?" asked Hershleder. "What wouldn't he understand?"

"Why I'm drawn to you."

Drawn to him? Jodie Fish was drawn to Hershleder, an insecure, selfish, unemotive man? Itty wasn't drawn to him.

"Honestly, David, our friendship has nothing at all to do with him," said Jodie.

Their friendship had nothing at all to do with Jack, except everything. Because wasn't Jodie Fish leaving her boyfriend out of something significant? And isn't that the essence of an affair? The act of leaving your partner out of something very, very significant? Hadn't he, Hershleder, left his own wife out of almost every significant event in his own life? It was as if during all their years of marriage he'd been having a liaison with his own mind.

"Do you think that's wise?" Hershleder asked Jodie Fish, but she just shrugged her shoulders.

"Sometimes you know you're making a mistake, but you're compelled to make it anyway."

Hershleder could relate.

Leave Jack out, they did. They left him out completely. They went on in this way. Days turned into weeks, weeks shaped and formed into months, Hershleder and Jodie Fish and their illicit trips out to Long Island, the hours in the diner, the cup after cup of bad coffee. When winter came, they often skipped the cemetery altogether but still drove the long drive out to the red Naugahyde booth out of some strange sense of rhythm, of necessary beats, the Jell-O gone the way of warm apple pie by then, the coffee now hot cocoa.

They met on Thursdays, in the afternoons, after Hershleder had seen to his private patients. Thursday mornings were mornings that Jodie Fish taught up at Columbia, so she was too tired anyway later in the day to get any actual work done on the book she had been contracted to write so long before that she wasn't even sure that the publisher was still in existence. For sure the money had run out.

They talked about this, their work, the inevitable frustrations. They talked about their relationships, his kids, the fact that Itty had miscarried, how Jodie Fish despaired that she would never have any children. They talked about what had led each of them out to the cemetery so many years later in a search for reassurance from the one person who had loved them the most. They talked about the people they had failed, and the people they were failing still, and how they each had failed just about everyone they knew, until it was Jodie Fish who came up with the rather optimistic observation that they had not yet failed each other.

"Wait," said Hershleder. "We've only been hanging out together a couple of months."

Jodie Fish laughed out loud at this, but Hershleder was serious. He'd failed everybody.

"For me," said Jodie, "it's all about my mother. Like I couldn't separate or something, and neither could she. My mother couldn't separate from anyone or anything, and so when she died I wasn't a full person, because only a less-than-full person would continue with my life. I love Jack, I love him, but with each day that passes I don't get any closer to getting the things I want."

"Which is what?" said Hershleder.

"Well," said Jodie, "now that you mention it, I'm not

exactly sure. I've got the career. What I think I'd like is the husband and the children."

"I had that," said Hershleder.

They were silent for a moment.

"It's my mother's fault," said Jodie. "Let's blame it all on my poor mother."

"No," said Hershleder, "no. We can only blame you on your poor mother. Let's blame me on mine."

"Bung-o," said Jodie, and she raised her coffee cup for clacking.

"Bung-o," said Hershleder, raising his own cup for her toast.

It amazed him how well he and Jodie Fish got along.

"Hey, Jo," said Hershleder, "why do you think it's so easy for me to talk to you? I can barely talk to anyone."

"Well," said Jodie, "even though we've known each other for a long time, we're not exactly weighed down by a ton of baggage or the perils of daily intimacy. Look at it this way, I'm your taxi driver, your bartender, the stranger you want to divulge all to, except I know you, I know where you're from and I care about where you're going. I'm also your long-lost girlfriend from summer camp. Plus, I'm here now, but you don't really ever have to see me again. That is, if you don't want to."

Jodie Fish took a long pull on her glass of water.

"Or," she said, "I could have just hit you when you were finally ready to talk."

"Wow," said Hershleder. "You're smart."

"Sure," said Jodie. "Of course. I've always been smart, but you were always too busy trying to get into my pants to bother noticing."

"Well, look," said Hershleder, sitting up now, sitting up and noticing, "if you're my long-lost girlfriend the drunken taxi driver, then perhaps I can bore you with a really weird chapter of my life story."

"Sure," said Jodie, "but remember the meter's running."

"You sure like to flirt, don't you?" said Hershleder.

"And what do you think you've been doing, David Hershleder?" asked Jodie Fish, flirtatiously. She was playing with a saltshaker.

He'd been flirting. He didn't know he could.

He decided to change the subject.

Hershleder began to tell her about his crazy trip to Europe, about his obsession with LeClerc. He went on and on; he was trying to explain the adult he had become, a person he felt he had recognized for the first time in Paris, a man he did not like. "This is pretty weird," said Hershleder, "but without LeClerc, I didn't know who I was. But who wanted to know me? I mean, most of it is ugly. I mean, now I realize I went there to find something true, something beautiful, to find something beautiful to bring back. But I'm all fucked up, I'm—"

"It's all right, David," Jodie interrupted him. "You don't have to turn cartwheels, I understand. My mother was a survivor, too."

Hershleder was silent for a moment. Bergen-Belsen. He'd forgotten.

A few tears slipped out of Jodie Fish's eyes and plopped onto the Formica table.

Hershleder touched one with his finger. It was still warm.

"I'm afraid I've lived a half-life," he said. "A life frozen in motion."

"You sound like her," said Jodie, and another tear slipped out.

Was it her own mother she was referring to? Or was it his?

"I remember when we were in high school," said Jodie, as if she'd read his thoughts. "The half-life stuff, the life frozen in motion. You said she said she didn't want you to be like her."

His mother was always saying things like that. Jodie Fish had known her, she'd listened to her talk. Jodie Fish had known his mother when his mother was almost young.

Hershleder felt kind of drunk.

"I can't believe you remember what I said. I can't believe I even told you that, even."

He said *even* twice, like a little kid.

What would she think of him? That he was sincere, wide-eyed, trustworthy? That he was an immature, stupid idiot?

But Jodie Fish graced Hershleder with her smile. She seemed very wise and very sensitive and very special at that moment. Even radiant.

Hershleder stopped there—his hands were shaking—and called over the waitress, who poured them both a warm-up. He stirred two packets of sugar into his cup and then peeled open and stirred in half a dozen mini Coffee-mates. He did this because he didn't dare look at her. Would she notice that he was acting crazy?

He put down his spoon.

Hershleder said, "I want to confess to you."

He didn't drink that coffee. He just stirred and stirred it until all that sugar and creamer lumped together into something sickening and solid that weighed down his coffee spoon.

"The night my mother died was the last night of Christmas break my senior year in college."

Actually it was two nights before the last night of Christmas break, but that's not what Hershleder had told his mother.

"You see," he said, "I wanted to get away from her."

He had wanted to get away from her, which was the God's honest truth. He'd spent most of his vacation on a ski trip hanging out with Kahnny. Was this the very same Jewish ski weekend where he and she had rolled around a lot with their clothes on?

Hershleder looked up tentatively to see if any of this registered, but Jodie Fish just nodded. Instinctually? Or did she simply want to appear supportive?

When he'd gotten back to the city, he'd decided to bunk over at his room at his father's. He'd not wanted to stay with his mother at all.

She had a little apartment in those days, somewhere on the Upper East Side, in the Eighties, by the river. Yorkville—what an irony. How fast she fled when she heard German spoken in the small shops. How quickly she learned to frequent the delis and the chain stores, the yuppie and Korean markets. She lived in a studio, an efficiency, whatever they called it at the time. Mrs. Hershleder was saving all her money for her tuition. No point in wasting it on some fancy residence. She didn't believe in alimony. She didn't believe in taking from the husband who had given her next to nothing of what she'd needed during all those lonely married years. She'd recently embarked on a

Holocaust Studies program at City College. Who cared that her apartment was no bigger than a postcard? She was spending all her time in the library anyway, and she was hoping to get ahold of an old piano. Where could she have put it? As it was, there was barely enough room for Mrs. Hershleder and her books and her records and her *tchotchkes.* In his defense, it occurred to Hershleder now, there really was no room for *him;* if his mother had wanted him to stay, she would have provided a place for him, alimony be damned, but Hershleder was getting ahead of himself here.

She cooked him dinner. Boiled chicken and soup on her gas burners; she hated that little oven. They had a pleasant enough conversation, Hershleder and his mother; each talked about what they had learned in school, not so different from the old days.

Now Hershleder told Jodie Fish that he wished he could remember some *something,* some very important clue, but he couldn't. It had all seemed the same to him; his mother was sensitive and worn and pale, although at times in the evening she glowed a bit too brightly; and she loved him with an obviousness that hurt.

Jodie Fish said that that was it in a nutshell, what made him want to stay away. She'd loved him too hard and too much and too obviously.

He was twenty-one and still a boy then. Now, of course, all he wanted in the world was to be loved too hard and too much and too obviously.

"Ma, I have a long ride back up to school," Hershleder said he'd said. "We're leaving at six A.M. . . . in the morning." He added these last qualifiers for her benefit, believing, like his Itty, in the persuasive powers of specificity.

"I was hoping that you'd stay with me, Dovidil," said his mother. She pointed to her bed. "We could have a good old-fashioned slumber party."

This stunned him.

"I don't know why, but I was stunned," Hershleder said to Jodie Fish in their booth, in their diner, some eighteen years later.

Jodie Fish nodded her lovely head—she was getting lovelier with what looked to Hershleder like a growing interest in everything he said. Was she trying to make him love her?

His mother had been trying to make him love her. His mother had said, "I'll make waffles in the morning."

Was this enough of an enticement? What could Hershleder have done? How was he to know that his mother was to die soon? She'd looked so healthy, painfully thin perhaps, maybe a little drawn, but she'd always looked thin and drawn—that was the way she was. And she seemed too smart, too unfinished, and too unrealized for an early and lonely death. She looked like a nagging parent. What had she meant, anyway, by her invitation? That she'd sleep on the floor? That he'd sleep on the bed? Vice versa?

Or did she mean the worst? Hershleder and Mrs. Hershleder, side by side, she facing one wall, he facing the other, nothing improper really, except that they'd be sharing the same bedcovers?

Consider the permutations, Hershleder said to Jodie Fish, and feel yourself squirm.

"Nah, Ma," he said he'd said. "I really got to get going."

"Of course you do," said his mother. She kissed him a bunch of times, on both cheeks, and she stroked his right arm from his shoulder to his elbow. Then he left. But not before she made him promise to send her some copies of the correspondence of Hannah Arendt and Martin Heidegger; Cornell had a special collection on microfiche. So she was planning ahead, a detail that made Hershleder conclude his mother still believed in the luxury of prospects.

It must have been sometime that night that she died, although it wasn't until much, much later that the neighbors made a call on account of the smell, and the police broke the door down just like they do in the movies.

"I don't know," said Hershleder. "I keep wondering. I mean, it had been so many years since she slept in a bed with somebody . . ." Hershleder trailed off here. He couldn't believe what he was saying. He couldn't believe that he could trust anyone enough to reveal this information.

"It's okay, David," said Jodie. "You and I are friends."

"Do you think that's what she wanted," asked Hershleder, "that's why she wanted me to stay? I know for a fact she was lonely. Do you think if I stayed, she wouldn't have died, alone there, that way?"

Jodie Fish reached out her hand, covering Hershleder's clenched fist with an embracement of her fingers.

"I never told anybody that she asked me to stay before," said Hershleder. "I don't think that before this even . . . I actually even remembered her asking me." He opened his fist here, during the ellipsis, in the downtime of the line, and

Jodie Fish interlaced his fingers with her fingers, giving his hand a compassionate squeeze, a tiny little heart-pump of pressure.

• • •

The rest of the evening Hershleder and Jodie Fish drove around looking for the right place. The Freeport Motor Inn and Boatel was near the water, and in winter, with Amy Fisher safely ensconced in the Bedford Correctional Facility, it looked sufficiently desolate. Still, there was that nice bright AAA sign hanging out over the doorway to the front office, which Hershleder found reassuring. He went inside, topcoat collar huddled up against his neck, head bent against the wind, beard rippling slightly with the currents, while she stayed behind in the car. Why? Was she embarrassed? Did she suddenly feel like the sixteen-year-old she would always be in his memory?

Inside Hershleder charged everything, taking the room a week in advance, as if it were possible that there would be no vacancies when they returned. Why did they plan ahead that way? So that they couldn't turn back?

They returned. He was afraid that they would exercise good judgment, that their consciences would take hold, that they wouldn't have the heart, but they returned in a week's time. What did Jodie Fish tell her boyfriend? That she was doing a reading at an upstate college? What did Hershleder tell no one?

Once again, Jodie Fish stayed put in her father's Volvo. As Hershleder leaned into the wind, fighting the elements during his brave passage to check-in, a blue van drove by outside her passenger window with one, two, three little fat boys (the tiniest guys in car seats, one to a row, each at a window seat), all sucking on their thumbs. They ticked off the moments that he waited before venturing into the motel office. One, two, three.

It took no time at all once he entered, because they'd prepaid everything. When Hershleder exited the motel office, he held the key up in victory for Jodie Fish to see. There were details that nobody else on the planet could be concerned with: the way he held that key up in the air as if they'd won something; the slow, determined way he walked to their room as if he were counting the steps to their short future aloud; the smile he displayed when he stood out in that cold, cold wind, waiting for her to drive up; the patience with which he watched her try to park the car, and then how he opened her door, slid her over and got in, how he parked her car for her.

They entered the motel room, Jodie Fish and David Hershleder, two Yids cheating on their goyishe partners. He flicked on the lights. There was a beaten-down shag rug, twin doubles, and long, thick drapes made up of what appeared to be water-resistant sailcloth. Hershleder watched Jodie Fish rub that fabric between her fingers; was it to anchor her to something? And then they both quietly disrobed.

Hershleder naked. Hershleder naked in the Freeport Motor Inn and Boatel, Hershleder naked on Long Island with a woman who was not his wife! He felt thin—that is, thinner than he was before. His torso was long, perhaps longer than his legs if you were to fold him in half—which is what he wanted Jodie Fish to do, he wanted her to fold him in half and in half again. His chest was covered with soft, curly black hair—a spiral or two of it graying—hair that rode his belly down to his genitals, and it was a little concave, his chest was, and his belly just the tiniest bit sloped out. Jodie Fish stared at this and the thickening slow rise of his penis. It was as if she had never seen a naked man.

She herself was creamy and soft, abundant and beautiful, to him anyway, in the light that slipped in from behind the curtains.

She was at the point where she looked better naked than in underwear. There with Hershleder, Jodie Fish didn't seem to care. She wanted him to see her. She leaned forward, her long, full breasts swinging slightly, and turned on a little lamp. This gesture alone touched Hershleder's heart. When was the last time a woman offered herself to him as a gift?

He reached out his hand, lifted her left breast, the way he'd always done with Itty, and put his other palm underneath, where he knew it would be warm.

Later, after they did all that they could do standing up with a man who is six foot two and a woman who is five foot five, after they did what he could do kneeling, they fell to the bed.

After two decades of his wanting her, Jodie Fish seemed to be wanting him. She motioned for Hershleder to turn her over, so he did, on that coarse, plasticated bedspread. It seemed that she wanted him to turn her over—that is, it seemed like it might have hurt her, for she gave a little gasp—and Hershleder wasn't sure if she really liked it, but that she wanted Hershleder to turn her over just the same and screw her up the ass. By the time that was done, they were giggly and sore and oily and exhausted and definitely showing their age, so they lay in bed and compared their sags and their scars and their lumps and they laughed over them. In the hour or so it took Hershleder to get hard again, he and she couldn't extricate themselves from each other's arms, not even to get up and go to the bathroom.

There was a clicker nailed to the end table by the bed. A TV rested below a mirror on a bureau directly across from them. They clicked from news to soap opera to talk-show channel. Just as Hershleder began to swell long and low again, a face filled the screen, a face selling floor wax or maybe too-tight jeans, a familiar face with a dark mole beneath pink lips on the left-hand side of that lovely, lovely face—one a musician might sight-read and play. "It's Maria," said Hershleder. "Maria," Jodie Fish repeated after him. "Maria, maria, mareeah." And the name stopped being a name, but became a sound, and then not a sound but a gesture that Jodie Fish made with her lips on Hershleder's neck and then with her lips on Hershleder's mouth and then with her tongue on Hershleder's tongue. And then, when he was inside her again, he said, "Make me come, make me come," into Jodie Fish's neck and she obeyed him.

• • •

The next morning they awoke, showered, hugged. "Baby, give us a kiss," said Hershleder. *Give us a kiss!* (Was this one of Kahnny's old lines? Had the Kahn-man ever deigned to use it on her?) Then they went for breakfast at their diner. A square of hard, bright sunshine sat on the table between them. How it glinted off the silver. Neither Hershleder nor Jodie Fish could eat a single bite. They were shy with each other. While first thing in the morning Hershleder had felt terrific, now that the day was under way he was feeling increasingly less great. He wondered, after the contortions of the night before, if it hurt her to sit on that stiff banquette, and while they sat there not eating, he wondered if she could feel him dribble out of her, blot through her underwear, and run down her pants leg. They had used no birth control as far as he knew. Would he end up giving her the child that she wanted to the point of desperation?

God, he hoped not.

He had slept with another woman. A lovely woman, an old friend, a new friend really, but a woman who was not his wife. Separated or not, Michael or not, Hershleder felt like he had strayed.

Hershleder looked at his bacon and eggs. He looked up at Jodie Fish, who was shifting in her seat, staring out the window.

"Hey," he said.

She turned her gaze to him. She smiled a half-smile—that is, her front teeth bit down on her lower lip.

"Hey yourself," she said. "How are you?"

He reached out his hand; she reached out her hand, too, and met his, somewhere in the center of their table.

"Okay," he said, "I guess."

"You feel guilty," she said.

Hershleder looked at her admiringly. "How come you always know what I'm thinking?"

"I do not," said Jodie Fish. "I just feel totally guilt-ridden myself. I can't believe I did that. I can't believe I had a one-night stand."

"A one-night stand?" said Hershleder.

"Jack goes away for a week, and what do I do? I live out some adolescent fantasy."

"A one-night stand?" said Hershleder.

He looked down at the table.

"Come on, David," she said. "It wasn't anything. I mean, it was *something*. We took each other from a to c, if you know what I mean, but it wasn't anything."

"I don't know what you mean," said Hershleder.

"Yes you do," said Jodie.

But he didn't. Before Jodie Fish he had never cheated on his wife, and before Jodie Fish he had never told anyone the stuff that he had confessed to her last week. In fact, Hershleder had never done half of what he'd just done with Jodie Fish with anyone else in his life. Could this awful tangle of tactics and emotion be a form of love? Or had they both just gotten what they could?

Jodie Fish was a proponent of the latter. Hershleder knew. He knew her now. He knew her from sex, from conversation, from where God himself must have inscribed this knowledge inside his bones, from what he saw refracted in his internal mirror. For the first time in a long, long time, Hershleder had seen into another person's heart.

It was a lot like his.

He looked up. Everyone else in the diner was eating their

breakfast. Bacon. Eggs. Sausages. Everyone else but her and him.

"Maybe you fall in bed with just anyone all the time"—Hershleder's voice was trembling—"but for me this was something real and it was big."

"No," said Jodie Fish. "It was small, Dave. It was so small it was almost nothing."

8

In Paris, LeClerc had been right on time. At precisely six p.m., he'd walked up his pretty Parisian block to his little limestone building. Hershleder knew this because he'd arrived at least half an hour earlier and had been waiting for him.

Josephson showed up at 5:45, as promised. Perhaps he truly had understood how much was riding on this date. They'd stood side by side in nervous silence. It felt as if not just Hershleder's legs, but all of him, had fallen asleep; he'd tingled and burned; even his bones and teeth had itched inside him. His eyes skittishly roamed the streets. The fading horizontal light of sunset cast inky shadows through the iron filigree that laced its way around the little balconies on the next building; their terraced floors looked like some intricate tattoo. Hershleder had noticed this as he looked up from his watch and down the block and then down at his watch again. So it was at exactly six o'clock—Hershleder could pinpoint the time precisely—when he spotted LeClerc a long way off, as just a jogging dot against the sideways glow of the horizon.

"Is that him?" Hershleder asked Josephson, leaking Josephson out of his hangover. Josephson grunted in begrudging recognition.

From their vantage point down the street, this much was clear as LeClerc moved in close and closer yet: He was a short, slight man, fine-boned, with a face that rapidly came into focus, a face that appeared to be etched into place, his skin so translucent it seemed as if one could reach in with a pair of tweezers, fold back the tissue, and delicately lift his skeleton out intact. LeClerc's thin, ashy hair looked freshly trimmed, revealing the pale, slightly moist inroads of his forehead as if they were exposed to the atmosphere for the first time. It flew up, LeClerc's hair did, at the smallest breeze, lifted even from the tiny bounce of his measured gait.

While he made his final approach toward them, Hershleder noticed that there was something no-nonsense about the way LeClerc moved forward in the world, something strained and contained and precise; the same descriptions applied also when LeClerc stood at rest, in front of them. So it made sense that the chemist was dressed in an old but tidy jacket and tie—no overcoat despite the chill—and that the sleeves of that same jacket swallowed up his shirt cuffs, and that his shirt cuffs rattled around his wrists; he was that small and that delicate.

And tight, LeClerc was wound tight. He looked like a good candidate for spontaneous combustion.

In his imaginings, Hershleder had conjured up a more disheveled type: a scientist, someone not unlike himself, with dark-rimmed glasses, who flipped his comb-over from side to side, perhaps even a pocket protector. A guy wearing a patterned sweater. A guy with some heft to him, a guy with bulk.

But if LeClerc weren't dressed so carefully—in browns and grays—if he weren't put together so impeccably—collar starched and buttoned down, the two flaps of his tie pinned into one long neat arrow pointing at his belt—his clothing might have worn like an adult suit on a boy.

The evening light was blue and light blue. Hershleder shivered on the sidewalk.

LeClerc nodded at Josephson. Josephson nodded back at him. There was obviously no love lost there.

An awkward silence followed, but LeClerc broke the ice. He offered up his own hand to Hershleder, and Hershleder reached out his hand, too. The two hands met, suspended in the dying light like a cheap hologram, a talisman, a token on a keychain, a commemorative memento one can purchase at a gift shop.

Surely, at another time, in another place, their two hands could easily have been raised in anger, maybe even in the course of violence, of explosive violent action. But Hershleder sensed none of that potential charge. LeClerc's fingers were long and thin, and the skin that enwrapped the bone was cool and papery; it felt clean; his hand felt just-scrubbed and cool and dry. That is, the tips of his fingers felt this way to Hershleder, for the tips of his fingers were all LeClerc offered up to him, to Hershleder, who at that moment felt freakishly sweaty and large-palmed. The chemist's press was swift, finger pads to finger pads, and as Hershleder gazed down into the palest blue of LeClerc's eyes—so lightly tinged by pigment, they held the cast and color of white marble, blue-rinsed—LeClerc retracted his fingers and then the hand slid back down by his side once more, and his jacket sleeve dipped down to swallow it.

LeClerc blinked, releasing Hershleder's stare, and in this moment of demesmerization Hershleder grew acutely aware of his own rudeness, so he coughed to cover up. LeClerc, in French, invited the men inside. At least that's the way it appeared to Hershleder, because the chemist, while pronouncing something difficult to decipher, gestured with his arm, and Josephson harrumphed in response. LeClerc pushed open the heavy wooden front door—which took some effort—leaking yellow house light into the cool blue air. The three men climbed the steep staircase, LeClerc taking out his keys on the fourth-floor landing. He jangled them together all the way up the next flight. The sound they produced was immensely irritating, punctuated that way by the syncopation of their heavy footfalls and the silence that pulsed among the three of them. The men marched on in size order, LeClerc first, Josephson second, and the comparatively tall Hershleder bringing up the rear. By the time of their arrival, Hershleder had transformed into a hulking, awkward giant, and was awfully short of breath.

LeClerc himself was so unflappable he didn't appear to take in any lungfuls of air at all; rather, he seemed to exchange oxygen and CO_2 through some epidermal osmosis, the way a plant would. That might account for the cool, dry texture of his skin. Not that Hershleder was reducing LeClerc to something vegetative; especially in these circumstances he wanted to be certain to see every person as a person, to have all individuals weigh the exact same weight on his private scale.

He wanted to behold them like a true observer, borrowing the eye of God. God would love each and every one of them the same way: LeClerc, Hershleder, and the brain-injured, nutty Josephson. Hershleder had learned this theory in his nonsectarian public elementary school, and trusted it, even though everything he'd seen and heard and smelled and touched in life had taught him that no one is equal in any way.

They reached the top. LeClerc inserted the key; the three men entered an attic apartment. A studio, an atelier. A one-roomed sloping cathedral, with walls and ceiling meeting up at odd and unexpected angles. The place was large and largely empty and painted white; the walls were bare, as were the scarred wooden floors, and even the windows felt naked and unshuttered. A drafting table faced one wall, a desk turned its back upon another. There was a single office chair on wheels that probably rolled back and forth between the two work spaces; what wax was left on the planks of flooring that lay between them had long ago been worn into tracks of chalk.

The inky stain of the advancing night seeped in through two windows, chasing out the light, one at the front of the studio, the other at the back. The windows were large, and the ceiling, at least at its apex, was quite high. There was a bookshelf tucked under a low angle of the ceiling where it met up with a short wall. There was a door that led to a bath. There was an electric teakettle that sat on the top of said bookshelf.

Period.

No place for Hershleder or Josephson to sit, no place to hang a hat, even.

"He got rid of the fucking couch."

Vintage Josephson. And then in French: "Jacques, blah zee blah zee blah."

Hershleder wondered if Josephson didn't also curse in foreign languages.

LeClerc nodded, reached out his arms for their coats, which Hershleder and Josephson handed over. LeClerc disappeared with those coats into the bath. He came out again to get the teakettle and then went back inside to turn on the tap.

"He can't live here," whispered Hershleder.

"A fucking microorganism couldn't live here," said Josephson. "The place is too goddamn sterile. He lives downstairs. He and his wife have two floors, not that I've ever been issued an invitation. Mr. Sterility here's afraid I'll contaminate his chairs."

"Oh," said Hershleder. He looked around the studio awkwardly, not sure at all about what to do with himself.

LeClerc reappeared. Plugged in the teakettle, opened a desk drawer and took out three teacups, a little silver bowl filled with cubed sugar, and a pair of silver tongs. He lay this spread attractively atop the bookshelf. He motioned to Hershleder to sit in that one chair. Hershleder politely gestured no-I-couldn't, but LeClerc swept his arm forward, insisting rather graciously.

"What is this?" said Josephson. "Welcome to fucking mime country?"

Hershleder glared at him. LeClerc glared at him. The two men nodded at each other; Josephson was exactly what they needed, a common enemy.

"Okay," said Josephson. "Let's get the show on the road, all right?"

All right indeed, all right with everybody. The whistle blew. LeClerc poured each of them some tea and lifted his practically hairless eyebrows ever so slightly when Hershleder held up three fingers for three sugars. Then LeClerc gracefully leaned against the desk. Hershleder rolled back and forth in the one and only chair as Josephson began the difficult task of simultaneous interpretation.

It took a while to get things going. Hershleder had spent the better part of the afternoon walking the streets of Paris while putting together a little prepared speech; he delivered that speech now. In fact, he was rather long-winded about it. Not since his days as president of Arista at the Bronx High School of Science had Hershleder ever made such a longiloquent presentation. He went on and on. Mom. Dad. The peculiarities of growing up in the diaspora. The spectacular attempt at genocide. The casualties of every generation that followed the generation that was directly victimized. He was curious, he said, about how one could deny these horrors in the first place and then go on to find the courage to re-research what he had originally believed, to reevaluate some of the tenets upon which he'd built his historical perspective.

Here, Hershleder's mouth filled with saliva; a little bubble seeped out the left-hand corner. He wiped his lip with the edge of his thumb and swallowed. He swallowed again for insurance.

Yes, he was curious. Definitely curious. He guessed that

was why he was here. He was curious about how a person can have the guts to rethink his life.

Now Hershleder gathered his own courage and looked up; until this point he'd been alternately studying his chest and the plain, hard-worn wooden floor, those chalky tracks from desk to drafting table that circled back and around again. He looked LeClerc in those pale blue eyes, LeClerc staring straight back at him, while Josephson rattled on, Hershleder hoped, doing his words justice, although for all he knew, Josephson was telling LeClerc that Hershleder had a proclivity for humping sheep.

"What exactly are you telling him?" said Hershleder.

"Exactly everything you told me," said Josephson.

The room was quiet.

"Arista?" queried LeClerc, as if to prove his point.

"Tell him it's not worth explaining," said Hershleder, two or three tears now rolling inexplicably toward his chin.

The tears made LeClerc uncomfortable. Not Josephson; tears on Hershleder's chin did nothing to him.

LeClerc rolled one hand in the air, stiffly, from the wrist, as if he wanted to push them all away and ahead, into the divergent pathways of their futures.

"C'mon already," said LeClerc via Josephson. "Get the fucking lead out."

"Is that what he really said?" said Hershleder.

"No," said Josephson. "No, what he really said was, 'Where does this asshole want to begin?' "

Hershleder shrugged helplessly in the blue wash of the

spreading night. It was so shadowy in the room now, the rolling hand glowed opalescent, and Hershleder could barely make out LeClerc's face, just the faint outlines of a skull gleaming dully in the dark. It was a face that haunted its own body.

"At the beginning," said Josephson. "Aren't you the guy who does research for a living?"

At the beginning. Hershleder nodded. I would like to begin at the beginning.

LeClerc walked over to the entranceway and flipped on the overhead switch, and the flash of light, it hurt their eyes, catching the men by surprise, all three of them off-kilter.

• • •

He'd heard of Villard, the famous French revisionist, that's all, but he had not known or really ever thought much about the debate. His lack of a position was challenged by his first visit to the camp.

"When was that?" queried Hershleder via Josephson.

"On vacation," LeClerc via Josephson rapidly responded to him.

"Why a death camp?" Hershleder pressed him.

"I'm a chemist."

Pause.

"For a chemist, it's a natural curiosity."

LeClerc had been to the camp twelve years before, and again two years later, and then in the past ten years, half a dozen other times. He knew more about the structure of those buildings than probably did its original architects, if any could still be found to be alive and living in the open.

"Or in Paraguay." Josephson added his own aside.

But in the beginning, on vacation with his wife, LeClerc was as ignorant as the rest, so he took the tour.

A docent had guided the LeClercs through artifact upon artifact, the barracks and the barbed wire, the barren yards, the mass grave sites, the infamous group showers; it was at the showers that LeClerc's interest piqued. He was a man who liked to figure things out for himself. LeClerc had not believed the docent's laconic guided tour of the showers; he didn't buy any of it. For one, where was the blue coloration, the residue of hydrocyanic acid that resulted even when Zyklon-B was used simply for delousing?

"It'd been forty years. Plus, every idiot knows it takes larger amounts of cyanide over a greater period of time to kill a louse than it does to kill a human."

Josephson.

"Shush," shushed Hershleder.

LeClerc raised those hairless brows another time, as if to ask: Do you, or do you not, want me to continue on here?

Hershleder shot Josephson a warning look. Then, to LeClerc: "Please begin again. Please."

LeClerc continued. It was his wife who had stumbled on a whole set of revisionist publications and had presented three or four of them to him as a gift. LeClerc, intrigued, was hungry to know more.

"France is as good a place as any for these things. So is

Southern California. Idaho. Germany, yes and no. It is against the law in Germany to publicly declare a revisionist argument, but as we all know, laws are not everything. I stayed put in Paris, did a lot of the work here, out of my own home. Information—that is, theoretical information—was not so hard to find. There's a lot been written, you see, and for those not so scholarly inclined, there are the videos."

"I've seen them, man," said Josephson. "They're seductive as hell if you're a racist and a moron."

"I found that with a little bit of hunting, there were people willing to talk. Several were chemists like myself. As you know, theoreticians hold somewhat different concerns than we scientists."

Here LeClerc gave Hershleder a little collusional nod of the head. It was a gesture Hershleder found himself appreciating. It cemented the fact that each took the other seriously. It flattered him.

"You are up on all the arguments?"

Hershleder nodded yes. "But what about the chemists?" How different were these men from a researcher like himself?

"We began to meet regularly; one could say we'd formed a little club. They decided to make me their emissary; I conducted the formal correspondence."

Here LeClerc modestly cast his eyes downward. "You know, it is often hard to find a scientist who can write well."

Hershleder nodded yes, yes, this was true.

"They raised the money to send me on several fact-finding missions. I searched out copies of the original plans, the shipping orders, the architects' correspondence. I toured and toured the camp, noting each and every deviation from the engineers' drawings and the actual physical plant. I read and reread everything I could find that was written on the subject, Villard and all the others. I was most thorough."

Hershleder nodded; he'd read the others, too. He would have liked to stop here and ask LeClerc what he had thought, about the readings, about Villard, about what kind of man this revisionist was, about the why of all of it, but it was this type of digressive behavior that often got Hershleder into trouble. One couldn't ferret out everything; there was no time. Yet there was time, later, for other trips, for a possible exchange of letters, perhaps even some transatlantic phone calls. There was just no time right now. Isn't that the paradox of life, limitless time in the future, no time at all in the present?

He had to keep his eye on the ball here, stick to his plan, as meager as it was, and his hypothesis: that some catalytic something had completely altered LeClerc's committed revisionist path, that some catalytic something had completely changed LeClerc's gestalt. Wasn't that what Hershleder really wanted, to extract and isolate that catalyst?

As for Josephson, he just seemed restless. He was stripping down his cuticles. He used his teeth.

"The purpose of the project was to prove what it ultimately disproved, to illustrate the impossibility of the gassings. As you might guess, I myself found my own conclusions rather surprising, and in my community there was more than a little dismay once I began to relate my findings. However, I believe that these findings are completely substantiated and irrefutable. I explain my methodology quite clearly in my book. You have read this book, yes?"

"Yes. Cover to cover." All 1,039 pages.

LeClerc seemed pleased.

"My biggest problem was the inner workings of the gas chambers. I did not understand how these units could function efficiently without endangering the workers that manned them, or even what kept the facilities from exploding. So I worked through the official documents and did my own redrawing. Would you like to see my charts and graphs?"

Hershleder responded, "I would be delighted."

Out came the charts, the graphs, the drawings, the years and years of correspondence. All neatly cataloged inside of LeClerc's locked desk drawers. At one point, LeClerc went back into the bath and came out with three more cylinders of plans. The two men spread them out against the drafting table. Hershleder asked many questions—the flow of this, the draw of that—and LeClerc illustrated on the paper with his hands, those cool, bony fingers acting like fine pointers. Hershleder was always grateful for the opportunity to learn.

The hours passed. LeClerc worked carefully and methodically in his efforts to fully explain each arising obstacle and the choices that were available at the time to neutralize them. A lot of effort had gone into the whole endeavor. This was obvious.

Somewhere in the midst of all of it, Josephson stopped his pacing and sat down on the floor.

He was a good teacher, LeClerc. Really rather patient with Hershleder and his inquiries. At only one point did he appear to get a tiny bit excited, and that little rise of blood pressure had to do with the genius of a downdraft and the inherent beauty of a pipeline. The inarguable grace of an equation when it worked.

Much of this information was not new to Hershleder. But it was reinforcing, if chilling, to have it all explained to him, LeClerc demonstrating the placement of the faux showerheads, the hooks hung upon the wall, the changing chambers where the prisoners disrobed. He relayed the entire process of extermination from the delivery of the "substances" to the removal of the "products."

Those were his terms, LeClerc's, and for the moment Hershleder noted but did not challenge them.

• • •

It was midnight by the time they took their first break, LeClerc exiting into the bath for several minutes of water-running. Once they resumed, it was two A.M. before Hershleder looked at his watch again.

"One could not help but concede that the Nazis had been clever."

This last line was a direct quote from LeClerc via Josephson, who repeated it in English with a bitter smirk. But Hershleder had learned hours before to look at LeClerc himself while Josephson was translating, in order to avoid as much as possible Josephson's unavoidable bias. Hershleder looked at LeClerc the way he would try and focus on an actor while simultaneously reading subtitles whenever Itty dragged him to a foreign film.

LeClerc himself did not smirk. LeClerc was too exhausted. He blinked and blinked politely to keep himself awake. Hershleder should have been more of the same, considering he also had jet lag to contend with. But Hershleder was too agitated, too frustrated, to be exhausted.

It was late. Josephson had flattened out completely in a supine position on the floor, holding his weary head up with the short stack of his fists. Hershleder kicked Josephson out of his stupor.

"So what made you change your mind?"

The weary LeClerc looked puzzled.

"Ask him again, ask him again," Hershleder prodded Josephson.

"What made you concur that the gassings occurred, sir?"

LeClerc stared at Hershleder as though he was an idiot.

"The facts. I studied the facts."

The facts, the facts. Hershleder knew from facts, he knew from a ton of them; he was buried in facts, he was paralyzed by the lot of them. But he was also painfully aware that knowing the facts wasn't always enough, that sometimes the facts just lay there cold and congealed and leaden. That identifying the problem doesn't always start the solution. That information itself isn't everything.

A person needs an ineffable something to kick him into gear so that he can begin the long, terrible task of making use of what he's gleaned. Treatment is built this way, thought Hershleder, treatment and relief, in medicine, in science.

Hershleder turned to Josephson. "I don't get it."

"Don't fucking look at me. I never got this entire stupid project."

"Stupid? You spent a whole year of your life on it."

"Yeah, well, my spiritual mother," said Josephson. As if this phrase alone explained everything.

"What the hell are you talking about?" said Hershleder.

"My spiritual mother. She was the project's editor. So how could I refuse? And then once I got near this revisionist crap," Josephson shuddered, "the bastards sucked me in."

"My mother, too," Hershleder said. "She was obsessed with this stuff."

"Sure. Of course she was. The Nazis stole her future and then the deniers robbed her of her past. Of course she was obsessed. She wanted to recapture what God had originally inscribed in the Book of Life for her. You know, what he intended, before her chapter got revised."

Hershleder felt tired enough to cry.

"You didn't even know her," said Hershleder. "How come you get it? How come you get it when I don't?"

"Why don't you get it already?" said Josephson. "Survivor shock. It's like a disease. Grief. Trauma. Mourning. And let me tell you, it can be inherited. Look at you, you're fucking riddled with it, pal, you're a fucking goner."

Hershleder stared at him.

"Don't give me those cow eyes, Hershleder," said Josephson. "I've been listening to you guys go on and on for hours, pipes and drafts, products and substances, like a pair of goddamn robots. What the hell's happened to you? What are you denying? What is it you can't face?"

"I'm not denying anything," said Hershleder.

"Yeah?" said Josephson. "In the past few hours did either one of you ever once mention fucking people?"

No. They had not. Hershleder shook his head no to this.

"Ever hear about eyewitnesses? Partisans and liberators? Anne Frank and her goddamned diary? Your own fucking mother?"

"Don't talk that way about my mother." Hershleder was instantly back in the schoolyard. But Josephson, as always, was on a higher plane.

"Would your goddamned fucking mother need LeClerc to explain to her the practical aspects of how the kid down the block was rounded up, selected, gassed, and then incinerated? Of all the questions she must have had, do you think those are the ones that plagued her?"

Hershleder was quiet.

"Christ, Dave. Why do you think they deny all this stuff in the first place? So they can do it again, right? That's why I study them. I want to be ready. I want to be the first warrior in the front lines of the apocalypse."

Josephson was panting heavily.

"It's time, *it's time, Dave,* to take a good look at yourself. Who's the real revisionist here, you or him?"

• • •

It was five o'clock ante meridiem. Outside were the first pearly shadows of morning light. Exhausted, the three men, each in his own corner, sat quietly, lost in the thought patterns of his own making.

Hershleder did not know what he felt about any of this. Sure, he believed in scholarship, in data; he believed in black and white. Sure, he believed in being armed against the far and fascist right. Therefore, if p, then q; he believed in fighting fake fire with real fire.

Q.E.D.

But was Josephson really right? Had he, Hershleder, really come all this way just to join forces with LeClerc in the practice of erasure and denial? Was this, like his trips home to Larchmont, just another pathetic attempt at undoing something he did not like? Who would he be now if his mother had lived a different life? He would be a different person.

There was nothing Hershleder wanted more. He put his head in his hands.

"You're right," said Hershleder to Josephson.

Now Hershleder turned to LeClerc. "And you're right."

He stared from one man to the other. He felt rather rabbinical when he said this. He wondered how he ever, ever thought any of this could possibly relate to him, to David Hershleder and his tiny, personal problems.

He said, "I must be out of my mind."

Josephson and LeClerc nodded sagely at this remark. They nodded in tandem for the first time that endless night.

Josephson turned to LeClerc. He spoke in French, translating immediately afterward for Hershleder.

"C'mon, Jacques. I want to know now, too. Why did you really start this whole business in the first place?"

LeClerc sighed loudly. It was late, very late, so late that it was early. He appeared to have had it with these guys. Slowly, as if he were talking to a retarded child, LeClerc spelled it out for them.

"I'm a scientist; a scientist doesn't accept blindly; a scientist needs evidence. Proof. Now the world has proof, proof that is unshakable. Now, when a Villard, a whoever, tries to stir up trouble, you have my study, the LeClerc study, you have all you need to refute them down on paper. I don't understand you people. One would think you might be grateful."

LeClerc went back into the bath and came out again with their coats. At this point, even the socially inept Hershleder and the socially inept Josephson knew enough to note that they had overstayed their welcome. Yet even Josephson wasn't ready to give in. They kept waiting, unsatisfied, for an answer they could buy: They waited for him a full five more additional long and silent minutes.

After all those hours of cooperation, those extra minutes proved unendurable, so wearily, LeClerc gave in.

"I don't like Jews," he said in English.

Hershleder and Josephson both stood. It was time to go.

• • •

Paris, France. Hershleder wondered if there might be any other city in the world that felt quite so haunted in the morning. Maybe Hiroshima or Dresden or Sarajevo or Beirut, South Central L.A. or Red Hook, Brooklyn. But in their guilt and haunting, could any of these cities feel so polished and so elegant? Hershleder and Josephson passed shop window after shop window outfitted with the most beautiful ladies' shoes. They looked like sleek, sensuous cats preening on their pedestals. The air was chilly, but fragrant with the scent of baking bread and freshly brewed coffee, with the spices of autumn and winter's first tentative sparkly breaths.

Hershleder and Josephson walked briskly down the sidewalk. For five blocks or so, neither of them spoke. But when Josephson stopped, reaching into his pockets for a cigarette, Hershleder got up the nerve to extend his own palm and asked if he could bum one.

He stood posed on the street like a beggar.

Josephson looked on him with pity. Then he shook out two filterless French cigarettes. He turned his back to the wind, struck a match, and cupped it with his fist. Hershleder, with the cigarette stuck between his lips, leaned the tip into that small flame and sucked in. The paper curled, retracting from the heat, the tobacco catching and then burning. Smoke bloomed out of Hershleder's nostrils; he shot it forth like that old Times Square Camel smoking billboard.

"Aaaach," said Hershleder.

He was tired.

The match blew out, so Hershleder offered up his cigarette and Josephson took it, pressing ember to end and returning it again.

"I love my wife," said Hershleder.

"I know," said Josephson, sounding like he did.

They walked on silently for a few more moments. Then, "I feel like I've spent the last twenty-four hours treading water," said Hershleder. "Longer. I feel like I've been treading water longer."

Josephson shook his head.

Hershleder took another drag on his cigarette. He stopped and turned to Josephson. He said, "You can't will yourself an epiphany, can you, Dave?"

Josephson said nothing. What was there to say? The sky streaked pink and gray with wild bleeds of orange; the buildings hung back gray and black and blurry like charcoal rubbings of unmarked graves. The men were cold, and the world was soft, too soft: Its core was bleating faintly, whimpering in pain.

• • •

A waste of time and a waste of money. That's what the Kahnman said. "The things I do for you, Hersh," Kahn said, pushing back his airplane seat and cracking a half-smile.

They were mid-flight. They were hovering over the Atlantic Ocean, Hershleder and Kahn in row eight, Josephson reclined in row nine, tapping his knee against the back of Hershleder's seat, Hershleder too deflated to even bother to turn and scold him. Overnight, he'd officially entered middle age.

He was returning empty-handed. He didn't have anything to offer up to anybody, much less to Itty and the kids, which was why, he told himself, he'd started with all this garbage in the first place.

"Come on, Hersh," said Kahn, "buy your oldest pal a drink."

Hershleder bought Kahn and Josephson rounds for the rest of the journey. He owed them that much; it was the least that he could do. The Davids all drank Seven-and-Sevens—that is, until Hershleder vomited into a little paper sack while they were endlessly circling New York Harbor.

While he puked, Kahn held his head.

It had been a long history of head-holding for Kahn. A master, Kahn was practiced at this action of accompaniment; his fingers grappled behind Hershleder's ears, his palm flush and cool against the spreading Hershleder bald spot. With a fillip of expertise, Kahn even patted Hershleder's knee while he was spewing, and then again when Hershleder was wiping his mouth with Kahn's very own silk hankie, and then again while Hershleder restuffed that hankie back into Hershleder's pocket. Kahn even patted Hershleder's knee when Hershleder leaned back in his seat and closed his red, red eyes, as red as if he'd been sobbing.

Kahn patted Hershleder's knee. The Kahn-man could be like that sometimes.

• • •

Back in New York, Hershleder said good-bye and good luck rather quickly to Josephson, who, after all that endless above-ground circling, had to scramble to make his connecting flight. He went running down the corridor, with Hershleder calling, "Good-bye and good luck," right after him, making Josephson even more eager to flee as fast as possible, his wick bouncing behind him like a little winning flag.

After that, and after thanking Kahn for being his best friend for life, after quietly confessing that he, Hershleder, didn't deserve him, after putting Kahn in a yellow cab and slipping the cabbie fifty bucks, Hershleder did not see Kahn for a long, long time. When he got home to that little studio apartment, he did not call Itty or his sisters, his aged father and his stepmother—a woman he rather liked; he did not even pick up the phone and dial his own children.

None of these people bothered to reach out and touch Hershleder either. Perhaps Kahn had fended them off. Perhaps even in his hurt, Kahn had known enough to tell them all to give Hershleder a little room. The guy needed the equivalent of a psychic refractory period.

Or perhaps they'd just grown used to his absence. Without communication, this much was hard to tell.

Even though he missed all of them, Hershleder did not call anyone whom he loved or anyone who was even vaguely connected to him for weeks and weeks. For months, even. Long enough to grow a full beard and to have it professionally trimmed and trimmed again. What he did was return to his routines.

Hershleder went to Bellevue, to Inge and the shreds of his position. Days in and out this go-around were as similar (and as varied) as days usually were at the hospital. On the second Tuesday of every month he'd have a grand rounds; he supervised students on Mondays and Wednesdays, spent Thursdays reluctantly with his handful of private patients. Whatever time he could squeeze out of the rest of the week was devoted to the EEG lab and his research. Maple Syrup Urine Disorder, dystonia, the death studies, brain birth.

In the evenings, he caught up with the medical journals, went through stacks of his mounting bills. Eventually, Hershleder signed himself up for a debt consolidation plan, and while what he owed was considerable, what he spent these days was the opposite, living as he did a spartan existence. In a year or two, he would be back to his normal set of payments: car, house, day camp.

In the mornings, Hershleder slept late for him, then bought each of the three early editions of the papers and went to Veselka's just for toast and coffee, no longer possessing much of an appetite for Eastern European breakfasts, and no more going to the movies. He was sick of nostalgia and miracle cures. Those ridiculous epiphanic moments. What did they have to do with his reality? He was the same as he ever was, only more so. Plus, he couldn't stand the thought of the Kips Bay theater without Maria. So he did his work. He did his work.

What else could Hershleder do but work and work harder? He was old and getting older to have learned so very little about how to live a life.

• • •

It was during one of these working days, a Thursday, in between appointments with his handful of private patients, that Hershleder stumbled upon Maria's niece and another chaperoning female adult—a cousin, aunt, or mother; she bore the requisite big hair—in the Bellevue hall. He actually, literally stumbled upon her. It was Inge's lunch hour. She and Louie had retired into a spare examination room, so in an effort to avoid the pain that accompanied his own desire and longing, the envious Hershleder roamed the halls. The little girl was appropriately child-size, and Hershleder hadn't exactly been looking where he was going. He smacked right into the kid, and the kid began to cry.

"Oh, my God," said Hershleder. "Oh, my God. I'm so sorry," Hershleder apologized.

The woman picked up the little girl and let the child sob into her shoulder.

"Somebody's just a little overtired," said the cousin, kindly.

"I'm so, so sorry." Hershleder patted the kid's skinny, ribby back, and at his touch the little girl switched shoulders, hiding her face from his.

But oh, the dusty milk of the child's skin, the neck so moist and white. How he wanted to run his finger down it, and lick up her sweat like frosting.

The cousin said, "Somebody's just a little bit sick of hospitals."

Hershleder nodded; he could relate.

"I think it's time to go home."

The kid agreed, nodding her head yes, yes, into the wet and loving shoulder of her relative.

The young woman smiled at Hershleder, who continued standing there in the hall, and when he didn't say anything more, she started walking toward the elevators. In a few more uninterrupted seconds she and the child would disappear, out of his life, out of his sight.

Separation anxiety: a refugee legacy.

How could he let her go?

"Hey, hey you, hey, tell me, how's Maria?" Hershleder called this after her, his heart thunking wildly. Anything at all to stop her in her tracks.

The young woman spun around, surprised. Surprised, she said, "Maria? She's doing good. She did a commercial, and now she's up for a bit part on a soap."

Hershleder nodded again, truly pleased for her.

The young woman smiled, the full-flower of the situation dawning on her, blooming for her, and when Hershleder saw this, the act of dawning, the young woman in full and dawning bloom, he let some of his own situation infectiously dawn upon him as well, for no other reason than that he was jealous: He was jealous of this young girl with a halo of recognition lighting up her pretty face. She was back-lit and beatific, the child limp and peaceful in her arms.

If he'd been a member of another order, another faith, he might at that moment have thought of the Madonna, but being Jewish and half-orphaned, Hershleder turned his mind and his heart to his own mother.

"So, it was you, huh?" said the young woman, so wise and strong and holy.

Hershleder nodded yes. Yes. Yes. It was him.

"It was you."

• • •

That afternoon, Hershleder headed out to Long Island and the cemetery where his mother was interred for the first time since they buried her. It was a wet, cold, raw day, and not much of what he expected to have happen to him happened to him there. Instead, he met up with Jodie Fish, his old girlfriend from summer camp. They had a flirtation, followed by the briefest of affairs. A one-night stand. This was made quite evident the morning after—that is, when Jodie Fish spelled it out for him—and then there was a long, tense ride back into the city, and a cordial but stiff parting of the ways. A whole week went by after that and then another and Hershleder did not hear a peep from Jodie Fish—not that anyone in their right mind might think he would.

Why should he hear from her? He'd not exactly picked up the phone to call the girl himself. He'd thought about writing her a letter, sending a card, a note, but he'd taken none of these steps toward furtherance or reconciliation. Every day when he checked the mailbox in his lobby, his heart did a little skip, but Jodie Fish had not bothered to write Hershleder either. Perhaps this was because there was nothing more to say. Perhaps this was because they had said it all already.

It was a Thursday, first thing in the morning. Hershleder was in his office waiting for one of his handful of private patients. The guy was always late, but on this specific Thursday he was already late by three-quarters of an hour, and Hershleder was trying to decide whether or not to bail, wondering if the guy would show.

He was thinking about Jodie Fish, thinking about how quickly she had entered his life, and how even more quickly she had left it, left him, and he she, and how damned depressing it was now, on top of everything else, to have to feel lousy about her as well.

He was sitting at his desk, a mahogany desk, a doctor's desk; he was surrounded by cups of sludgy coffee. The liquid was so vile—the surfaces filmy and streaked with clumpy white—that Hershleder had to look away. He looked down at his shoe. A bow was tied, a little lopsided, out of his shoelaces.

He was a lousy shoe-tier. He'd always been that way, as a child and now that he was pushing forty. Something about not getting that knot tight enough, something about the two loops drooping and uncoiling and then him tripping and falling on his face. He didn't remember tying that shoe himself that very morning, although he knew that this was the most likely scenario, as there was no one left on the planet these days who would deign to tie it for him.

This had not always been true. When Hershleder lived at home his children had fought over the task of tying his shoes; how far had he strayed? When they first met, when he and Itty were dating, how many times had she stopped him while they were out in the street so that she could quickly knot up his loose laces? From summer camp to med school, there had always been some girl willing to kneel at his feet, finding him attractively incompetent. Jodie Fish, for example, Debbie Schwartz's friend, sensitive Jodie Fish, the Kahn-fucker, Hershleder's confidante, his soul mate. Jodie Fish, who had just dumped him. And at the Bronx High School of Science, once during an Arista meeting, Kahn himself had tied Hershleder's laces together around the rungs of Hershleder's presidential seat, so that when Hershleder stood he pitched forward and fell face first into a crowd of geeks.

It was his mother who first taught him this fine art. They'd gone down to the Stride-Rite on Fourteenth Street and bought a pair of shoes. P.F. Flyers. Then they'd gone home and practiced, twisting, threading, pulling through, and looping. When he'd finally gotten it right—a bow just like this same bow now, which drooped slightly to one side—his mother acted as if he'd just found the cure for cancer.

"Two floppy ears," she'd said, "just like a little bunny. You're a very special boy, Dovidil," his mother said to him, over and over again, and he believed her.

In a way, that was what had both made and ruined his life. He'd believed his mother when she told him he was special. Had she been lying? For he couldn't tie a shoelace to save his life.

His mother, the one who abandoned him, who sentenced him to the life of a half-life, a life frozen in motion; his mother, Adela Hershleder, who opened her little oven, laid down a towel, laid down her head, and turned on the gas.

Hershleder looked at his shoe. He looked at his shoe again. Hadn't he always known this to be true? Why now, at this peculiarly simple moment, had he chosen to remember it?

He'd left his mother that false final night of Christmas break, the final night he'd failed her, and gone back across town to the room he bunked in at his father's. He'd spent the next day goofing around the city with some old pals from his high school. On Friday the eighteenth, he and his ride, this guy Sean McCarthy, had gotten a late start. He and McCarthy got a late start and then lost a bunch of time eating dinner at the Roscoe Diner. They each had an order of the diner's deep-fried French toast and, still hungry, ended up splitting a big Greek salad. What a vile combination.

Hershleder could remember what he ate for dinner eighteen years before, but he couldn't remember tying his shoe that very morning. He could remember that dinner because it had been nauseating but still satisfying—he and McCarthy had gotten stoned the minute they drove over the bridge.

They were twenty-one and twenty years old, respectively.

McCarthy sang Sinatra's "New York, New York" and Springsteen's "Born to Run" at the top of his lungs for hours on the interstate. The radio was out. It had driven Hershleder a little crazy, but it was McCarthy's car and Hershleder was McCarthy's passenger, so he hadn't said anything.

When Hershleder finally got back up to Ithaca, it was rather late at night. And cold. It was freezing. By accident, he'd left his dorm window open during those very coldest of winter months, the whole damn Christmas vacation. He remembered now, so clearly, as he looked down at his shoe, a nice shoe, a shoe tied sloppily, that as he entered his floor, he'd heard his own phone ringing, ringing, down the hall, and so he jogged toward it, knapsack and duffel bag flapping clumsily, slowing the poor kid down.

One of his dormmates had stuck his head out of his own attic single and said, "Could you pick up already, Dave? All that ringing's driving me crazy."

So when Hershleder flung his door wide, he couldn't for a split second decide whether to pick up the phone or to close that open window. Sure, he wanted first to be a good neighbor, to be popular, to be liked, but it was so very cold in there, in his dorm room. His nuts retracted; they shrunk to half their usual size.

Hershleder remembered now, eighteen years later, that after that moment of indecision, he'd opted for the socially responsible choice; he dove for the phone, ignoring that frosty window, so that while he sat on his bed, ear to receiver—his stepmother saying "Thank God" at the sound of his breathless hello, and passing the phone to his waiting father—Hershleder felt like he was sitting in a path of blasty ice. He felt like he was sitting in front of an open Sub-Zero freezer with a fan directing all that freezing air right at him, as if all that freezing air was funneled through a spotlight, a spotlight that had trapped and frozen him in its glow. When his father told him what his father told him, eighteen long years ago, it was so cold in his dorm room, it was so cold in Hershleder's cold, cold dorm room, that ice crystals formed on the tips of his eyelashes. This was true. Ice crystals formed on Hershleder's eyelashes because he himself had turned into a monster with ice for blood. His father told him what his father told him, and this was Hershleder the ice monster's first response:

"Fuck her."

Fuck her, fuck her, fuck her.

Fuck her.

Hershleder looked down.

His shoe was brown.

9

THERE IS NO REVISING ANY OF THIS.

On Wednesday, January 16, 1975, Adela Hershleder did what the Nazis could not do: She finished the job for them. She opened her own mini-oven, spread a towel across that grimy little half-door, laid down her head, and turned on the gas.

This is fact and inarguable. No longer was there any point in running away, denying or rewriting it. There had been no accident or leaky pipe, no rupturing of either a cerebral or aortic aneurysm, as Hershleder had later reported conflictingly to his wife and Kahn and the friends and relatives who knew all of them—his father and his stepmother and his sisters, co-authors in this sloppy conspiracy. Another heart-mind dichotomy.

Adela Hershleder.

She had been smart, sensitive and whiny and depressed and self-sacrificing and easy to delight; and she suffered.

His mother.

He'd refused his own mother when she'd asked him to stay the night. After Paris, Hershleder had been ready to tell this to somebody. All that struggle and survival leading up to one desperate act all alone in her lonely apartment without a son there to comfort her.

He'd confessed much of this to Jodie Fish, but not all of it, and to cement the confession, he'd slept with her, letting sex do what sex does, letting it open him up to the best and the worst of himself. Hershleder confessed to Jodie Fish and he took her to a motel and he slept with her, which made him feel human and very much alive, and at the time, well, it had been kind of nice.

Now he wanted to go home.

• • •

Grand Central Station. Restoration. The terminal was covered with scaffolding—a vaulted, soaring amphitheater in the middle of a much-heralded steam-cleaning. As with that famous Sistine Chapel, the ceiling kept reappearing in patches brighter and renewed. Hershleder craned his neck, and for the first time that he could remember, he could even see some stars. They were patterned out like the winter night sky, which was heavenly.

Hershleder bought his ticket and made his way to Track 11.

"Smoke," hissed the young man in a black concert T-shirt. "Thai stick, dust, coke."

Hershleder nodded his hellos, but he did not stop.

"Hey, man," said Mr. Black Concert T-Shirt. "Where you been?"

Hershleder shrugged. He did not know a simple answer to this question, but he was touched, so he gave the guy a two-fingered salute before moving on. It was nice of Mr. Black

Concert T-Shirt to have noticed Hershleder's absence and to graciously welcome Hershleder back to the fold. Would that when he arrived in Larchmont an hour later, his own family would be so moved.

An aproned man was selling newspapers on the platform and Hershleder was tempted to pick up a copy of *The New York Times,* but isn't that where his troubles began, or at least a small-big part of them? There was something to be said for willful ignorance. He'd already bypassed the Oyster Bar, and so here, too, he walked on.

Hershleder entered the train at the first car. Outside the terminal it had been a dreary March morning. Not rainy, but with the promise of rain, and even in that gray tunnel the air felt pregnant and damp. Hershleder slid into a seat, knocking over an empty box of Dunkin' Donuts with his feet, and stared out the thick, scarred train window. The light above flashed on, then off again. It would be a few minutes before the train started up. The car was empty, so there was no stranger to focus on, no old neighbor to chitchat with, no parent of a college chum to be polite to, no teenage couple arguing so passionately that one would feel envious and compelled to eavesdrop. There was none of this. No diversions.

Hershleder was on his own.

He stroked his beard. Even with the rug burn long healed, Hershleder hadn't had the heart to shave it off; it's a rare pleasure in life to find a growth that can be charted.

Of course, there was another bearded wonder for Hershleder to contend with—Itty's boyfriend Michael. Would he be waiting there in Larchmont? After this long, impossible journey, would Michael, her lover, be standing in the doorway like a sentry to stave him off?

The lights flicked on again, the bells ding-donged, and the doors shuddered shut. The train to Larchmont lurched out of Grand Central Station and through that long, dark, skanky tunnel. Michael. 13-9-3-8-1-5-12. For the first time Hershleder understood why his small son Jonathan talked and thought in numbers. In some way it made things easier. Like his dad, there were probably a lot of things Jonathan did not want to think about. How could a parent save his child from this dismal inheritance? Especially a parent who for all practical purposes had abandoned his son?

Who knows? But he would do his best; he would make it up to him. David Hershleder, M.D., divorced or not, Jonathan's 4-1-4, he would try anything. Anything! He wanted so much to be a good father.

Maybe it was too late; and then again, maybe it wasn't.

Hershleder leaned his forehead against that filthy window and watched the world fly.

• • •

She was sitting on the porch. He had called her from the station. No more surprises; no more passive aggression. He wanted a fair fight; he wanted resolution. For once in his life, Hershleder wanted a thing resolved. She was sitting on the front steps waiting for him. Itty in a turtleneck and sweatshirt and a pair of thermal leggings. Even from down the block as he approached her, she appeared surrounded by her usual cloud of dust. She was hunched over, her hands between her knees to keep them warm. She wore a pair of Hershleder's old house slippers that flapped around her small feet and thick knitted socks of the pepper-and-salt variety, the kind hippies wear with Birkenstocks.

Itty. Her hair was loose and antic, the red and golden curls rippling slightly in the slight breeze. She released one hand to knot it up, but the hair almost instantly worked itself free again. It had always had a life of its own. There were weeks, Hershleder remembered now, that Itty hadn't even bothered to comb it out. Why should she? It uncombed itself so quickly.

Buster was lying at her side. When he saw Hershleder turn up the Hershleder walk, sidestepping the Casa Hershleder sign, the Dalmatian tensed, making as if to bolt for him, but Itty grabbed the collar quickly and held the dog down.

Itty, his wife! His estranged wife. She was sitting on the steps, the steps of the house that had once been their house; it seemed such a long time ago. She was protecting Hershleder from the wrath of what by all rights should have been his dog.

Hershleder slowed and sat next to them. He raised his hand, offering it up for Buster to sniff. After a moment or two, Buster calmed a bit; perhaps, Hershleder could only hope, the dog recognized his scent. Then Hershleder scratched behind the Dalmatian's ears, trying his best to befriend him.

Buster's muscles rolled back, he relaxed them; he folded down onto the ground so Hershleder could pet his spotty coat.

"Good boy," said Itty. "You can never move too slowly."

Was that last line directed to Buster or to him?

How many weeks and weeks and months had it been? How long since Hershleder had last gazed upon her fully? Itty was still beautiful, he reassured himself, but there were new crinkles around her eyes and a web of lines that worried across her forehead. This much aging was inevitable, although it was still surprising. She hadn't been frozen in time! She hadn't been frozen in time without him there to fully gaze upon her. Itty was getting older, too; he wasn't the only one in this family who was getting older. So many invaluable moments he'd thrown away like trash.

"I dig the beard," said Itty.

She smiled at him, a tentative half-smile, and Hershleder noticed a little streak of white extending from a corner of her mouth, a little streak of something white and crumbly. It sat lightly atop the down of her cheek like a bit of lace.

Toothpaste.

Like most people, Hershleder had often wondered why he had been put here on this earth, what was the divine purpose, the master plan, behind his bewildering existence. The chance of his birth alone seemed so minuscule and so unlikely: a German mother and an American father born to a Russian and a fugitive from the Austro-something Empire. What were the odds, really, of her egg meeting his sperm and spawning in Queens, of all places, during the most repressed and boring decade of the century?

These unimaginably large odds first occurred to Hershleder when he studied reproductive science in the ninth grade. Later, in social studies, when they sketchily covered recent European history, he'd realized that the chances of his mother's surviving the war at all had been frighteningly tiny. At that point in his life he'd decided that he had been put here on this earth in order to justify her survival. He decided to follow in his father's footsteps and become a physician, to earn back the privilege of his birth.

But now as he looked at his estranged wife, Itty, her smart, good, talented, and loving mind wrapped in a knot of curls, clay dust and unspecified schmutz adorning her stretchy outfit, that streak of old white toothpaste dappled against the graceful curve of her downy cheek, he realized that he had been born for the purpose of taking from and giving to this woman. So what, their actual marriage had been sorely wanting; what mattered now was that for the first time in his life all the things a marriage could honestly be seemed within his grasp.

"There's toothpaste on your cheek, Itty," said Hershleder.

Her eyes opened and her hand fluttered up. She pressed a dirty digit to her tongue. She rubbed the toothpaste away with that one damp, clayey finger.

"There's so much I have to tell you," said Hershleder. "I don't quite know where to begin."

"How about in the middle?" Itty smiled at him.

Hershleder's eyes filled with tears. His hand trembled, so he buried it in the dog's fur.

"It's okay, Dave," said Itty. "I'm listening."

Hershleder told and Itty listened. He told her about California and Paris. He told her about his own attempt to deny all the lousy things that had happened to him, and how in a horrible, perverse way, he had been attracted to what LeClerc had originally espoused. "I was revising history," said Hershleder. "My history. I shut myself off, I even turned away from you. In fact, I was a lot like that anti-Semite LeClerc, except that he could face up to the truth."

"Seems to me that you're facing up to it now," said Itty.

"I guess so," said Hershleder. "I mean, it's kind of you to say so. I mean, Itty, more than anything, that is what I want. . . ."

"Breathe deep," said Itty. So he did.

When he caught his breath, Hershleder continued. But when he got to the part about his mother, again his voice grew halting. And again, Itty interrupted him.

"Dave, I'm not an idiot."

The tone of her voice, a bit hard to read here, did not sound to Hershleder's searching ear to be unforgiving or unkind.

Itty knew! Of course she knew; she had known all of it instinctively for a long time. For many years she had known but still waited patiently for Hershleder to fill her in like a real husband.

Now, even though it might be too little too late, she still heard him out. She listened. She was that way, Itty. When he was finished, she shook her lovely head.

"I always wondered what it would feel like to hear you say it to me out loud."

"And?" said Hershleder.

"It's harder than I thought," said Itty. "Everything about life is harder than I thought it would be."

It was cold out there on the steps, but Hershleder didn't dare suggest that they go inside. Rather he breathed in the moist, muddy smell of that damp, desolate bridge between winter and spring, the season with no name, no holidays, and little pleasures of its own. When he was a boy, he'd always thought of it as a season of potential, of promise, all about the future, heralding times to come, but Hershleder didn't want any of that potential business now. It was noonish. The sun should have been high, but there was no sun, no clouds even, just a fine and consistent gray light that swaddled everything in neither-here-nor-thereness, but in a gentle and breathy complexity.

The wind blew. It blew Itty's hair into her face. She tucked a lock behind each ear, but the curls just sprang away again.

"Oh, Dave." Itty sighed. "Where have you been? Where have you been all of your life?"

A perfect come-on line for Hershleder. He almost cracked a joke, but one look at her expression told him that Itty was sincere.

How could he sincerely answer her? For most of his life, Hershleder had been in a place he had never really known or explored and could no longer even recognize, and he didn't even need to know from any of it anymore, except to let it serve as a reminder of what he did not want.

Now he was here with her. Right now with her, with Itty.

What could be more thrilling?

Hershleder knew that at some point soon—because the air was so chilly and the wind was kicking up—he would be asked by Itty to move, either to come inside that closed front door or, in all likelihood, he would be sent away maybe once and for all down the block from his own stone Tudor. Still, the moment itself seemed more than just a touch miraculous; it seemed right. It seemed right that now, in this very instance, he should be sitting on the steps, here together, with her.

For this much alone, David Hershleder was happy.